# BRUJA

## AN ALPHA GIRLS NOVEL

### AILEEN ERIN

INK MONSTER

# INK MONSTER

First Published by Ink Monster LLC in 2015

Ink Monster LLC
100 Commons Road, Suite 7-303
Dripping Springs, TX 78620
www.aileenerin.com

ISBN 9781943858422

Covers by Ana Cruz Arts

## ALSO BY AILEEN ERIN

*For Annabelle Sunshine Latcham.*
*Mama misses you every day.*

# CHAPTER ONE

"CLOUD. WAKE UP!"

My brother's voice called from beyond the haze, yanking me from my dreams.

"Cloud! You're having a nightmare. Wake up. Now." He shook my shoulder.

A sharp inhale rang out. I didn't realize it was me until a second gasp racked my chest. *This has to stop.* I swallowed down the fear and panic that were drowning me.

"Claudia?" He finally used my real name, worry thick in his voice.

I blinked as the dream faded and reality set in. "I'm fine." I didn't dare tell him that my body felt like lead, and I was more than a little nauseated. I swallowed and took a deep, steadying breath. It was dark and the floor was cold under my feet. "Where am I?"

"The hallway. I was up reading and heard you crying."

I wiped my face and felt the tears wetting my cheeks. *I'd been crying?*

"Come on. This way."

He turned me around, and I followed clumsily. My body wasn't reacting right.

*Luciana.* Just thinking her name caused goose bumps to break out over my skin. The oath I'd taken still bound us together. The other members of the coven had each taken one, too, but Luciana had threatened my family—my mother—until I agreed to a more invasive one. It allowed her to draw on my ability to strengthen others' magic. Any time she wanted, she could suck me dry for a power boost. Even though I'd left, the oath was still there, and I had to focus—and be awake—in order to stop her from using it.

I stumbled into my temporary room—one of the guest rooms reserved for visiting wolves on the floor above St. Ailbe's infirmary. My vision blurred as I tried to imagine what Luciana had been doing with my power just then. How tainted was my soul now?

I sank down onto my bed before I might faint. Since I left the coven three days ago, Luciana took control of me every time I fell asleep. She no longer cared about getting my consent before using me for her black magic—not that I'd given much consent to begin with. But now...

I'd been trying to stay awake by reading spell books from the wolves' library, but I'd obviously failed. The dim bedside lamp was still on, but I needed it to be brighter in here. "Do me a favor and turn on the overhead light?" I asked Raphael.

Light filled the room, revealing the tiny, twin-size mattress with clean white sheets. There wasn't anything to complain about but, still, the room felt utilitarian. The house we grew up in was a bit more...colorful. Filled with different scents and textures. At the very least, Mom was always burning sage for protection. I'd kept that going after she left. Without the scent, I found it hard to settle down at night.

St. Ailbe's was only a few miles from home, but it felt

2

infinitely farther. The werewolves didn't like scents. I could understand that with their sensitive noses, but some accent pillows or art on the walls wouldn't kill anyone.

It wasn't just the lack of decor in the guest rooms. The differences between the wolves and the coven seemed vast. Although there were times I really felt connected to my cousin Teresa. Sure, she was only half-witch now, but she seemed to understand me, too. I was glad I'd gotten to know her better these last few weeks, even if it had happened under the worst of circumstances. The wolves and witches were going to war, and I'd turned my back on my coven—on everything I knew—to stop Luciana, the evil woman who'd changed our coven, *La Aquelarre,* into something so dark that remembering the role I'd played in her rise to power made my chest ache.

I wanted to make amends, but now I was in Teresa's territory and everything seemed a little out of my control. Even my own body. I ached for something familiar. Something more than just my twin brother.

I brushed my sweat-soaked hair back from my face as I tried to regain some sense of composure.

Raphael settled down beside me, and I scooted over to make room for him. "This is the third night she's drained you," he said. His deep voice was a contrast to my higher one. Just like everything else, we were the yin to each other's yang. The balance. It made sense. We were twins. Although he liked to make it known that he was older. By minutes. But that was what counted to him—specifics. He was an exact kind of guy.

And he was right.

A few of us had turned against Luciana and she'd never let go of that betrayal. Especially not mine. Luciana wanted me back. She didn't care as much about the others, even though they'd taken their own oaths. As far as I knew, they weren't having the nightmares. Luciana wasn't using them for their abilities. But she was haunting me. Draining me. I feared that no matter how far I ran, no matter how fast, she'd never stop.

Every time she did a spell, she drew on my power to make it stronger. To make her stronger. My leaving had left her in a power deficit. The second I was asleep, my consciousness relaxed, and she could use my powers to boost her own. It was causing nightmares, making me sleepwalk and cry out in the night as she siphoned away my energy, but I wasn't about to go back to the coven. Not even to put an end to this.

I'd find a way to break the link. If I didn't, it wouldn't matter anyway. Because I'd be dead. Either way, Luciana wouldn't be getting what she wanted.

The crisp sheets crinkled as I lay back against my single pillow. "I'll be okay. It's just a few bad dreams." We didn't have total ESP, but we knew each other well. Ridiculously well. We finished each other's sentences, knew when the other was hurt, and definitely couldn't lie to each other. It never worked.

"Whatever she made you say in your oath, it's obviously much stronger than what's standard. We're working on breaking ours—hell, Shane's is already broken just by the force of his counteroath—but yours... It isn't normal. She shouldn't be able to do this to you, and it's scaring me." He paused. "You have to break this oath before it kills you."

I rolled my eyes, trying to act as exasperated as possible. "I'm not going to die." I tried to make it sound like a ridiculous idea, but my brother was always too smart for his own good.

Raphael shifted just enough to look down at me. His black hair was sticking up at odd angles, which meant he'd been asleep. He always knew when I was having a bad dream. Our twindar was strong, no matter what else was going on.

"Your skin is pale and the bags under your eyes have gotten darker every day. You're losing weight. She's sucking you dry. Don't think I haven't noticed."

I suppressed another eye roll. "I wouldn't dare call you anything but observant."

"Don't get sarcastic with me. This is serious."

"I know." If anything, I was more aware of that fact than he was.

"She's using your oath for more than she should. The bitch will bleed you dry if we don't stop her."

*Please, Raphael, tell me something I'm not fully aware of.*

I looked into his eyes. They were the same dark brown, almost black, as mine and nearly the same shape. Mine were a little more round, giving me an innocent look. The kind of look that no longer fit me. "I know better than you what Luciana is capable of doing." I'd even betrayed my own cousin's trust trying to stop her.

"I think you should consider this trip to Peru. Putting some distance between you could weaken her hold."

I shrugged. "I'm not convinced that distance will help."

"It can't hurt, that's for sure."

"Raphael..."

"Cloud..."

I couldn't help the little smile that came out at his nickname for me. He used to make fun of Mom with it. She *hated* when people called me Claw-dia. She'd say, "Cloud-ia. Like a *cloud.*" I didn't really care how people pronounced my name. There were bigger things in life to worry about.

"And what about Mathieu?"

I groaned. "What about Matt?" He hated being called Matt. It was petty, but I refused to call him anything else.

"He's been calling my cell."

The guy was such a jerk.

"He's a jerk," Raphael said, and I snorted. *Twindar alert.* "But if he knew what Luciana was doing to you, he might help. As far as he knows, you're going to marry him."

The thought of asking him for help made me want to throw up. Besides being too young for marriage at only twenty years old, and not loving—or liking—him at all, he was the kind of guy who truly thought that a woman's place was barefoot and pregnant in the kitchen. I wouldn't survive a marriage like that.

Or maybe he wouldn't survive it.

Either way, it was another thing I'd given up to keep my family safe from Luciana, and another thing I had to free myself from. "I think you're forgetting that I'm trying to get out of marrying him. Asking him a favor would be a horrible idea. He'd take it as confirmation of our engagement."

"I know you don't want to marry him, and I don't want you to. Just tell him you need help, and I bet he'll come through."

Nope. Not going to happen. The situation with Matt was complicated enough already. I'd been an idiot and agreed to the match that Luciana wanted. But, in my defense, I'd met him four years ago, when I was young and naive. I'd been unhappy with my situation, and he knew it. He swept in like he was going to save me. He was going to take me away from the Wicked Witch and bring me to live with his coven just outside of Windham, New York, when he became their leader. For all of about five minutes, everything seemed perfect. We even had the same interests.

Then I found out Matt was full of lies. He didn't like classical music. He didn't like classic literature. He wasn't saving me from anything. I'd been set up. And when I tried to get out of the agreement, he'd really shown his true colors. Douche extraordinaire.

But hate was too tame a word to explain how Raphael felt about Matt. When he found out about the engagement, he just about lost his mind. That he was telling me to go to Matt now was a true sign of how worried he was.

"If you're not leaving and you're not going to ask Matt for

help, what are you going to do?" Raphael paused, but not long enough for me to answer. "Because you can't go on like this. You won't survive it."

"I'll figure something out. You know me. I always do."

Raphael pinched the bridge of his nose as he squeezed his eyes shut. He only did that when he was so frustrated he wanted to strangle me.

"Look. They have different books here. And Tía Rosa will help, too. I bet she knows how to get away from Luciana. I'll find a way. Don't doubt me now. I can't do this without you."

After a moment he dropped his hand. "You're probably right."

"Probably?" It didn't really matter which part I was right about. Just that I was right.

"We'll go see Tía Rosa tomorrow, but if she says you should go far away, then I think you should reconsider Muraco's offer on Peru."

*No way, big brother.* "That wolf is old and insane. You heard him. He wants me to go to Peru alone and find some sort of mages that haven't been heard from in a century. Me? Hiking through the woods? Alone. *In Peru.* Is it just me or does that sound like a disaster waiting to happen?"

Raphael snorted. "When you put it like that..." He paused. "But how can we defeat Luciana if she starts summoning demons again? Especially if she's using your abilities to boost her spells? We don't have the knowledge or power to kill that kind of evil and neither do the wolves. She'll slaughter us all."

I suppressed the shudder that wanted to roll down my spine. "We'll find a way. We don't have any other options." To be honest, I wasn't sure what we were going to do, but I'd gone my whole life following other people. Doing what they wanted. Trying to save everyone and only hurting people in the process.

I was done with that.

Yes, we needed to stop Luciana, but I wasn't convinced that rushing off to Peru because Muraco said so would solve our problems. I couldn't take his offer seriously unless he had a more concrete goal, like a weapon he knew where to find or a source of white battle magic that was free for the taking. But wandering through the mountains to find mages who may or may not exist and may or may not deign to help? I just didn't have time to fool around like that. None of us did.

Raphael stood up. "Fine. I'm going back to bed." He started for the door then paused. "Are you going to be able to sleep?"

*Not a chance.* "Sure."

"Liar."

I threw my pillow at him. "Go already." I paused. "But, actually, give that back first. That's my only pillow."

Raphael shook his head and tossed it gently back to me. "'Night, Cloud."

"'Night, Turtle."

He shook his head again as he closed the door. He didn't like being reminded about his former obsession with a certain quad of humanlike turtles.

Once he was gone, it was quiet again, and I wished he hadn't left. I knew Raphael was just in the room next door, but the walls were so thick that being here was like being in a tomb.

*I guess that makes having horrible, screaming-bloody-terror nightmares not so embarrassing.*

I huffed and the sound echoed against the walls. I wanted to sleep. Exhaustion pulled at my body like a ten-ton weight, but I was afraid of what Luciana would do with my powers when I slept. I didn't dare let myself close my eyes, but no matter how hard I tried to keep them open, they grew heavy. Sleep tugged and I barely managed to shake free from the next nightmare before it swallowed me whole.

I threw off the covers, walked to the tiny window, and slid it open. Sticking my head out, I breathed in the familiar scent of the forest. We might be miles away from the compound, but it was the same forest. It had the same cedar trees. The same sounds of night.

Two floors below me, wolves prowled through the St. Ailbe's campus. I'd never been here until a few days ago. The campus was bigger than I'd expected, but completely hidden from the road. It had to be. The werewolves liked their privacy. *That's one thing we have in common.*

One of the wolves circling the quad below noticed me leaning out the window and headed my way. I was breaking the rules. The campus was on total lockdown, with patrols going night and day as the wolves waited for the next attack from Luciana, but I couldn't help myself. I would've liked to go out and sit in the quad in the moonlight—maybe even do a cleansing ritual—but the wolves wouldn't let me outside. Not at night. I'd found out the hard way that leaning out an open window was enough to upset them, but I'd suffocate if I didn't get one clear breath.

The wolf stopped at the bottom of my window and looked up at me, tongue lolling out the side of his mouth. A bright yellow aura of power surrounded him, marking him as a werewolf. All wolves glowed yellow to me. Some so pale the color was almost white. Others so deep and dark it was nearly brown. If I was right, this was one of Teresa's friends. Christopher? I couldn't tell one wolf from another, but his aura... the coloring seemed right. He howled up at me, and I waved.

As if on cue, Christopher yipped at me. I started drawing a protection knot in the air in front of the window. I moved my finger through the air, drawing a complicated pattern as I willed the magic to work.

*Thick as glass and strong as steel. Nothing shall pass through this seal.*

The words didn't really matter, but I needed them to focus my will. I wasn't sure why I liked to rhyme my incantations—I wasn't a fantastic rhymer—but it made the words feel important, which made them stronger.

I stopped the knot in the same place I'd started it. That was the one thing that I couldn't mess up. The ends had to align or it wouldn't work. The knot glowed brightly in the air for a second before dimming.

There. It was done. "All safe now. No need to worry about me," I said.

Christopher tilted his wolfy head to the side and yipped again before starting away.

At least he trusted me enough to let me use my magic. I rested my arms on the windowsill. I had a lot to accomplish in the coming weeks—at least I hoped I had weeks... I couldn't predict how fast Luciana would work against us.

The pressure would get to me if I let it. Instead, I tried to breathe through the stress. Being away from Luciana was a good thing. The first step to getting everything put right.

Thank God Teresa had shown up when she did. She'd been a little later than I would've liked, but that was better than not coming at all—which had been a real possibility after she was bitten and turned from our future coven leader into a full-time werewolf.

To be honest, I was a little jealous. She'd gotten to live a normal life until a few months ago, while I'd been struggling with the Wicked Witch. I didn't begrudge her that...much. I wanted what she had. A life. Real friends—not coven members who were trying to suck me dry. A boyfriend who would do anything for me, instead of Mathieu le Douche.

My shoulders were so tense that I could barely roll them back. *So much for breathing through the stress.*

The one thing I couldn't forget—that I couldn't *let* myself forget—was what I'd done to get here. Taking that stupid oath in the first place so that Mom could leave the coven. Doing Luciana's bidding until my soul was blackened. Then manipulating my cousin so that she'd be forced to stay at the compound. She'd been stripped of her powers—tortured—because of me. And getting Daniel killed...

I owed both of them. And no matter what—by the time this all ended—I would repay the debt. So help me God, I would settle it or die trying.

# CHAPTER TWO

AS MUCH AS I'd hated being confined to the coven compound, I'd always felt at home there. It *was* my home. Everything I knew was there. Every*one* I knew. And they all knew me. I'd never been an outsider before. I was from one of the oldest coven families and I had a secure place there.

At St. Ailbe's, I definitely felt like an outsider.

No one would talk to any of us *brujos* except Teresa's friends. The rest of them gave us a wide berth. We were unknowns. I understood that. But still, there were eight of us and loads of them. Which meant that we ended up going everywhere in a group. Raphael was half-convinced that if we separated, the wolves would attack. I didn't think that was likely, but if I were being honest, we'd betrayed our own coven. The wolves knew that, and if it came down to a fight... They might not make the distinction between good witches and bad witches.

*I've already lost one friend. I can't lose anyone else.*

I swallowed my grief. I'd cried all day after Daniel died, but now I had to keep going. His death had stopped Luciana's attack. For all her evilness, she still loved her son. As much as someone like Luciana could... But the quiet after the battle wasn't going to last. The nightmares alone proved she wasn't sitting still. She was going to come after us, and now she wasn't just drunk on power, she was angry, too. Her ally had killed her son, but there wasn't a doubt in my mind that she believed the wolves and those of us who'd left her were at fault.

Now we had to be ready for whatever hell Luciana was going to throw at us. When this was over—when Luciana's threats weren't hanging overhead like an anvil about to crush us —I'd give myself more time to grieve for my closest friend. For now, I had to ignore the ache in my heart.

*I miss you so much, Daniel.*

"Ready to go?" Raphael said as he stuck his head through the doorway.

I'd showered over an hour ago, and it was past time for my morning cup of coffee. "I'm ready whenever everyone else is." I flattened my hands against my short jean skirt.

"Everyone's good to go. We're just waiting for Cosette."

I grinned. How fey of her to take the longest.

"I'm ready," Cosette's voice rang out from the hall. "I've been ready." She appeared in my doorway, her aura a glittering rainbow. The first time I'd seen it, I'd stared, dumbfounded. I'd like to be able to say that I didn't feel that way every time, but that'd be a lie. I was used to seeing different colored auras around witches, depending on what kinds of magic they specialized in, but her aura was breathtaking. Like holographic glitter. A bright shining silver, but then all colors of the rainbow all at once. It was unlike anything I'd ever seen.

"Oh... Well..." Raphael said as he practically drooled.

I raised a brow at him. He knew she was majorly off limits. Cosette was always vague about her background, but I'd spent enough time with her to read between the lines. She'd never revealed what kind of fey she was or where her abilities lay, but

I could sense the undercurrent of her power. It was *a lot* of power. She had to be much deeper into the fey courts than she let on.

Cosette flounced ahead of us, all tall and willowy in a miniskirt and tank top. Raphael tilted his head to stare at her butt.

*Gross.* I shoved past him, shooting him a look. "No," I mouthed over my shoulder.

He shrugged.

Lord help me. Raphael getting tangled in fey intrigues was the last thing I needed to worry about. Cosette was on our side, but Raphael wouldn't last a minute in the fey courts. Because of his straightforward nature, he'd never learned how to be diplomatic about things. And, if what I knew about the fey was right, they were all about politics.

As we followed Cosette outside, the group was quiet. I scanned my friends' faces as we moved across the well-manicured quad. Yvonne looked tired, but that could just be because she was older. Her hair had turned gray before I was born. This was a stressful situation for us, but that was possibly more true for her. She'd betrayed something that she'd spent her long life supporting.

Elsa was quiet, but then again, she was always quiet. Now the way her shoulders hunched and her feet dragged along the freshly mowed grass told me this quiet was different than her normal demeanor.

Dark shadows hung under Tiffany and Beth's eyes. Only Shane had managed to break his oath, and I was beginning to wonder if he'd even made an oath to begin with. The rest of us were lagging light-years behind him.

It was worse than I'd thought. I'd assumed Raphael looked tired because he kept saving me from my bad dreams in the middle of night, but what if that wasn't it? Was he hiding the effects of his own oath from me?

I barely held in a frustrated sigh. No wonder he wanted me to go to Peru. He knew that I'd saved our parents from Luciana. It pissed him off. He hated them for leaving, but he'd push me away if he thought he could save me from sacrificing anything else. And I would. I'd go back to her if that meant saving him.

There was no way I was going to Peru now. Not when my brother was in danger and trying to hide it from me.

"It's Samhain today," Elsa said.

I stumbled for a step before catching myself. *How did I miss that it was Samhain?* It was an important holiday. The coven always celebrated it with a feast and a nighttime ritual. It was a time when the veil between our world and the next was thinnest.

"Do you think we should do something for it?" Beth asked, turning to me.

I hated to let anyone down, but I doubted that the wolves would let us outside in the middle of the night to do any magic. "Not this year, but next year—we'll make it good."

No one questioned it, but the silence from the others spoke volumes. I ignored it. There wasn't anything I could do. Not right now. We had so many other things to worry about right now.

As I stepped into the cafeteria, my anxiety rose to a record-breaking high. The way everything stopped as we entered made me beyond uncomfortable. The students paused with their forks halfway to their mouths, staring so hard that their auras washed over me in a wave of golden-yellow energy. Even the man flipping pancakes at the grill station stilled to study us.

Raphael was right. The wolves didn't trust us, and I didn't blame them. Helping them once wouldn't erase all the animosity they felt toward us. But they hadn't bothered us. Yet.

From the way they watched us and kept us separate, if we stepped even a little out of line, they'd be all over us before we could breathe a word of protection. Raphael stepped closer to me, and it seemed like we were on the same page as usual. With our seven witches and one semi-fey against hundreds of werewolves...

It was only when Cosette stepped into the room, her head held high, that the rest of us felt confident enough to enter. I wasn't sure how she did it—maybe it was the fey in her—but she always commanded a calm, confident presence even in the tensest situations.

She nudged my shoulder. "Want to split an omelet?"

"Sure. Should I go with you?" The werewolf guys weren't shy and a few of them were eyeing Cosette like a different kind of meal.

"I'm not worried about a few wolves." She gave an enigmatic smile as she flipped her dark blonde curls. "If anything, they should probably be afraid of me." She strutted off to the omelet station like there wasn't an army of Weres ready to pounce on us at the slightest inclination. The one thing I knew for certain was that fey didn't lie. So the wolves probably *should* be afraid of her.

That thought instilled a little more confidence in me as I started off toward the fruit station. As long as Cosette had our backs, we should be okay.

Raphael grabbed my arm, stopping me before I got very far. He was still following Cosette with his eyes. "Shouldn't we all stick together?"

As much as I agreed with the safety-in-numbers defense, I didn't want to show the wolves any weakness. Cosette had set the tone, and now we just needed to maintain it. "I'm grabbing some fruit. Why don't you get some food, too, and then we'll find a table? Teresa is bound to be here soon and—"

"I'm here!" she said from the doorway.

Her long hair hung in loose waves down her back. I'd swear her skin glowed, and her body... I'd kill for that. She liked to say that it was because she was a wolf, but she'd liked running long before she was bitten. I was curvy. I'd never get rid of my hips, even if I starved myself. And why go through life being hungry all the time? Life was too short to care that much. Still, everytime I saw her, I felt a little twinge of jealousy. Seeing Dastien hovering behind her only compounded the feeling.

I pushed away all those green-tinged emotions and focused on my brother. "See." I shoved Raphael in the direction of the food. "Go get your breakfast."

The one thing that St. Ailbe's did amazingly well was food. From the hot- and cold stations to the short-order cooks, there was enough here to feed the entire state of Texas, and all of it was delicious. Still, I was always surprised that with as much food as they put out, none of it seemed to go to waste.

*These wolves can definitely eat.*

Shane and Elsa stuck close as they navigated the food lines, but he kept looking around, probably searching for Adrian. I wasn't sure what was going on with them, but Adrian was the only wolf who actively sought us out. He had a little bit of *brujo* blood and said he wanted to learn more about his magic lineage, but the way he and Shane kept exchanging looks...

If my gut was right, I was sensing definite chemistry between the two of them.

"You sleep okay?" Teresa said as she came up to me. She wore a T-shirt that was brightly printed with cover art for a band I didn't recognize.

"Sure."

She sniffed. "That was a lie."

"Good job," Dastien said.

I grinned up at him. His short, inky black hair curled around his ears. His smile showed off two way-too-sexy dimples. Not to mention that he was tall enough, big enough to make any girl feel taken care of. Add to that his bright amber aura, and he was too much. In the category of completely drool-worthy. Plus, he treated my cousin well. There was nothing better than a man who wanted to coddle his lady, yet gave her all the power in the relationship. That was infinitely sexier than the guy I was supposed to be with.

I allowed myself another split second to envy what my cousin had before moving on to admiring it.

"Don't be condescending," Teresa said.

"Tessa. I'm honestly telling you that was good. You're using your nose."

She sighed. "It wasn't all nose."

I had no idea what they were talking about. Trying to follow their conversation was extremely difficult at times. It was like I was missing pieces of it.

"I've been trying to get her to be more like a wolf," Dastien said when he noticed my confusion. "She should be able to smell people's emotions. Especially lies." He said the last while looking at Teresa.

I glanced from one to the other. "You can smell a lie?"

"Dastien can. Me... I rely more on hunches. But I'm getting better at it." She paused. "Nice deflection. I'll ask you about the sleep stuff later. If I don't eat soon, I might die."

"*Chérie*. You're not going to die."

"You tell that to my stomach."

They bantered back and forth almost faster than I could keep up with. Their auras glowed brighter as they walked. Meshing together. Bouncing off each other. I could see the deeper connection that their bond provided. That little bit of green envy eased its way back up my spine, and I headed to grab some fruit before the feeling could take over. I was happy for my cousin. Not jealous. Happy.

By the time I found the table, people were staring again. I didn't mind speaking to people or being friendly, but some of the stares felt more than a bit hostile. That I didn't like at all.

I sat down next to Cosette, who was already exchanging not-so-subtle smiles with a table of Cazadores across the room. At least *someone* was enjoying the attention. "Anyone else feeling like you're living in a glass bowl?"

Teresa sat on my other side. She had four plates filled with food balanced on her tray with one giant glass of orange juice. "I've been stared at most of my life. Before, people didn't like me or thought I was a weirdo. Now everyone's more interested in a friendly way. Mostly." She paused and looked around. "They're curious. Just don't let it get to you." As she spoke—still glancing around the room, a wave of golden energy passed from her to the gathered wolves. Everyone starting moving—going about the day—in an answering ripple.

"Thank you." The list of things I owed her for was growing by the second. I wasn't sure how I'd ever pay her back. Especially after what Luciana had done to her...

"No problem."

"I don't like the stares," Elsa said. She was so petite that even with her striking brown eyes and dark brown pixie cut she usually managed to get overlooked. But she liked it that way. "It's impossible to stay hidden."

A few more wolves sat down at our table—all of them Teresa's friends. I liked Christopher the best of the boys. He was really fun and easygoing. Talking to him was effortless.

Adrian sat down next to Christopher, and I nearly groaned. It wasn't that I didn't like him, but he was so desperate to learn from us that it made it hard to talk about anything but magic. I liked to think I was more than just a *bruja*. More than just the sum of my abilities.

Admitting that even just to myself felt rude. Here I was, taking protection and hospitality from the wolves, and then begrudging them for wanting to learn more about me. It was the lack of sleep. If I wasn't careful, I was going to start being openly cranky. Not acceptable.

Meredith was hilarious. I wished I had the guts to dye my hair fun colors. I'd met her a while ago, before Luciana shut down all relations between the young wolves and coven members. I'd always wondered what happened to her, so getting to know her again was nice.

Christopher threw a biscuit at Teresa, shocking me out of my reverie.

She caught it and looked at it almost like she was surprised it was in her hand. "Don't throw food at me."

"I just find it funny. All you witches think it's such an adjustment being here."

She threw the biscuit back at him a little harder. "Shut up. It was a hell of an adjustment and they've all gone through some rough things to get here. Don't be an asshole."

I felt my cheeks heating at her language.

"I think you're embarrassing your cousin, *chérie*."

"Sorry," she said to me.

"No. It's nothing." I cleared my throat and handed Cosette a bowl of fruit. In exchange, she slid half the omelet across to me. I took a bite and nearly moaned. It was delicious, filled with asparagus, avocado, onion, and cream cheese. Not a combination I would've ever picked, but it was great. "Now this is amazing." I drank a sip of coffee—which was brewed to perfection—and energy started coming back to me. I was going to have to carry around a cup of this all day to stay awake and alert.

"Knew you'd like it," Cosette said.

"It's a perfect omelet."

"Are there veggies in your breakfast?" Christopher said. "That's just wrong."

"You're awfully cheery for this hour," Teresa said.

"I got up earlier and went on patrol with Adrian and Dastien, so I'm much more awake than usual. This is my second breakfast," Christopher said proudly as he shook his long blond bangs out of his eyes.

Teresa snorted. "What are you? A hobbit?"

I couldn't help but laugh at that. I covered my mouth with my hand. If anything, being with the wolves was interesting, and the constant banter kept me from thinking about Luciana...

*Great. Now I'm thinking about her again.*

I dropped my fork with a clank and took a long drink of my coffee. When I set it down, everyone at the table was looking at me. "What?"

Teresa cleared her throat. "You know, if there's anything I can do to help—"

"Don't worry. I'll be fine." Raphael muttered something but I didn't need to hear it to know what he was saying. "I'm going to try a few spells to break our oaths. I was reading a book before bed last night, and it mentioned a combination of ingredients I haven't tried yet. That could make the difference we need." I took a bite of my omelet, but it suddenly had no flavor.

"Do you think you can break it?" Teresa asked.

"I think so." I cleared my throat, trying to sound confident and probably failing. "I've only tried a few spells, so there's bound to be one that works eventually."

"I wish I could help," she said.

Teresa's skin might be glowing, like every other wolf's, but her eyes didn't hold their usual lightness. "Are you doing okay?"

She shrugged. "Sure."

Dastien reached over and grasped her hand as Teresa stared

hard at the table. I'd always thought she was invincible, and she made it seem like everything that had happened to her was no big deal. But it was a huge deal. And it had only been a few days. I'd be stupid to think that she wasn't still dealing with the repercussions.

"Don't worry," I said. "If this next spell doesn't work, I might take a trip to see Tía Rosa later."

"That's actually a really good idea," she said. "She'd definitely help. And it'd be good to see Axel."

Meredith clapped her hands. "I'm liking this. I haven't been off campus in forever. Let's ditch class today."

Adrian laughed. "You haven't been to class in weeks. What's the point in starting now?"

Teresa shrugged. "I don't know. College?"

Christopher laughed into his cup of coffee. I guessed the wolves weren't big on advanced degrees? I would've killed for the chance to go to college, but Luciana wouldn't let me off the compound. I'd tried to convince her to give me Internet access for an online program, but that hadn't flown either. After this I was going to have to figure something out. I had zero life skills and no home. The wolves wouldn't let us stay here indefinitely.

"Well," Teresa started as she pushed away from the table. "We're going to need to take at least two cars. I'll drive, and who else?"

"I'll drive," Donovan said as he walked up to the table. "You won't be leaving here without me."

Meredith sighed. "I won't die if I'm out of your sight."

"Maybe, but I'd rather not have you in any more danger. All right?" Donovan was shorter than the average wolf, but for some reason that didn't matter. He had so much power, it came off of him in waves, even in his human form. He commanded a presence that had nothing to do with the way he looked physically, and everything to do with what he was—one of the Seven. One of the most powerful werewolves alive.

Watching how these men treated their mates made me want a guy of my own.

But I needed a life first. My own life. Not one tied to Luciana. Or the coven. Or even my brother.

Most importantly, I needed to break ties with Luciana so that we could all get some sleep. "Give me a couple hours to try and figure this out. If I haven't found a solution by then, we'll leave for Tía Rosa's."

Teresa nodded. "Sounds like a plan."

I stood up, leaving behind my barely eaten omelet. My stomach was in knots and I couldn't stand to eat one more bite. Even though it was involuntary, in a way I was still helping Luciana. No one really knew how bad it was except my brother. If I didn't find some way to break the oath soon, the wolves would find out what was really going on and they'd have a whole new reason to hate me.

# CHAPTER THREE

THREE HOURS LATER, I was standing in the closet that housed the pack's spell supplies. They called it metaphysics, which was laughable. It was magic and had almost nothing to do with science.

*Wolves.* I shook my head.

I scanned the shelves again, not believing that they could be missing sage. It was the base of almost every spell I did. I always had at least four bunches on hand at all times. But there wasn't a single solitary leaf in this so-called supply room. I hadn't noticed it was missing before because I'd been trying crazy spells full of odd ingredients.

How was I supposed to break this oath if they didn't even have the most basic supplies?

The shelves were carefully organized. Labels marked every vial and bottle. And it was alphabetized. I went back to the r's and stopped at the t's. Saffron. Safflower Oil. Sago Palm. Salamander. Salicin. Salsafy. Salt. Saxifrage.

"Son of a—" I cut myself off. I didn't like cursing. Those words were too overused. Except in this instance, I couldn't think of anything else that suited the situation better.

*If you don't have anything nice to say, don't say anything at all.* I tried to live by the Peter Rabbit rule. But sometimes it was hard.

I stepped out of the room and nearly walked into Cosette.

"Hi," I said, trying not to sound suspicious.

Besides the use of their supply closet, Mr. Dawson had loaned me one of the classrooms where the wolves attempted spells. The others had been helping me, but Cosette had disappeared after breakfast without a word of explanation. Not that she owed me any, but something was going on with her. I had no idea what it was, but I'd seen her storming off, gesturing wildly as she spoke on her cell phone.

"I found this book." She held out a leather-bound square without any other explanation.

*She was helping me?* I realized my mouth was hanging open in shock and closed it. Cosette had been with the coven for three months. In that time, I'd gotten to know her as much as she let me. She wasn't usually helpful. Sometimes she seemed frustrated by it. Almost like she knew more than she let on, but couldn't let us in.

From what I'd pieced together, fey rules were hard to live under, and Cosette was having an especially hard time with them.

I took the book from her as we walked to the classroom. "Thank you."

She gave me a small nod. "There's a part that you might find interesting. Read Chapter Seven."

I flipped through to the first page of the chapter. The subtitle read "On Breaking Blood Oaths." *Wow. When she helps, she really helps.* "This is fantastic. Thank you."

"Don't thank me yet," she murmured so low I almost didn't catch it.

*What did she find?* I narrowed my gaze and started scanning the page. Raphael came to stand beside me, reading over my shoulder. The second I read the part she was talking about, I slammed the book closed, placed it on the table, and stepped away. I wanted no part in any of that.

I met Cosette's gaze. "No. No way."

She shrugged. "I know it's not ideal, but what you're all going through is horrible. The best I can do right now is give you a real option."

Yvonne came closer. "What is it?"

"Yeah," Tiffany said, as she came over to look. "It can't be that bad. I mean...it's not evil, right?"

Cosette shook her head, and I closed my eyes, rubbing the bridge of my nose. "No, it's not evil," I said.

The rest of the group had tramped over to the table, all leaning over the book. I knew from the dead silence when they reached the part that I had.

"You can't... We can't..." Yvonne muttered.

"It worked for your cousin," Cosette said.

"We're witches," Beth said. "We don't just mate with fey or any of these other creatures they mention here. Has anyone seen a djinn before? Do they even exist anymore? And if we agreed to mate with a wolf, wouldn't they have to bite us? I don't want to be a *wolf*. I'm a *witch*."

"It doesn't say anything about changing over," Tiffany pointed out. "Just that the new bond would override any prior claims."

"Is that really possible?" Raphael said, and I spun to stare at him. He held up his hands. "I'm just wondering. You could form a mate bond without being a werewolf?"

He couldn't possibly be considering this.

"I thought to succumb to the pack, you had to be a wolf," Shane said.

"Not necessarily." Cosette tucked her hair behind her ear.

Her aura glittered as she moved. "Packs and covens of the past intermixed enough to follow a single leader. Tessa isn't such an anomaly if you dig deeper."

This was ridiculous, and I still got the feeling that Cosette wasn't revealing everything she knew. "This is a nonissue. Unless anyone has clicked so well with one of the wolves that you really think you're mates? Because unless you're basically two halves of a soul, it won't work." I couldn't speak for the rest of them, but I wasn't binding myself to anyone unless it was my soul mate. Who might not even exist. I'd already made a mistake taking an oath to the wrong kind of person, and I wouldn't redo that particular mistake just to get out of this.

Elsa shrugged. "They've given us such a wide berth, it's not like any of us would know if one of them was interested in us in any way other than guard duty."

"You'd know if they were interested," Cosette said.

I blew out a breath. "Well then, it doesn't apply to any of us. Thank you for trying, Cosette."

"You really shouldn't thank me." Her jaw clenched and for a moment, I thought her aura flickered, but it steadied into its usual glitter before I could be sure. "But more knowledge is never a bad thing."

She was right, but as I looked around the room, I noticed hope dwindling. We'd been at it for three hours, and weren't any closer. The past two days had been failures, and the way today was shaping up, it would be more of the same. Unless we did something different. "Shane, you broke your oath, right?"

"Yeah, but it wasn't much of an oath. I'm not sure it even counts."

"What do you mean?"

"Well, I'm the youngest of all of you and I don't have much power. Luciana didn't seal it with blood, so deciding to leave the coven was enough to shatter it."

The shock I felt was mirrored on everyone in the room. "She didn't bind it with her own blood?"

He huffed. "No. At the time, I was insulted. She didn't want to bleed in order to lock me in. It was like I didn't matter. But now, I'm kind of glad she didn't. No offense, but what you all are going through..."

"None taken," Raphael said. "So, what now?" My twin looked at me like I was supposed to have a plan.

I didn't know what to do. I'd led them away from Luciana to here, and now they were all suffering. I was the worst leader in the history of leaders. I needed to fix this.

It was time to try something different. "I think we owe Tía Rosa a visit."

Yvonne gave me a small nod. "I think that's very wise."

If I were wise, I would've thought of going to her days ago. "Okay. I'll tell Teresa, and we'll head out."

Tía Rosa was really my great-aunt. She'd left the coven when my grandmother died because she couldn't abide taking orders from Luciana. I hadn't heard from her since, but Axel and Teresa had. They'd even been to her house.

If anyone could help us, Tía Rosa could.

IT DIDN'T TAKE LONG to get out to Tía Rosa's. We caravanned in three cars with plans to meet Axel there. The wolves separated us witches among Donovan, Teresa, and Christopher's cars. If Meredith hadn't been so excited to leave campus, I would've thought that they didn't trust us to come back.

Which was silly. Because we had nowhere else to go.

So there we were. Meredith and Donovan. Teresa and Dastien. Christopher and Adrian. And seven *brujos*. Cosette had decided to stay at St. Ailbe's for reasons she didn't explain, as usual. Whatever she was doing, I liked to think she was helping the only way she could.

In the meantime, I'd promised to stop Luciana, and I planned to stick by that promise. We just needed to break these oaths first.

Tía Rosa's house was small but cute and cozy. The garden looked natural and full, but not overgrown. It was an organized chaos brimming with herbs and plants used in spellcrafting. I was drawn straight to the large sage bush. I tore off a leaf as I walked by and ran it between my fingers, feeling the smooth texture before bringing it to my nose. I inhaled deeply and then slowly let out my breath.

Scent memory was a force to be reckoned with. Sage always made me think of Mom.

"You're thinking about her again," Raphael said beside me.

*Stupid twindar.* "Yeah."

"I don't know why you still care about her. If she was any kind of a mother, she never would've left."

That wasn't fair. "You know I made her go."

He shook his head. "Even after all these years, you still defend her. She was weak. She gave you up to Luciana, sold you for her own freedom." He looked away from me, but I could feel his disgust as if it were my own. "She was a horrible mother."

"She *is* a horrible mother. *Is.* Not *was.* She's still alive."

"She might as well be dead."

I hit Raphael's shoulder. "You don't mean that."

"Yes." His voice held a level of finality that chilled me. "Yes, I do."

The door swung open, cutting off my response. Not that I had a good one. We'd had this fight a million times before.

A little lady stood in the doorway. A pair of glasses hung around her neck, dangling from a beaded necklace. Her curly white hair was cut short, and her back was hunched a little. She smiled at me, and I smiled back automatically.

"Not all mothers are strong. And when placed in a tough spot, not all mothers choose the right thing for their children," she said, her voice rasping. "That doesn't mean you can't love her or wish for things to be different."

I sighed. "Hi, Tía Rosa."

"I wondered how long it would take you to come visit me." She opened the door wide. "Come in, everyone. It's past time for a chat."

After a few days at St. Ailbe's, being at Tía Rosa's was a shock of scent and color. The smoke of the incense burning on her side table made me feel at home. Holy candles burned. Embroidered pillows nearly covered the couch.

My other cousin, Axel, Teresa's older brother, sat on one of the other chairs. *"Hola, primo,"* I said.

"Hey," he said, standing to greet us all.

Rosa bustled toward the kitchen and brought in a pot of tea before hurrying back and forth with a tray full of cups and saucers.

She made sure everyone was settled with a full cup before sitting in a well-worn chair beside the couch. She waved me over to sit down next to her. "So, you've finally broken ties with Luciana?"

I carefully set my teacup on the coffee table. "That's the problem. We're all bound by our oaths to her."

"Leaving the coven did not break your oath?" Rosa frowned, forming a deep line in her already wrinkled brow.

"No, ma'am," Shane said. "Only mine was broken that way."

Tía Rosa turned to Yvonne. "What's happened?"

Yvonne wrung her hands. "It's worse than what you predicted. So much worse."

Tía Rosa seemed to crumple. Her wrinkles looked a little deeper than they had a moment ago. "I had hoped I was wrong."

"I should've listened to you," Yvonne said. "I wanted to stay and help the younger ones, but all except these few chose to follow her way of thinking."

Tía Rosa took my hand in hers. Her skin was so thin that it felt soft and papery. If I wasn't careful, I worried I might hurt her. She patted my hand. "I'm sorry I have no good news for you. If Luciana bound your oath by blood, then there is little you can do. Barring extreme circumstances, it will only be broken when she chooses to release you."

I swallowed. I couldn't accept that. Not and live. "No. That can't be the answer. I just—"

"Maybe we should let the wolves bite us," Beth said.

"What?!" Teresa said. "No. That's a horrible idea." Dastien muttered something I couldn't make out. "Sorry, but it's a horrible idea. I'm okay with being a wolf now, but it wasn't an easy transition and I almost didn't survive it. I was out of it for a week. And it didn't get easier after I finally stabilized. Honestly, sometimes I still struggle with it. It's not something to jump into."

"But if that's the only choice?" Meredith said. "Why not give it a try if they're volunteering?"

"No," Donovan said. "Tessa's right on this one. 'Tisn't something to jump into lightly. I've seen even born wolves go mad because they couldn't handle the first transition. That's why we have places like St. Ailbe's to help normalize the transition. It would be too dangerous for one who's unprepared, especially with no mate to serve as anchor."

"But it worked for Teresa," Beth said.

"Yeah, because I had Dastien. Right?"

"Right, *chérie.*" He cleared his throat. "I held her for days while she slipped between human and wolf, unable to hold either shape. It nearly killed her." He gave a Gallic shrug. "And it's worth noting that biting Teresa is what set off this whole chain of events. Biting more witches could add fuel to the fire that Luciana's trying to start."

"I don't know. I hope the other covens can see through Luciana's crap, and I'd rather have a chance than the alternative." Beth cracked her knuckles. "And trying would be taking a step to fixing this. Staying like we are isn't working for anyone."

Everyone started talking all at once. But Tía Rosa had left me a clue. "You said barring extreme circumstances." I spoke loudly and the others quieted down. "What might those be?"

Tía Rosa coughed, and the wheeze made my lungs ache. "The wolves are right," she said when she had her breath back. "Becoming a wolf would break it, but it is dangerous. There are some other supernaturals that might help, but only at a great cost. Most likely a cost higher than any of you would be willing to pay. Otherwise, you must bind to a stronger witch to override the oath, but I know of no such one as long as Luciana holds your power."

I shook my head. "And Teresa doesn't count?"

"No. She hasn't fully come into her powers yet, and by the time she does, it might be too late."

Yeah. That would've been too easy. "Then I don't know anyone either." On her own, Luciana was hardly the most powerful coven leader, but with the forces she'd been drawing to her, and all the energy she'd drained from me these past years...

The truth was exactly as I'd feared. My own power was locking all of us in.

"What if you broke your oath?" Raphael said. "If you could get free, the rest of us could bind to you to break ours."

I laughed with frustration. "Sure. Fine. Great. But we're facing the same problem either way. I can't break my oath." I'd hoped to at least free the others, but we all knew that Luciana had bound me the tightest. It would be that much harder for me to break from her.

"What of Peru?" Donovan asked.

"You mean Muraco's quest?" He had to be joking. "There's nothing solid there." I'd rather do my grasping for straws here, surrounded by my few allies, than alone in a foreign country where there was no guarantee I'd find anything to make the trip worthwhile.

"Bear with me for a second."

I took a breath and let it out slowly. "Okay."

"Muraco says he knows of mages who can fight the kind of magic Luciana is wielding. If you find those mages, and if they have that kind of magic, then it stands to reason that they might also be stronger than she is. Then you could break your bond and return not only with the magic we need to fight Luciana, but also with the ability to save your coven members from their oaths."

I shook my head. "I don't want to disrespect you or any member of the Seven, but I heard a lot of ifs in there."

"I understand that," Donovan said. He was getting emotional, and his Irish accent was sounding a little more, making his t's sound harder than normal. "But there's not much choice, lass. Turning you into a wolf isn't an option, so you're going to have to find one of your own that will break it."

I blew out a breath. "There's one more option."

"What's that?"

The others knew Cosette was fey, but they had no idea how pure her blood was. They'd assumed she was lesser because she was here with us, but a lesser fey wouldn't have an aura like hers. Not that I was an expert either, but I could tell she was special. "There might be a fey we can ask." At the very least, she might give us more information if we asked directly.

Raphael grabbed my arm. "No. If she could break it, she would've offered already."

"It might not be that simple." I shrugged, not wanting to give away any more of her secrets than I already had. "There's no harm in asking and if she can't help, then I'll think about Peru." As brave as I liked to think I was, I wasn't deluded enough to believe I could go through with being bitten. I didn't have a mate to anchor me, and after being bound to a fiancé I didn't want, I wasn't about to tie myself to some wolf on a whim.

No. If Cosette couldn't help, then I'd sit down with Muraco and try to get some specifics out of him.

As the rest of them finished their tea and visited with Rosa, I said a prayer. *Please, for once, let me find the answers I need.*

# CHAPTER FOUR

THE AFTERNOON HADN'T TURNED out the way I wanted, but that didn't mean something couldn't change. We stopped for food on the way back, and the sun was setting by the time we pulled through St. Ailbe's gates.

I'd been quiet all through the drive. The trip into Austin hadn't been a total waste of time. I knew more now than I'd known before. And knowing was half the battle.

The next step was getting Cosette to either help or point us to the fey who could. But something told me Raphael was right —if she could've done more, she would've done it already. She'd witnessed enough of Luciana's type of witchcraft to claim that the fey would be on our side when the next battle came. Days had passed and she hadn't said a word about any of her people headed this way, so I could only assume that there were other forces at work.

Maybe I hadn't said the right thing. Offered up the proper incentive to get her to work her magic on my behalf. Fey liked to make bargains—or so I'd read—and I'd rather end up bound to Cosette than to Luciana or any of the alternatives.

As I broke away from the group and headed toward the

quad, the others were making plans to go to the library. Do some more research. If I'd learned anything about Cosette in the past few months, it was that she liked being outdoors. And since coming here, she really seemed to like being around the wolves. She'd go wherever they gathered.

Going on that instinct made finding her easy. Ever since we'd gotten here, the girl had been a magnet for the wolves. She lay sprawled on a blanket in the center of the quad, wearing large headphones and tapping her fingers as she flipped through a magazine. A ray of sunlight shone down on her, creating a sparkling prism effect on her aura. It was almost blinding.

All around her, wolves prowled. Oh they were pretending to do other things. Two guys chatted, shoving each other. One seemed to be doing some homework. A few others shared a pizza. But they all were watching her. Only half-participating in what they were doing.

*So much for asking her for help in private.* I gathered up my courage and sat on the blanket.

She slid off her headphones and then closed the magazine as she sat up. "How did it go?"

I swung my braid over my shoulder. "Not great."

"So, what are you going to do?"

*Here goes nothing.* "Tia Rosa did say that some fey have the ability to—"

"No."

Wow. I hadn't expected much, but being shut down before I could even ask? "I understand if that's not something you can do, but if you could point me—"

"I'm not able to help you with that right now." She twisted the cord of her headphones so tight around her finger that the tip went red, cutting off her circulation. "And believe me when I say that's not the answer I want to give."

Now that I was listening for it, I could tell how carefully

she'd chosen those words. She was only saying she wouldn't help now. Not that breaking the oath was outside her power. "Let me rephrase then. Would you be able to break the oath if your circumstances were different?"

"You're learning how this works." Cosette perked up so quickly that a few of the wolves forgot to act and stared outright, but I was too busy concentrating on her to pay them much attention for once. "I'm not allowed to answer that question."

But that was an answer in itself, wasn't it? "Then you could—"

"Still no." She gave her head a sad shake, and her voice was gentle. "I'm bound as tightly as you are, just to a queen instead of a crazy witch."

"I thought the fey would be on our side." She'd said as much. Unless Cosette was lying about not being able to lie? I hoped not. I was already a little hurt that none of this had come out sooner.

"So did I." Cosette slumped back onto the blanket and her hair pooled around her in a mass of curls. "But the courts want to stay neutral. Because I'm—" Her voice choked off and she made a frustrated noise at the back of her throat. "If I did what you wanted me to do, I'd have to take a side."

There was one more hope dashed, but I seemed to be losing them left and right today. I still couldn't give up. "If your queen does nothing, she could be doing all of you more harm than good."

"That's basically what I told her." Cosette fisted her hands in the blanket. "The battle that's coming is about more than witches and wolves. If I step out of line now, she'll summon me home and I'll be no help to anyone later."

"I see." Except I didn't see at all, because it sounded like she was saying she *could* help—she just wouldn't where I was concerned.

"Claudia..." Cosette sat up, rubbing at her temples. "I have no intention of letting you, yours, or any of these wolves die, but I can't act yet. And I know you well enough to know you wouldn't ask me to if you knew what it would cost."

I brushed my arms against the chill settling into me, trying to convince myself the feeling was just from the sunset. I understood what it was like being bound by hard rules better than anyone. Getting angry with Cosette would only make me a hypocrite.

That didn't make her words any easier to swallow. I had a solution. Right here. But I couldn't use it.

She glanced up at the sky and then started gathering her things. "Let's get in before the moon comes up."

"Right." Cosette's audience of wolves was finally dispersing and none of us would be allowed out here after nightfall. I brushed off my skirt as I stood. "Thank you for being as honest as you could be." And at least she didn't intend for any of us to die. It was a small comfort, but it was better than nothing.

"Please stop thanking me." She let out a sad sigh. "I don't deserve it and the habit's going to get you into trouble if you keep looking for help from the fey."

"What if I asked your queen for help?" I didn't know which court Cosette was aligned with, but surely if I went to the top of the hierarchy, I could get what we needed. None of us would be able to stay neutral once Luciana started pulling demons into the world. It had to benefit the fey to help our cause.

"Don't even suggest that." Cosette took a last glance at something in the air and then grabbed my arm to hustle us both off the quad. "She might take you up on the offer, and she'd require much more than a blood oath in exchange."

Cosette's shudder passed through my arm and that response struck a chord. If I added up what she'd said and hadn't said, and combined it with her aura, then I had one more question to ask and no reason not to finally let it out. "How closely are you related to your queen?"

Her long strides faltered, and that alone was enough of an answer. Close enough that I wasn't going to get a straight response out of her.

"No one ever thinks to ask me that," Cosette said. "What makes you ask?" She slowed to a stop as we entered the courtyard.

"Mostly your aura."

"You don't give yourself enough credit, Claudia." She tilted her head to the side. "I truly believe you'll figure this out."

We'd see how much credit I deserved. Maybe I was over-reaching by asking for help from the fey when I hadn't explored all the options closer to home.

It was time to talk to Muraco about Peru.

I SAT CURLED up on the couch in St. Ailbe's library into the wee hours. Muraco had gone on a hunt. Apparently he didn't like sticking close to one place. He'd become a bit of a loner in the past century, as Mr. Dawson had put it.

*Century. I laughed as I picked up the next book. Sometimes I wonder how much weirder life can get, and then it just gets weirder.*

I'd taken to studying all the books on witchcraft that St. Ailbe's had on hand. Luciana had kept us all ignorant of some things. She didn't want us gaining too much power and fighting her. Now that I intended to fight her, I had to make up for lost time. Reading kept me busy and awake when all I wanted to do was sleep. Plus, the library had a fancy coffee machine. Caffeine was essential to my don't-fall-asleep plan.

I stood up, stretching my tired muscles. Everyone else had

gone to bed hours ago, but that was to be expected. I checked my watch. 3:00 a.m. Only a few more hours until daylight. For some reason, it was easier to stay awake when it was light outside.

I walked over to the shelves and scanned for anything that seemed interesting. My vision was getting blurry from lack of sleep, and I was starting to feel more than a little loopy. After so many hours awake, it was almost like I was living in a dream. I jumped up and down, trying to gain some energy. Maybe another cup of coffee would help, too.

I headed toward the machine, grabbed a fresh mug, and started pouring the thick brew.

A siren went off and I jumped, spilling some coffee on my hand.

I froze. For a second, I thought I'd fallen asleep, but the burn on my hand meant that I was awake.

*Fire?*

No. I didn't smell any smoke.

Then panic gripped my chest. Luciana?

*Samhain.*

*Oh no. Not yet.* It was too soon. We weren't nearly ready.

I dashed to the door. The halls of the academic building were quiet, but the siren kept going. As soon as I stepped outside, the stench hit me.

Vampires.

It was an attack.

And all my potion vials were in my room where they did me absolutely no good.

*So stupid.*

The alarm shut off, leaving only the snarls and shrieks and chaos of the fight.

Wolves fought together, pressing back a swarm of vampires. Thirty or forty of them swarmed across the campus, attacking from every direction I could see, and their rotting meat stench made me clap a hand to my nose.

The wolves were winning. Killing them off one by one. Without any of my potions, I wasn't much help against them, so I stayed back. I drew a few knots in the air. Spells of protection and stealth and agility. I pushed the magic out to cover the wolves as I watched, waiting for an opportunity to jump in where I wouldn't be in the way.

Time seemed to slow as three figures dressed in white stepped off the path that led to the parking lot.

*No way. They wouldn't do this. Not on my watch.*

I sprang into action. From this distance, I couldn't see who they were, but it didn't matter. I ran across the quad, drawing a knot of protection on my chest. A vampire moved toward me, then stopped as the protection hit home. I dodged the fighting wolves. I couldn't fight the way they could. My getting involved that way wouldn't do anyone any good. But the coven members that were starting toward the wolves—

Them, I could stop. I wouldn't let them any closer to the wolves. Not while I had breath left to spell them with.

"Claudia," Teresa's voice rang out, but I didn't stop. "Wait."

Something grabbed my shirt, pulling me up short. I spun around. "What?"

"You don't want to see this."

I turned back around as I heard Raphael cry out. "Daniel!"

*My blood ran cold. No. She wouldn't do that. She couldn't...*

Raphael and the others ran outside, racing across to the figures in white.

"No. It's not possible." I couldn't believe what I was seeing. Daniel was there. He was one of the people in white.

But he was dead.

*Oh God.* The only way to make the dead walk again was to

possess them with some nasty demons. Daniel was a monster now, but my brother hadn't realized that yet.

I couldn't stop it. I was too far away.

Raphael reached Daniel and froze. Daniel's shoulders were hunched over, making him seem smaller than usual. His usual spiked hair was limp. He leaned toward Raphael and I knew something bad was about to happen unless I found a way to stop it.

I grabbed Teresa's hand and pushed what little energy I had left into her, amplifying her werewolf abilities. "Run. Fast. Don't let him kill my brother."

In a flash, her aura brightened until it was like staring at the sun. Her form shimmered—clothes falling to the ground—as she changed to wolf while running across the grass. My eyes couldn't keep up with her. One second she was in front of me, and the next she was gone. She jumped on Daniel, knocking him from Raphael, but it was too late. Raphael screamed, and I could almost feel Daniel's teeth as they ripped into my brother's arm.

I took off running as fast as I could, wishing I had even half Teresa's speed. Pure terror clawed at my gut. This wasn't happening. I couldn't let this happen.

When I got close enough to make sure I wouldn't hit any wolves, a spell formed on my lips and I flung it at the two standing figures. Girls. Sadie and Antonia.

The spell hit its mark and they stumbled back.

Daniel was on the ground. Not moving.

He was dead. He should've stayed dead. Not been corrupted by Luciana's evil magic.

"Come back with us," Sadie said as she pulled herself to her feet. "Luciana can fix your wound."

"Never!" Raphael struggled to get up, cradling his arm against his chest.

Relief made my limbs shake. He was okay. He wasn't dead. He was going to be fine.

"None of us are ever going back there," Raphael said.

The wolves howled, and I noticed the quiet that had fallen over the rest of campus. The vampires must all be taken care of because the wolves moved to form a tight circle around us.

"Take them to the feral cages," Mr. Dawson said. He wore only a pair of gray sweatpants as he stood among the wolves. Two more men came running, wearing the same clothes.

"That's not a good idea," I said. I didn't know what these feral cages were, but I wasn't sure they were strong enough to hold a witch. "They'll be able to—"

"No. I'll sedate them," Dr. Gonzales said, appearing at Mr. Dawson's shoulder with a black messenger bag slung over her shoulder. "They won't be able to use their magic if they're unconscious."

The two girls held each other as they were led away by the two men, six wolves, and Dr. Gonzales. They headed toward the building where classes were held. It seemed odd, but a groan from Raphael and I forgot all about them.

"Let me see it," I said as I knelt next to him.

"Daniel... He..."

"I saw." No magic that animated the dead was good news. But this... This was beyond bad.

Green oozed out with my brother's blood.

"Let's get him to the infirmary," Mr. Dawson said. "Dr. Gonzales can look at the arm when she's done with the others, and we can see what we can do."

I swallowed down my fear. "Okay." I didn't say what I was thinking, because I wanted to hope and not scare Raphael any more, but if the bite was infected, it was infected with something that medicine wouldn't fix.

A hand came down on my shoulder and I looked up to see Yvonne. "One step at a time."

"What should we do with the body?" Mr. Dawson said as he motioned down to Daniel.

I looked at what was left of my friend. We'd grown up together. Played together. Studied together. But this... This wasn't my friend.

This was an abomination.

His skin had turned gray with patches of black. His mouth foamed white. Blisters covered his arms. And that was just what was visible. I stepped closer and choked at the foul stench of sulfur.

He held no aura. No soul. Whatever had been animating him was gone now.

"Burn it," I said, and then I turned my back on him.

I had to focus on what I could do. I'd been too late to help Daniel, but if my brother was hurt, there wasn't anything I wouldn't do to save him.

# CHAPTER FIVE

"YOU SHOULD GET SOME SLEEP," Dr. Gonzales said and I nearly laughed. I'd used magic tonight—sending my already depleted energy reserves so deep into the red that my body literally ached all over from exhaustion, but sleep was not an option. Especially not now.

"I'll be fine," I said. I was sitting in the only chair in the tiny room. The hospital bed took up most of the space. A small table sat beside it with the lamp on dim, providing the only light. There was a small bathroom behind me, and a wall of cabinets took up what room was left.

Raphael quietly snored as the pain meds worked their way through his body. It had taken twenty stitches to fix up the mess that z-Daniel had made. Meredith called him that. Z for zombie.

Only it wasn't zombie so much as demon. I'd made that known, but according to Meredith, d-Daniel sounded more like a stutter and way less cool. If he had to be brought back like that, the least we could give him was a worthy nickname. Again, according to Meredith.

What we called the abomination that Luciana had created

didn't matter to me. What really counted was that Raphael was all right.

"Well, if you're going to stay in that chair the rest of the night, there are blankets in the cabinets." Dr. Gonzales moved toward the door. "I'll be just down the hall. Shout if you need anything."

I nodded, not looking away from my brother. "Thank you." I sat there, as still as I could be, until she left. Then I scooted the chair closer until I could rest my forehead on the bed.

The wolves had to sense what was wrong with him. I could only smell it when I was this close, but the scent of sulfur surrounded my brother now, and it didn't take a genius to guess what would happen next. My brother would be just like Daniel. Luciana wouldn't be satisfied until her twisted magic took everything from me.

What would I have left when she took Raphael?

Goose bumps ran up my arms, and I went to the cabinets on the other side of the bed. It took me three tries, but I found the blankets. The wolves liked to run the air conditioning in the infirmary a little more than I was comfortable with.

Or maybe I was still in shock.

The door opened and light filled the dimly lit room. "Hey," Teresa said.

*Oh God. I'd forced her change. She was going to be mad at me.* "Hi."

"How is he?"

I sank down into the chair with the blanket bundled in my arms. "Not good."

"I heard Dr. Gonzales cleaned the wound and stitched it."

I nodded. "She did a great job taking care of him, but she can't fix this."

Teresa sniffed and I finally turned and met her gaze. Her

eyes were glowing, meaning her wolf was close to the surface. "Is that sulfur?"

Tears welled, and I tried to blink them away. "Yes."

"Oh shit," she said as she sat on the end of the bed. "This is really bad."

"I know." A single tear managed to slip free, and I quickly brushed it away. I couldn't break now. I had to be strong.

"Do you think..." Teresa started and stopped. I waited for her question, but I could guess what she was going to ask. I'd been asking myself that same question.

"Do you know what's going to happen to him?" she said finally.

"I don't know for sure, but... Did you see Daniel?"

"Yup."

I gave her a level stare.

"No. No. That can't happen."

I shrugged. "That's my best guess. Although nothing is certain. If I can find a way to stop it, then he could be back to normal in no time." That was a long shot, but I had hope. I cleared my throat. "Thank you. I'm sorry I used you, but—"

She sliced her hand through the air to cut me off. "Don't even. God. Whatever you did boosted my power to like the umpteenth degree. I never felt so strong or so fast before."

I nodded. It had cost me a good dose of energy that I didn't have to give, but if it had stopped Daniel from killing my brother then it was worth it. At least now I had a shot at figuring out how to save him. Undoing some nasty magic was far better than trying to fix a ripped out throat. That was impossible to fix.

Thank goodness Teresa wasn't angry. "Well, I'm sorry I didn't ask your permission."

"It's fine. But now I know why Luciana wants you back so badly."

I sighed. "Yeah." Would I go back? If she promised to save Raphael, I wouldn't have a choice.

"I know what those girls said, but take it from me. Trusting Luciana isn't a good idea. No matter what she promises."

"But if she can save Raphael..." I reached out, cradling his hand in both of mine. "I don't know that I could risk his life."

"Don't even—"

A cell phone rang, and I recognized Raphael's ringtone. That was his phone.

"That's why I came down here. Not just to check on you, but Raphael dropped his phone in the quad and it keeps ringing." She pulled his small flip phone from her pocket and handed it over. "It says Matt."

I groaned. He was probably the last person I wanted to deal with right now.

"Is that the douche bag?"

I laughed. "Yeah. That's the douche bag."

"Why is he calling your brother?"

"Probably because I don't have a cell phone."

"You don't have a cell phone?"

I took the phone from her and it stopped ringing. *Saved by the bell.* "You remember the amazing cell reception at the compound."

"Right. I wasn't thinking. Of course. Why would you have a cell if you couldn't use it?"

"Exactly." I held up the phone. "But this is Raphael's. He left the compound every day for work so it made sense for him to get one. Clients needed to get in contact with him. But Luciana never let me out of her sight."

The phone started ringing again. I didn't bother reading the caller I.D.

"You going to answer that?"

I didn't want to. Not even a little. "If he calls again, I'll pick it up."

She grinned. "Makes sense." She motioned back to my brother's sleeping form. "So how do we help him?"

I leaned back in the chair. "I have no idea. That kind of black magic is so far out of my knowledge base. I'm hoping that the demon didn't fully infect him, but I won't know until he wakes up, and I'm not waking him up. Not yet." I chewed on my lip. "Is Muraco back by any chance?"

She shook her head. "He's not expected back until the afternoon. Why? What are you thinking?"

"Honestly, I don't know what I'm thinking. But if Raphael needs white magic to fix him—and I have a feeling that's what he might need—then I'm going to have to go to Peru."

"All signs are pointing that way. You can break your oath there. You can fix Raphael there. And you can find magic to help us there."

I nodded. "I noticed that, too. Powerful signs happen in threes. I was told three times in twelve hours that I should be in Peru. I don't like to ignore the spirits when they shout at me." I didn't want to pry, but had to ask her... "Have you seen anything about this?"

She cringed and looked away from me. "Not really anything helpful. I'm sorry. Ever since...you know...it's been hard. I feel like I'm blocked. It's probably just psychological, but I'm worried that—"

The phone started ringing and I wanted to chuck it across the room.

"You don't have to answer it," Teresa said.

"He'll just keep calling." But boy did I *not* want to answer it. "Hello." I held my breath as I waited for his response.

"Claudia? Finally. What the hell is going on down there?"

I didn't know what to say. Or where to start. "A lot is going on."

"I heard from Luciana. She's freaking out. Whatever this little rebellious phase is, you should get over it and go home."

*Rebellious phase?* He made it sound like he was so much older than me. And he was. At thirty, he was exactly ten years older than me. It made him extra gross for getting engaged to a sixteen-year-old at twenty-six. Not that the age difference was the problem. It was more his lack of maturity. "I'm not going back to the compound. Not now. Not ever."

"But—"

"No." I nearly shouted the word. "You don't know what's been going on down here. And if you do, well then I'm even happier that we never got married. Because that's not going to happen. Ever."

He started yelling profanities, and I put the phone away from my ear.

"Hang up," Teresa said.

"I'm just going to let him calm down for a second," I whispered to her.

Her gaze narrowed as Matt let another insult fly. "You weren't kidding. He's totally a douche bag."

I smiled, and put the phone back to my ear. "Matt. Stop." I said the words calmly, and he actually quieted down. "Luciana is up to some bad things. Really evil. I'm going to do my best to stop her, and if you want to show up here and try to get in my way, fine. Good luck trying to get through the wolves, but if you want to try, I can't stop you. But no matter what you do, you're not going to change what I'm doing. Not at all."

He called me a word that I would never repeat, and Teresa snatched the phone from my hand.

She pressed End and snapped it closed. "And we're done with that guy. Jeeze. I thought I had a bad mouth."

I laughed. Big belly-jerking laughs. And boy did I need them. "You do have a bad mouth, but he's worse."

"No kidding." She stood up. "I'm heading to bed. You staying here?"

I nodded. "I can't leave him. What if he wakes up?" *And what if he's not himself when he wakes up...*

"I don't blame you. When Meredith was sick, I spent a little time in here. I know it's not the same. She's not my twin, but it was scary. And I felt responsible for fixing it. Just..." She paused. "Don't put too much pressure on yourself. You can't solve everything."

"Says the girl who's always rushing in to save the day."

She snorted. "As my father says, 'Do as I say, not as I do.'" She laughed at her own joke. "Try and get some rest."

She closed the door behind her, and I shook out the blanket, getting as comfortable as I could.

When I'd woken up, over twenty-four hours ago, I'd thought the day couldn't get any worse. Luciana was draining me and I was already exhausted and frustrated.

I'd been so wrong. It could always get worse.

I gripped my brother's hand, and prayed like I'd never prayed before, letting the words slip from my lips as I waited for the sun to rise, and hoping that the new day would dawn with some measure of answer to my prayers.

# CHAPTER SIX

"CLAUDIA."

Something jerked my shoulder and I sat up, blinking the sleep from my eyes. "Oh God. I fell asleep."

"Have you been in here all day?" Teresa said. Her hair was piled in a sloppy bun. She wore a pair of dark skinny jeans and a black T-shirt with a sunburst around the word "orb." I wondered briefly what that meant before remembering where I was.

The last thing I remembered was laying my head on Raphael's bed. I'd been praying, and then nothing. I completely passed out. "What time is it?"

"Just after two."

I quickly did the math. I'd slept like the dead for almost ten hours. With no dreams. The magic Luciana had cooked up last night must've worn her out. My body didn't seem quite as heavy as it had. "Wow."

"I came to tell you that Muraco is back. We were going to meet in the library, but I think you need food." She got that distant look in her eyes, which meant she was probably talking to Dastien via their mate bond. Her aura flashed with hints of amber, and then I was certain they were talking. "Okay. We're heading to the cafeteria instead."

My stomach rumbled.

"Come on." She pulled me out of the chair, and my limbs felt stiff and clumsy. Teresa laughed and pointed to my face. "You have a crease in your cheek from the blanket."

I rubbed my fingertips over the right side of my face. "I do. I was sleeping hard."

I quickly unbound my long, straight hair. It flowed past my butt when it wasn't braided, which was why I usually kept it braided. I ran my fingers through it, giving it a rough comb, before quickly braiding it again. I straightened my peasant shirt and pulled my skirt down, as it had ridden up while I was sleeping.

That would have to do. I'd take the time to shower later.

Before I left, I took one look at my brother and my heart sank. His skin was pale, with a sheen of sweat. "What about... If he wakes up and he's..."

"Dr. Gonzales is going to come in and watch him. If something changes, you'll be the first to know."

"Okay." I could deal with that. Leaning down, I brushed a kiss across his forehead and was surprised at how cool he felt. "Has Dr. Gonz—"

"I passed her on my way in. She says he's stable, for now."

"He hasn't woken up at all?" I'd expected to wake up when he did, but I'd been sleeping so hard, maybe I'd missed it.

Teresa shook her head slowly. "I'm sorry."

Fear for my brother and what might happen to him gnawed at me. I brushed his black hair away from his forehead. "I'll find a way to fix this, Raphael." It was a promise that I would do anything to keep. I hoped it didn't mean that I was going back to Luciana, but if that would fix him, then... I turned away from his bed. "Okay. Let's go."

We were quiet for a little bit of the walk, but Teresa broke the silence. "I know that it's going to be tempting to go to Luciana. I just... I'm really afraid of what will happen to you if you do."

I was afraid, too. But if it came down to it, I wasn't sure I could stop myself from going to her. "He's my brother. My twin."

"I know. And I'd do anything for Axel, but—"

"You don't understand." It wasn't the same. He was my *twin*. He was all I had left in this world. "He stood by me in that hell of a compound. He wouldn't leave. He sacrificed so much. And if I have to sacrifice to save his life—"

"No!" She spun, grabbing my hand and pulling me to a stop. "He wouldn't want you to do that. Even if it meant his life."

I wrenched my arm away from her. "You're not a twin. You couldn't possibly understand what that means."

"Maybe not, but I know what Luciana is capable of. I went to her trying to save Meredith, and if you remember that didn't exactly work out." She stared me straight in the eye. "If you try to go back to her, I will stop you." The words were calm and clear, and I knew she wasn't messing around.

My hands made tight fists. "You'll stop me?" My voice had gone cold, and I couldn't bring myself to care.

"I won't let you put yourself in harm's way." Her tone was soft and placating. The guilt at the harsh tone I'd used with her weighed heavy. She was being kind, and how was I repaying that? "If you need protection from yourself, then that's what I'll do. What exactly do you think will happen if you go back to her? Because I promise, it'll be nothing good."

I knew it wasn't going to be good. I'd lived there. I knew what she was like. But that didn't change the position I was in. "I'll do what it takes to help my brother," I said softly.

"I get that. But I'm your cousin and I'm going to help you

the best way I know how. I'm sorry, but I'm all you've got right now."

The truth of that sunk in and hit me hard. *Oh God. If Raphael dies, I'll be alone. Truly alone.* I bit my bottom lip to stop it from trembling.

"You're going to be okay, Claudia. I've been through my share of tight spots in the last couple of months—ones that I didn't know how to get out of. But I did. You will, too. You can do this. You can find the answer. Just don't give up. Don't go back to that woman. Find another way."

I met my cousin's dark brown gaze and found strength in it. In her. I wished I were as strong as Tessa. I had to try to be. I *would* save my brother. "Then I hope Muraco has something good to tell me because I'm barely hanging on."

"If he doesn't then we'll figure it out." She half smiled, just a slight tip up on the right side of her mouth. "I'm not really one to quote anything religious, but if all this crazy stuff doesn't make you believe in some higher being then I don't know what will." She huffed a little laugh. "I've found that when God closes a door, there's usually a window."

"And if there's a window, there's a good chance Tessa is jumping out of it," Meredith said from behind us.

"Shut up. I was trying to be serious," Tessa said.

"And I was being literal."

I raised a brow as I stared at my cousin. "You jumped out of a window?"

"*Windows.* Plural," Christopher said.

I turned to see the rest of the group joining us in the center of the quad. Mr. Dawson, Muraco, Donovan, Dastien, and Adrian. Along with Shane, Yvonne, Tiffany, Beth, Elsa, and Cosette. They must've left the library at the same time we left Raphael's room.

"For some reason, I'm not surprised to hear that."

"They're there for a reason," Teresa said. "I'm sure you'll find one or two to jump through before this is over."

Doubtful. I hated heights. "Literal windows, not going to happen. We'll see about the metaphorical ones."

"You'd be surprised what you're capable of achieving when you put your mind to it," Teresa said.

"So wise beyond your years, *chérie*," Dastien said as he put his arm around her. The group started moving toward the cafeteria again.

"Someone's gotta be wise in this relationship," she said as she elbowed him in the stomach.

He groaned dramatically and they started bantering again. I was getting used to this place. To these wolves. Growing up, I never would've thought I'd end up here. Even associating with the wolves was off limits, but here I was, living with them.

Life took unexpected twists and turns. It was all I could do to keep up with them lately.

When we entered the cafeteria, I was surprised to see so many people eating. With it being between mealtimes, I figured it would've been empty, but wolves were nothing if not a hungry bunch. There wasn't as much food out as they had during the three main meals, but it was more than enough for my purposes.

"Let's get some food, and then we'll chat," Mr. Dawson said.

While we were eating, the place cleared out. I wasn't sure if Mr. Dawson had said something to the others milling about or if they were just finished. Either way, I was thankful for the relative privacy. It wasn't that I didn't trust everyone in the pack... But I didn't really trust everyone in the pack. Not yet. But Teresa's friends, I trusted. They'd been warm and welcoming.

Now, I just hoped they had some brilliant ideas on how to save my brother. That seemed like a long shot when I wasn't even sure what was wrong with him.

I sighed and pushed my plate away. I'd managed half a

burrito, but I couldn't eat one more bite. Nerves made it barely possible to sit still.

Muraco cleared his throat and everyone quieted. His white hair was long and shaggy. He was the only werewolf I'd ever seen that actually looked old, which I was pretty sure meant he was ancient. His skin reminded me of Tía Rosa's—paper-thin and wrinkly. He moved slowly, pulling an envelope from the back pocket of his jeans and sliding it across the table. "I was away the last few days, working on something for you."

Something for me? Weird. I tore the envelope open and emptied its contents. It was a small navy blue book with the seal of the United States of America on the cover. "You got me a passport?" I wasn't aware that was something that you could do for someone other than yourself. And where had he gotten a picture of me? "I don't know what to say." Thanks didn't seem appropriate when I was more than a little worried about the ethics of it.

"I went by to see Raphael today."

He did? How many people had been in that room while I'd been asleep?

"And it looks like you need to find these mages quickly. Faster than before."

Right. But was that really the answer? I had to be sure before I went on the proverbial wild-goose chase. "Before I jump on the first plane out, you haven't told me anything about what I'm looking for, *who* I'm looking for, and how they can help me. I can't just go there and look around, hoping to stumble upon something. Raphael... He's—"

"Dying."

*I swallowed the lump in my throat. I will not cry right now. He's not dead yet. There's still time.*

"I will tell you a little about my country."

It was with those words that wolves around the table all took a breath and leaned in. Like they'd never heard anything about Muraco or Peru before. There was something about Muraco that made me want to listen to him, too. To trust him. And I definitely wanted to hear his story.

"In my country, we don't separate ourselves from other supernaturals. It's not normal for us to live the way you do here. All in your own compounds behind your own walls and fighting amongst yourselves. It's not right."

I bristled at that—who was he to tell us how to live—but remained quiet.

"Long ago, a wolf fell in love with a very powerful witch. She didn't turn, because she was happy with her life as it was, but they were mated all the same. Together, they formed a new way of living. Witches. Wolves. Fey. All living together. Having families. This is where I am from. This is how it should be. I've tried to tell the other packs, but no one will listen." He looked at Teresa and Dastien, who sat together, their hands entwined. "But they give me hope for peace in this part of the world."

He gestured with his hands, and his joints popped. "We lived together for some time before there was trouble. You see, not everyone lived in the villages. Some witches wanted to stay apart. Some packs wanted to roam. Some fey liked underhill better. But we all got along. For a time. Then the magic casters—mages, witches, wizards—whatever you want to call them, it's all the same—split away from us, breaking into two groups. Good and bad. The good ones practiced a pure white magic. They lived alone, like priests working their magic—meditating and praying. When things went wrong, people from all over the country, from other parts of the Andes, would come to seek their guidance. To receive blessings. It was said that their auras were so pure they glowed in the darkness. And sometimes, a witch from my wife's coven would decide that they wanted that quiet life and they would disappear to join." He sighed, and I looked at Yvonne.

Had she heard of anything like this? I'd have to ask.

"The bad ones," Muraco continued. "Well, they made evil things. Very evil things. We tried to stay away, but they attacked the village. We couldn't stand for that. For a few years, there was war. Light and dark. We helped fight these dark casters. The light won, but at a high cost. So many lives gone. And in the end, those white mages... They disappeared. The fight had taken too great a toll. I'm not sure if they lived on. If they had a quiet life in the wilderness or not. But their magic lives. At night, during the new moon, you can see it lighting up the mountain. This magic is what you all need now. Their white energy is the only thing that can fight the coming darkness." Muraco took a drink of his coffee. "This is the hard part. The finding of them. They might have left behind magic. Books. Or they might themselves be there. It was so long ago that I doubt they live now, but there's no way to be certain save to look, Claudia de Santos."

A shiver rolled down my spine at my name, and Muraco continued. "Your power may let you find them where I and others could not. All that is certain now is that dark magic was used to bring back your Daniel. I haven't seen the like of that in more years than memory recalls, but that is very much what those evil mages did. It took many years before the white mages found a way to fight such power, but they did. We do not have years this time. So you must go. Now."

Mr. Dawson cleared his throat. "What about her oath to Luciana?"

"What about it?"

"Do you think they can break it?"

He sighed. "As I said, they might not be there. She might find bits of their magic left behind. And I hope that is enough.

From what I know of oaths, what the girl needs to break the bond is already inside her. She gives the oath more power by believing in it."

He was wrong. Dead wrong. "No. She has a hold over me. She made me—"

"Oh, I'm not saying that the oath has no power. I'm saying that to break any oath you need either good magic to override it or the sheer force of will to overpower it. That's why some are easy to break. If the witch who did the binding didn't make it so strong, when the person leaves... Poof." He motioned with his hands. "It's gone."

"He's right," Shane said. "That's why I'm no longer bound."

"Exactly. Others, the witch wants to hold tight," Muraco said. "You have to overpower her. Or find some way to override it."

"Override it?" If this was the whole mating thing again...

"A bond like theirs will do it." He waved his hand toward Tessa and Dastien.

Yeah. Like that was going to happen. "So how do I find the temple of these white mages?" If they had a temple. I suspected it would be more of a ruin by now.

"Come with me if you want. I'm heading home tomorrow to gather others who might be willing to join the coming battle. When we arrive, a member of my pack will take you to where I last saw them. It's now a busy village, but you have the sight. If there is magic hidden in the forest, you will see it. Trust your instincts and follow them to find what you need."

"And what if I don't find it? What if there's nothing to find?"

"It's there. Believe it to be so, and it will be so."

I closed my eyes, barely able to contain a groan. I just had to will things into existence. Fine. Easy-peasy.

"I think this might be your best option," Teresa said. "And it would get you away from Luciana. Maybe that's far enough away that you can actually rest without her draining you. Just that might be enough to break the oath."

"Peru could hold all the answers," Beth said.

"Nothing is ever that easy," Elsa said. As usual, her few words cut right to the truth.

Everyone started talking at once. Witches debated with the wolves, and I leaned back in my chair, tuning it all out.

It wasn't their decision to make. It was mine. I had to figure it out.

The only other one at the table who was quiet was my cousin. Something told me she knew plenty about these tough decisions. She gave me a little nod, letting me know that she'd support my decision either way.

But I knew she didn't want me to go back to Luciana.

That was the easy route. Maybe not in the long term, but it would solve my immediate problems. Ultimately the cost of going back to her was high.

Peru, on the other hand, was the much harder route. The road less traveled. Literally. It could end up costing me everything, or if it worked and I found what we needed, I could save us all. Save my brother. And stop the witch I'd helped to create.

"I'll do it," I said it softly. The wolves heard me and froze. Turning to me. But my fellow witches didn't have their good hearing. They were still arguing.

I stood up from my chair, and its legs scratched against the floor. "I'll go to Peru with you," I said the words much louder this time so that everyone could hear. The last of the talk quieted.

Muraco nodded. "Wise decision. The journey will be difficult, but you will overcome."

"I hope so." I pushed down the fear that chilled my skin. "I really hope so."

# CHAPTER SEVEN

AFTER I DECIDED TO GO, the group sprang into action. Mr. Dawson ran off to make travel plans for me. Getting a last-minute plane to Peru wasn't an easy feat, especially since I needed to get on Muraco's flight. I didn't much care if I had to sit in the cargo hold. Now that I was going, I wanted to get there. Right away.

Then Meredith brought up the fact that I had nothing to wear but cut off skirts, flip-flops, and peasant shirts. I'd been in such a rush to leave the compound that I'd only brought essentials. Shopping was the last thing I wanted to be doing. I needed to spend as much time with my brother as possible before I left, but I had to be prepared for this trip. I couldn't hike the Andes in worn-through leather sandals.

After a quick trip into town, I had a fancy new backpack, running shoes, thick socks, and all the warm clothes I could foresee needing. Now I sat on the floor in my room at St. Ailbe's, trying to pack. The werewolves didn't restrict Internet access like the coven did, so I'd read a quick article on how to best pack a backpack. I'd never done anything like this before. Hell, until a few days ago, I'd hardly left the compound.

Apparently, rolling the clothes was the best way to get everything to fit. It seemed like a good idea, but the way I did the rolling, it wasn't working. If anything, the lumpy rolls took up more space. I let out a frustrated growl as I shook out the pair of pants in my hands and tried rolling them for the fourth time. Everything seemed lumpy this way, but what did I know about packing and going on trips?

I just needed to get this done already so I could go check on Raphael. I didn't have time to pack and repack this stuff over and over.

Someone knocked on my door. "Come in," I said, and looked over my shoulder.

Teresa peeked in. "Hey. Thought I'd see how it was going."

I dropped the pants I was trying to roll. "Horribly." I surveyed the mess in front of me. "I'm not sure I can fit all this inside. I've tried to whittle it down to necessities, but..." The plan was a little on the vague side, so I had to be ready for almost anything.

Teresa settled down on the floor next to me. "Can I help?"

"Please." I waved my hand over the pile of stuff. "I'm getting nowhere."

Teresa took the pants and started rolling them. Somehow they ended up in a tight log without a single lump.

"How'd you do that?"

"Practice. Axel was a Boy Scout for a hot minute." She snorted. "Anyhow, Dad worked long hours and couldn't take time off to go on weekend camping trips, so Mom went with him. I was too little to be left alone, so I was forced along. Not that I wanted to go. Nope. I like bathrooms with running water and bug-free beds. But some things stuck with me. Mostly packing and marshmallow toasting."

Wow. Boy Scout. I hadn't pictured her brother as someone

who'd get into that kind of stuff. "So you went camping but you didn't like it?"

"Exactly." She paused. "You're right. It's not all going to fit, but you don't need all this underwear."

Was she nuts? One week gone meant nine pairs—just in case I wanted to freshen up at night. And that was shorting myself a few pairs. I wasn't going around dirty. "No. I need these."

"This may sound gross, but if you're at a hotel, wash 'em in the sink. And if not, wear each pair twice. Once inside out." My face must've shown my disgust with her suggestion. "Trust me. You don't want to carry more than you have to. Every ounce counts."

I nearly laughed at how ridiculous this was. Even when it came to something as simple as packing, my cousin was so much better at it than I was. I'd feel more confident if she were going with me. "Are you sure you don't want to go, too?"

"No way. I got cornered into staying at the compound, but there's no way in hell I'm leaving St. Ailbe's again. I feel safer when I'm here. Even if we're constantly on watch, I have my pack. And there's no way I'm going anywhere without Dastien. Not only would he flip, but I don't want to be without him. He's my safety blanket, and after what happened, I need him."

I'd been so caught up in everything that had happened, I kept forgetting to check how Teresa was faring. When she was around Dastien, she seemed fine. Strong. But then times like this, she looked so fragile. Like if I breathed on her too hard, she might break.

Guilt weighed me down. Luciana had used some really dark magic to strip Teresa of her powers. She'd drawn Teresa's magic into little jars, using the energy to fuel her spells and summon demons from the underworld. I couldn't help but feel responsible. I'd needed her help, so I'd manipulated her to get her back on coven land any way I could. I'd told Luciana about the planned Full Moon Ceremony. It was my fault she and Dastien weren't fully bonded. My fault her powers had gotten stripped. My fault she didn't feel safe anymore. I hadn't intended for her to get hurt. I thought I had it under control. I thought I was looking out for her, but I'd never thought Luciana would go so far. But I'd been wrong. And Teresa had paid the price.

"You shouldn't second guess yourself," I said.

"I could've done a lot of things differently, but I was so focused on taking Luciana down that I didn't stop to think everything through like I should've." She grabbed a shirt and started rolling it. "Anyway, even with all this baggage, I thought about going with you, but right before I went to bed last night I had a little premonition. Vision. Whatever." She huffed. "I guess talking to you about being blocked loosened something. I was lying there with Dastien, thinking about everything, and... Well, it was a little one, but it was just enough to show me that if I go to Peru, bad things happen. It has to be you." She grinned and I was suddenly scared. That grin meant nothing but trouble. "Plus, I have a *feeling* you're going to meet someone there."

She had to be joking. "Please. I'll be too busy trying to find some possibly nonexistent mages—who *might* have the answer to saving my brother and defeating whatever Luciana conjures next—to breath, let alone time enough to flirt with anyone." The idea was ludicrous. "Trust me. Romance isn't anywhere on my radar." Especially when I was wearing my underwear twice.

"Are you saying that because of the douche bag?"

"No." That hadn't even entered my mind. Even after talking to him last night. "Honestly, there's only so much room in my brain. All I can focus on right now is finding the mages and getting back here as quickly as possible." Sure, I wanted what Teresa and Dastien had, but that was a useless daydream right now.

One day, it'd be my turn. But I had a lot to accomplish before then.

"I still say keep your eyes open. You never know what you might find."

"Maybe," I said to appease her and end this pointless conversation.

Another knock came at the door. "Can I join you?" Cosette said as she peeked around the doorframe. Her aura shone so bright I could almost see her pearly sparkle through the wall. "I need something to do."

I wished that lending me some of all that power was considered "something to do," but I couldn't waste time wishing for the impossible. Cosette had her own problems, and as tempting as it was I shouldn't expect her to put everything aside to fix mine. "Have a seat," I said.

Teresa's gaze followed her as she moved across the room. "Getting bored under the constant threat of attack?"

"Hardly." Cosette waved a hand as she plopped down on my bed. "That part makes me feel right at home."

"Well, don't get too comfortable," Teresa said. Her tone was surprisingly firm. "Mr. Dawson and the rest of the Seven have been looking for you all over campus. They want to talk."

"Which is why I've been avoiding them." Cosette tilted her head to the side as if brushing off the most powerful alpha wolves in the world was a perfectly reasonable thing to do.

"Why? If you can help us—"

"When the time is right." Cosette gripped the edge of the bed so hard her knuckles whitened. She was finally showing a little of what must be her real thoughts.

"You can't stay on the sidelines forever." Teresa crossed her arms as she stared down Cosette. She looked more than a little annoyed with the fey. "Not with what's coming."

That thought made me swallow hard. The evil wasn't coming. It was already here. Daniel was proof of that.

So was Raphael.

"I wasn't planning to." Cosette let out a heavy breath. "But I do what the queen says or I pay the price. For now, just think of me as an objective observer. Later..." She waved her fingers, letting us interpret her trailing words how we wanted. "Well, we'll see about later."

"What about your coven?" Maybe she was tied on the fey side, but the wolves would need more than the handful of us to fight Luciana and the allies she was probably gathering right now. Any help they could send would be better than nothing.

"They worship the queen." She shrugged. "They're not going to risk pissing her off."

A coven loyal to the fey? I'd never heard of such a thing.

"That's not normal, right?" Teresa turned from Cosette to me. "I'm still brushing up on this whole magic thing, but I thought *brujas* pretty much kept to themselves."

"We usually do." It was what I'd been taught. Most things didn't like what our magic could do to them. Covens kept in touch, but our ancestors had been hunted and burned for so long that keeping secret seemed the only way to stay safe. I'd never considered there being another way.

It gave me hope that Muraco wasn't totally insane with his stories about the ancient supernaturals mixing. If fey and witches could get along, then why not witches and wolves?

There was every possibility that the mages still existed in Peru. And if they existed, I'd find them. I had to.

"Either way, Mr. Dawson wants to—" Teresa's head tilted to the side and her aura flashed with bits of amber. There was no missing the change in her as her eyes slipped out of focus. She was busy talking to Dastien through their bond.

No matter how often I saw it, it surprised me. The *brujas*

didn't have anything like that. Our marriages were more human and normal than the mate bonds the werewolves had. Witches got married, divorced, cheated. I'd be lucky to click on more than one level with a guy.

Teresa stood up, dusting off her hands. "Duty calls. It seems the boys have found something in the woods."

I swallowed and took a breath before speaking. "Luciana?"

"Dastien isn't sure. He's in wolf form, so he's not communicating very well, but he says it smells bad."

"Bad?"

She shrugged. "It could mean anything." She pointed to the next pair of pants in my pile. "Just lay them on the floor and make them as flat as possible before you start rolling."

"Got it. Thanks."

"Yell if you need anything." She hurried out, already distracted.

When I was sure she was far enough away that she wouldn't overhear, I finally spoke. "Would it help you if I told her what I suspect about you?"

"I don't know." Cosette leaned forward. "What do you suspect?"

"That you're more than you say you are." I doubted "objective observer" touched the surface. She always introduced herself as part fey, but it finally struck me that she'd never said which part. I'd just assumed half or less. Part could mean ninety-nine percent. Or part fey and something else that wasn't necessarily human.

She smiled. "I could say the same of you."

I almost laughed. "Right."

"Don't worry about me and Tess." Cosette patted my shoulder and a bit of her energy crackled against me. Her power seemed bright and tranquil when I felt exactly the opposite. "If my plans work the way I hope... Maybe we'll be BFFs by the time you get back."

I wished I had that confidence. "Sometimes, I don't even know if she likes me."

"Claudia." Cosette dropped the curl she'd been playing with. "Everyone likes you."

I tried to roll up the pants, failed, and tried again. "That's in no way true. Plenty of people don't like me."

"Name one person."

"Jemma."

"One *person*." Cosette flopped down on the bed, somehow making the movement elegant as she propped her head on her hands. "Not one comically jealous witch. She just wants Matt and, honestly, you should ship him back to her already. You're too good for both of them."

I'd been trying to do just that. I hoped that last night would get the message through and he wouldn't try to contact me again. "I did my best. I was probably ruder than I should've been." I flattened out a shirt and started rolling. "Teresa has a *feeling* I'm going to meet someone in Peru. How absurd is that? I'm trying to save my brother's life, not date."

"She might be onto something." Her aura glittered to the point that I thought some fey magic was starting to work, but it settled too fast to follow. Maybe that was just Cosette being Cosette. "I know I haven't been able to admit to much, but I always told you I had a form of Sight. You witches just assume that means seeing the future."

Didn't it? "What do you see about me?"

Cosette stared at me until I had to swallow down nerves. Maybe it was better not to know.

"The red string of fate. You'll find your destined person..." Cosette's voice dropped, turning more serious than I'd ever heard it. I wanted to hope, but I knew the bad news was coming.

"But I'm worried about your oath to Luciana. That tie could strangle you if you're not careful."

I couldn't get excited about a destined person when I was so worried about keeping myself and the people I cared about alive. "I'll figure out how to break it. It will be easier in Peru." And I said a quick prayer that I wasn't just trying to convince myself.

"I... Ugh." Cosette wrinkled her nose and said something in a language I'd never heard before. The words were beautifully fluid, but I could tell she was cursing. That much was universal. "I want to help. I really want to. I can't make any promises without binding myself, but I'll try. I don't want to see you getting hurt."

"I wouldn't want you getting yourself into trouble." Even though I was terrified of what might happen, I'd made the oath. I'd known the road I was heading down and the consequences were mine to bear.

"That's why I'm offering. It's easy enough to ask the little folk to watch over you, but be careful if you ask them for favors. If they follow the old ways, they'll try to take you for whatever they can get."

"Thank—"

"Claudia." Cosette held up a hand. "Chill with the human manners. If you're asking for something, bargain hard and make sure you know exactly what you're agreeing to. Never imply that you owe anything."

"Got it." I nodded, grateful even if she wouldn't let me say it.

"Good. Although depending how things play out these next few days, maybe I'll come running after you." She let out a sigh that sounded like a spring breeze. "Getting mixed up with the wolves is changing everything for both of us."

That was an understatement. I'd seldom left home before

and suddenly I was flying off to a foreign country, trusting the wolves to keep me safe, while I searched for ancient magic...

I said another prayer, hoping I had the strength to do this. Raphael's life depended on it.

Cosette might be worried I'd make an unfair bargain, but I was very close to being desperate. If it came to it, I was willing to give up anything that could save my brother. To save what was left of my coven and the wolves.

If I failed, Luciana's black magic would spread through all our supernatural worlds. Not even normal humans would be safe if demons came into being.

I'd do anything to stop that from happening.

# CHAPTER EIGHT

THAT NIGHT I couldn't sleep at all. Call it nerves or fear—from the effects of the oath or the upcoming trip or the fact that I was sitting beside my still unconscious brother. Or all of the above. I just couldn't relax enough to make myself actually sleep. I'd said all my good-byes at dinner, and the morning would be just Muraco and me. I'd start this journey on my own —the same way I'd finish it.

My mother had always told me to picture what I wanted; if I believed it to be true, it would happen. I'd been doing that all night as I sat in the chair beside Raphael's bed.

He hadn't woken up yet. No one knew what that meant, but it couldn't be a good sign. His exhale had taken on a rasping rattle that made my lungs burn in sympathy. But that wasn't the worst part.

His aura was changing. It was usually blue and purple with touches of white. Now, it was turning a muddy brown. It was like his soul was slowly disappearing. I'd cried a little at first, but as time ticked by I grew more and more determined.

I'd go. Find the magic I needed to save my brother and

defeat Luciana. Use the distance to figure out how to break Luciana's hold on me.

My backpack sat at my feet. I'd stuffed it until I could barely get the flap closed. I was showered. My hair was braided. I was as ready as I'd ever be.

When I shook off the sleepless trance long enough to check the time, I realized it had gotten away from me. Muraco would be here any minute now, and this might be the last time I saw my brother alive.

*No.* I stood up and paced away from the bed. I rested my forehead against the cool wall, trying to calm down but failing.

I couldn't think like that. I had to fix this. There was no other choice.

A soft tap sounded at the door just before five in the morning. I brushed my sweating palms on my jeans.

"Are you ready, child?" Muraco said as soon as I opened the door. His white hair stood out brightly against his darkly tanned, wrinkled skin. He was tall, but walked with a little bit of a hunch. His golden aura had threads of darker oranges and reds running through it. Most of the wolves here had very one-note auras, but his was rich and varied. The deeper highlights told me he was special. He had to be much stronger than he looked. And much, much older.

"Yes, sir."

He huffed and turned, heading down the hallway.

I leaned over my brother and kissed his clammy forehead. "Hang in there for me. Don't you dare give up."

With that, I hoisted my pack and started after Muraco. When I reached the door, I didn't dare look back.

The next time I saw Raphael, I'd be handing him the cure he needed.

A black SUV was idling in the parking lot. I didn't know which Cazador had to take us to the airport, but I felt a little bad about the early hour. I could've driven. I had a license. Not that I used it much... But I had it.

"You will do this," Muraco said when I got in the car.

I placed my backpack between my feet and buckled in. "Of course." I stared out the window as the car began to move.

*So long,* I thought to myself as the driver sped out of St. Ailbe's parking lot. Only the unknown lay ahead of me. Even with all my worry, there was hope. I just had to hold on to that feeling and not let go.

BY THE TIME we landed in Cusco, I was ready to be done traveling. It'd taken two flights and most of the day. Since Mr. Dawson had to get my ticket so last minute, I was at the back of the plane, while Muraco was at the front. I didn't mind, but now I was anxious. In all the rush, we hadn't coordinated where we'd meet after this last leg of our journey.

At least I'd found a new hope to latch on to. As soon as we'd taken off in San Antonio, I'd felt my oath to Luciana start thinning

I'd let sleep take me in the middle of the first flight, but I'd been in the aisle seat. The guy in the middle seat hadn't liked it when my head rested on his shoulder and he couldn't wake me. He'd been pretty upset.

Since I was on the aisle again for the second leg of the trip, I fought sleep the whole way from Lima to Cusco. I didn't want to cause another scene, but a handful of hours of sleep in the past few days made it extremely difficult to keep my eyes open. Thankfully, it wasn't a long flight.

I waited to exit my aisle, holding only my small purse. I texted Teresa quickly and then shut the phone off as the roaming warnings started buzzing in. I'd borrowed Raphael's cell, but I would pay the bill. It would be expensive if I wasn't extremely careful. I looked past the man sitting next to me to stare out the window as I waited for everyone in front to clear the way. The sun was setting outside the airplane window, spreading beautiful pinks and oranges across the sky.

"Ma'am?" the guy sitting next to me said, impatient to get out of the aisle.

"Sorry." I moved too quickly and tripped over my own feet. *Just the way I wanted to start this out.* "Sorry," I mumbled again to no one in particular and started down the aisle.

As soon as I crossed the bridge, the temperature hit me. *Cold.* I held my arms tight to my body. Even the air smelled different here. Thinner and crisper. The crisp part was fine, but the thin quality made it feel like I couldn't take a full breath.

I inhaled deeply, trying to get in more air, and failed. I'd never been at such a high altitude. Muraco had said to be careful and take it easy, but I didn't have time for that. I had to adjust quickly.

I stepped into the terminal and looked around for the old wolf, but Muraco was long gone. I couldn't find a hint of him anywhere. The mass of people moving up and down the areas between gates made it hard to really find anyone. Overhead signs pointed the way to the exit—baggage claim and car services—and I started along my way. At least I'd already gone through customs in Lima.

I searched for Muraco in the crowd ahead, but didn't see him anywhere as I walked forward. He must be waiting for me somewhere outside.

*He'd better be waiting for me somewhere outside.*

I made it to the baggage claim and grabbed my bag, hefting it onto my shoulder before continuing my search for Muraco. The closer I got to the exits, the more chaotic the airport became. Tour guides held up signs trying to get their groups together. Stands advertising different tourist attractions took up space along the walls, crowding me in as workers shouted about deals.

I thought I'd made it out of the worst of the mess when someone shoved a bowl of dried leaves in my face. "Coca leaves. Take some. *Gratis*. Free."

The bowl smelled of earth and something totally unfamiliar and I stepped back on instinct. The lady smiled at me, showing off a few missing teeth. She wore a beautifully embroidered full skirt. Her bright pink cardigan picked up the colors of the thread flowers. Her browned skin was thin and wrinkling, but she kept on smiling at me, holding the bowl, urging me to take what she was offering.

No witch with any common sense would accept unknown herbs from an unknown source. The lady seemed nice, and if she really was offering dried coca leaves, they weren't harmful by themselves, but that was the problem. They could have other herbs mixed in with them or be coated in something else. And even if taking things from strangers at airports wasn't stupid to the nth degree, I didn't know what she wanted me to do with a bunch of dried leaves. They didn't look particularly edible.

Yeah. I wasn't going to go down that road. "No, thank—"

"You should take some, princess," a deep, gravelly voice said from behind me.

*Nope. Not gonna happen.* I opened my mouth to tell that to the speaker, but as soon as I saw him I couldn't breathe.

He was the most gorgeous guy I'd ever seen. He grinned down at me, and I nearly melted on the spot. As it was, I was going to embarrass myself by staring. His hair was black and cut short, but it looked a little messy. Not like he'd spent all morning trying to get it right, but more like it was just naturally like that. Effortlessly handsome.

And his eyes...

They were so dark brown I couldn't see the difference between the iris and pupil. Like twin dark pools. If I wasn't careful, I could get lost in them.

I was inching my gaze down his body, taking in the lovely browned skin, when I finally focused in on his aura. Golden.

A wolf. Of course the mega hot guy was a wolf.

*Which means he's utterly off limits.* It was a good thing. That way I wouldn't be tempted. But as I looked at him, he was more than tempting. I should've been used to Weres after St. Ailbe's, but apparently I wasn't. He'd taken me totally off guard —so much so that I was forgetting to speak.

He cleared his throat and motioned back to the lady. "The leaves. They're dried coca—"

"I know what they are, but isn't cocaine bad? Plus, it's not good to take things from someone you don't know."

He laughed and I held my breath, not wanting to cover that beautiful sound. He picked a couple leaves out of the bowl. "Cocaine happens when you do all kinds of awful things to the plant, but this—" he held them up for me to see "—is natural. Helps with the altitude. If you're feeling dizzy or short of breath, then chew on the leaves, just let them rest in your mouth, or steep them into a tea. It's a local remedy." He stuck one into his mouth and chewed. "See? Perfectly safe."

I was definitely feeling dizzy and short of breath, but I couldn't say for sure if it was because of the altitude. "I'm fine."

He grinned, showing off a perfect row of pearly whites. "If you say so," he said as he moved past me toward the exit.

I stayed there, standing still as everyone else moved around me. I couldn't take my eyes off his back as he wove through the chaos, never bumping anyone, moving straight and confident.

My exact opposite.

The lady still stood there expectantly, so I took a handful of leaves against my better judgment and shoved them into my pocket for later as I thanked her.

When I turned back to the exit, my eyes found him again. He was looking back at me. Was I supposed to follow him? Did he know Muraco, or did he just enjoy watching my awkwardness?

I straightened my shirt, suddenly self-conscious. He winked and my cheeks grew hot as he disappeared through the exit.

*Way to play it cool, Claudia. I adjusted my backpack and started walking again. Next time you come across a guy like that, just move on. You've got things to do here. Raphael is counting on you.*

*And great. I'm talking to myself. In my head. Again. But still. Off to a great start.*

As soon as I passed through the sliding doors, the cool breeze hit my face. The air was noticeably thinner, making me feel seriously out of shape. I was no Teresa, but I forced myself to do cardio DVDs a few times a week. Apparently, that wasn't enough to survive Cusco. The leaves were in my pocket... But still, I couldn't put them in my mouth. Who knew where they came from?

I scanned the parking lot of the tiny airport. It was getting dark, and a sea of people milled. Some were picking up loved ones. Others were tour participants. Cab drivers shouted as they offered the rest cheap rides to hotels.

Where in the hell was Muraco?

I couldn't afford to mess this up. I didn't have time for this. I needed to get started looking for these mages.

Stupid. So stupid. I should've planned more. Asked more questions. He'd mentioned a hotel, but I had no idea what it was called. Was I supposed to get there on my own?

I should've convinced Teresa to come with me. She'd know what to do.

"You okay, child?" Muraco said, startling me.

My heart jumped into my throat for a second. The wolves were always sneaking up on me. I shouldn't flinch every time someone talked to me when I thought I was totally alone, but the reaction wasn't so easy to control.

*Thank God he hasn't left yet.* "Yes. I'm fine."

Muraco stood with a group of guys. They all wore jeans and fleeces. Most had a bit of shadow to their beards. From the way they watched me, it seemed like they were assessing me. Understandable. I was an unknown *bruja*.

All of the staring made me a little uncomfortable. They were so handsome that they made me feel self-conscious. They could definitely make a calendar of Peruvian hunks. Or more accurately, Peruvian werewolves. I knew Cosette would buy one.

As I took them in, my head started pounding. This time, I hoped it was from the altitude. I rubbed my temples in slow circles.

"Try the coca leaves. They'll help," said the hot guy from earlier. Even next to the calendar men, he stood out. His aura was so bright that if I looked too closely it felt like staring into the sun. With all that gold, he'd be a summer month for sure.

Mr. July?

"I'm fine," I repeated as I tried to stop with the delusions and focus on Muraco. The sooner I got to my hotel, the sooner I could get comfortable.

Muraco nodded. "This way."

The hot guy kept pace beside Muraco as I trailed behind. The rest of wolves spread out, surrounding us. As we wove through parked cars, an unusual gray and pink aura caught the corner of my eye. I tripped over my feet, and the hot guy caught my elbow.

*Oh no. It can't be...* I scanned the area as I gained my feet again, frantically looking for what I knew couldn't be there. I hadn't said anything to Matt on the phone about Peru. Had I?

I'd lost my temper, so maybe I had. But I didn't think so.

No. It couldn't be him. I was exhausted and seeing things. There was no way he could've made it here from New York faster than I had.

The guy shook my elbow, gaining my attention again. His eyebrows bunched together, forming a crease. "Are you sure you're okay?"

"I thought I..." I paused. No. It wasn't possible. "I'm sorry. Must be tired from all the travel."

Mr. July studied me for a second before nodding slowly, but from the expression on his face there was no way he was buying it. *Right. Werewolves can smell lies.* Thankfully, he didn't push me for a better answer.

"Let's get you to the hotel," his words were soft, almost like he was worried I'd break.

I smiled weakly at him. "Don't worry. I just haven't been getting much sleep lately. I'm sure I'll be right as rain in the morning." That wasn't a total lie. "I'm okay, though. Really." That was a half-lie, which meant it was also half-truth. I wasn't sure if it would "smell" right, but it was the best I could do.

"Mmm-hmm," he said as he guided me toward a group of silver vans.

One more glance over my shoulder confirmed that I'd been imagining things. I hadn't seen him. He didn't know I was here. No one knew but the wolves and my friends.

My hands shook as I tried to get my backpack off. One of the other wolves tried to help me with it, but one look from Mr. July and he disappeared into another van.

*What the...*

Mr. July stepped behind me, lifting my backpack easily from my shoulders.

*Why not let the other guy help?* Even after my stint at St. Ailbe's, wolves still baffled me sometimes.

"Hop in." He motioned toward one of the vans. The other wolves were climbing into the vans on either side of us, but Muraco got into the center van. I followed his lead, sliding onto the bench seat next to him.

The drool-worthy one threw my pack in the back of the van as I sat down and busied myself with buckling my seat belt.

Mr. July slid the van door shut and I jumped. I grasped my chest and then laughed softly at myself as he got into the passenger seat in front of me.

I was losing it. Imagining Matt here. The combination of high altitude and no sleep was a killer. A good twelve hours of shut-eye and everything would be okay.

For a second I relaxed back into my seat, and then I realized where I was. In Peru. With a bunch of wolves and not a witch or coven member in sight should I need one.

I glanced at the four wolves in the van with me. I sure hoped none of them were biters. Because as much as Teresa said she liked her new way of life, I really, really didn't want to be a werewolf.

Trusting these wolves would either be my salvation or turn out epically bad. With as much bad as I'd had thus far, I hoped I was swinging toward the good. But something told me I might not be so lucky.

Mr. July turned in his seat and gave me a wink.

*Maybe being a wolf wouldn't be so bad...*

He grinned, as if he could read my mind, and my cheeks grew hot. Then he started full-on laughing as he turned back to face the road.

*Oh boy, I'm in so much trouble.*

# CHAPTER NINE

CUSCO FELT OLD. Not like any place in Texas—with its freshly paved roads and new buildings. The ancient stone streets rattled the tires on the van. The tiny roads felt even tinier with the buildings crowding in against them. There was barely enough room for cars to pass, and with added pedestrians, I was convinced we were going to hit something—or someone—before we made it to our destination.

We cut through a little courtyard that was all lit up—it had to be the town center. A Catholic church took up one portion of the square. I made a note of it. I loved to sit in old churches. I didn't pray that often, but my soul felt quiet and relaxed in them. A fountain stood in the center of the square. Spouts of water flowed down from the top feature—a bronze man holding some sort of scepter.

People crossed into the street without looking and tourists and locals mixed together, enjoying the early night. It was nice to see so many people filling the square. The town felt alive. Vibrant. If my head weren't pounding with a headache, I would've asked to be let out here and walk the rest of the way. It was a shame just to pass it by.

"Almost there, princess," Mr. July said from the passenger seat.

"Princess?"

He turned just enough so that I could see his face. "I call it like I see it."

"Great," I muttered. He thought I was a spoiled rich girl. I was neither rich nor spoiled. Was that really the vibe I gave off? Maybe I'd been rude to him back at the airport?

Well, I couldn't change what must have been a bad first impression, but I could help how I acted from here on out. I had no idea what to call him. Something told me he wouldn't appreciate being called Peruvian Hottie. "We were never introduced properly. I'm Claudia de Santos. And you all are?"

"Pedrico," said the wolf sitting in the seat behind me.

"Andrés," said the wolf who was driving.

But Mr. July hadn't answered yet. "And what's your name?"

"Lucas," he said simply.

"Lucas?" I wasn't sure why, but it didn't fit him. Usually the name fit in with the aura. But not his. He felt more...handsome? No, that wasn't it. Regal? Not quite right. More something...

"Yup." He paused. "Why don't you believe me?"

I hadn't realized I was broadcasting my emotions. "I guess I figured you're Peruvian. Shouldn't you have a name more exotic than Luke?"

"No one calls me Luke. Ever."

I grinned, and it probably looked a little evil. Now I knew exactly what I was going to call him. Why I got so much fun out of playing on people's names, I had no idea. But, when given the opportunity, I couldn't help myself. "So, Luke. Where are we headed?"

He muttered something that I couldn't hear, but Muraco could. The old man started laughing—the sound was loud and wheezing—and the other two wolves in the car followed suit.

"What? What did he say?"

Muraco and Lucas—who were nowhere near the same age—looked at each other and started laughing harder. "Boys." Didn't matter how old they were, they were all the same. I leaned back in the seat and closed my eyes for a second, rubbing my temples. Being over two miles up was no joke.

We turned down what couldn't be considered anything other than an alley, and Andrés parked.

"Here you go," Lucas said.

The hotel looked nondescript from the outside. Only two large wooden doors—as tall as the first story of the three-story building—marked its entrance. A little placard to the side read Hotel de los Siete Cruzes.

*Finally. A place to stay still for a little bit.*

I hopped down from the van as Lucas grabbed my backpack. Muraco hadn't gotten out. The fear I'd felt when I thought he left me at the airport still lingered in the back of my mind. Being lost in a foreign country wasn't appealing in the least. I needed a little direction. A place to start my journey.

I cleared my throat as I stood in the open door. "So, uh, what...umm...tomorrow..."

He leaned forward and patted my cheek. "Don't worry, child. Andrés will be back—"

"I'll take her," Lucas said in Spanish.

"I thought you had things to do," Andrés said, also in Spanish.

I nearly laughed. They didn't know I could speak the language.

"Things have changed," Lucas said with a hint of growl in his voice.

What had changed? Was he reading me as some kind of threat?

Muraco's gaze met mine and he grinned. "Boys. The girl speaks perfect Spanish."

"Way to spill the secret," I muttered, and Muraco's grin turned into a laugh.

They switched to another language, whispering fast. It didn't take long before Muraco's grin faded and he joined in.

What on earth was going on?

Finally Muraco cleared his throat. "It seems that Lucas will be your guide during your stay."

*Mr. July was going to be my guide? No.* That wasn't going to work. "Are you sure? I mean, I'm okay with Andrés if that's easier."

"Eight a.m.," Lucas said, still growling a little. He came around carrying my backpack like it weighed nothing, but his voice softened. "Don't be late." He handed me the pack, and I nearly dropped it. I had for sure overpacked.

"He's not to interfere, but to help. Protect. The mountains are full of dangers," Muraco said. "This task is yours alone."

"Right," I muttered. No one knew more than I did what was at stake. If Lucas was going to be my guide, I'd make it work. And I'd focus every second on the image of my brother in that awful bed. "I'll be ready in the lobby before eight. Thank you very much for your help."

"Try the broth soup. It's good here. Especially if you're adjusting to the altitude." Lucas got back into the passenger seat as I slid the van door closed. "And try the coca tea." Andrés honked twice and then took off.

I was left staring at the entrance to the hotel. *Oh crap.* I didn't have a credit card. All the travel blogs said you needed a credit card for hotels. I'd thought Muraco would be staying here, too, but that was dumb. Of course he'd go with the pack. And I couldn't stay with an unknown pack any more than they'd want to host an unknown witch.

*It's fine. I'll figure this out. No big deal. Mr. Dawson had sent me on my way with a good amount of crisp Sol bills. Maybe they'll let me prepay for the night.*

I stood there, running through various scenarios, before I mustered up the courage to go inside. *No time like the present, Claudia.*

As soon as I stepped into the foyer, my breath caught. The entrance was ornately decorated, and huge wooden sculptures of howling wolves stood at either side of the door. A round marble-topped table decked with an elaborate flower arrangement took up the center of the lobby, and one wall had a fireplace surrounded by tables and chairs. The little sofas looked so plush that I could sink into one and fall asleep right then and there.

A woman looked up at me as I stepped to the check-in desk. "Checking in?" she asked in rapid Spanish.

I nodded. Being out of my element was making it hard for me to find my voice. I wasn't even on the same continent as my comfort zone.

"Name and passport, please."

"Oh. Right." I fumbled to get my passport out of my purse for her as the hotel's front door opened. A cold burst of wind hit my back, but I was too busy searching my seemingly bottomless bag to turn around.

"There you are," a voice said behind me. "You nearly lost me for a second when you left the airport. Thank God I already had my rental."

Everything went still for a second. It was like the world paused to take a breath while I cringed in horror.

*Oh no.* I squeezed my eyes shut. I was right. I did know that aura. It was one I'd never forget.

I finally found my passport and slid it across the counter to the woman.

AILEEN ERIN

"I flew all day to catch up with you. How could you leave the country without telling me?"

And that was it. There was no denying it. I couldn't stop my sigh. Even the sound of his voice aggravated me, but I was too tired to really fight with him. I shifted the pack on my shoulders as I turned toward him.

When I first met Mathieu, I'd thought his tall, lanky stature was handsome. Maybe he was a little too skinny for me—I didn't much like the idea of my future husband being thinner than I was—but he was a good-looking guy. His skin was tanned. His light brown hair had golden, sun-bleached highlights running through it. He liked to play sports in the summer, and always ended up looking like a beach dude, even though he lived in New York.

Now, whenever I really looked at him, I'd notice his hair had too much product in it, making it look greasy. And his pointy nose and eerie light green eyes reminded me of a snake. An upright cobra, getting ready to strike. Because he would strike. And when he did, my confidence would pay the price.

*Not today, Claudia. You're stronger now. You're not under Luciana's thumb anymore.* "I wasn't aware that I had to ask your permission."

"Maybe not my permission, but Luciana's."

That caught my attention. A sliver of icy fear ran down my spine. "How did she know I was here?"

He shrugged. "Does it matter?"

It most certainly did.

"She called me last night to tell me, and I hopped on the first flight out. I can't believe I beat you here."

I swallowed down the panic that threatened to take over. I couldn't let Matt see how afraid I was, but the knowledge made me cold. There was a spy at St. Ailbe's. Yvonne and the others

90

had all left the coven of their own accord. But they could be spies.

Or it was possible that a wolf who'd been involved in the attempted pack takeover was still backing Luciana. Either way, I needed to get to my room. I had to call Teresa and warn her. But first I had to somehow get rid of Matt.

"I'll give it to you, I never thought you'd go against Luciana. You're more ambitious than I thought." The way he leered at me made me want to puke.

"I'm not asking Luciana's permission for anything. Like I told you on the phone, I want nothing to do with her."

He crossed his arms and stared at me down his long, straight nose. "Breaking from her is dangerous."

I jiggled the backpack. "I know." He didn't have to remind me. I was on zero hours of sleep thanks to that stupid oath, and if I didn't do something about it, I'd die. And if I didn't find a way to fix my brother, he'd die, too. She was systematically destroying my whole family. No one knew how dangerous she was better than me.

The woman at the front desk cleared her throat. "Your room is ready. Señor Reyes has arranged everything already." I made a mental note to find out who that was and thank him as she slid a little envelope to me. "Room number is written inside." She glanced to Mathieu and back to me quickly.

I could've kissed her. Matt didn't need to know my room number. "Thank you." I grabbed the envelope, holding it close to my chest, and turned to Matt. "I'm going to my room now. Good night. Safe travels back to New York." *And please take a hint for once.*

Unfortunately, Matt's listening skills were as terrible as always. When I started down the hall, he did, too. *I couldn't keep going on like this with him.* I took a deep breath before squaring my shoulders to face him. "Look, Matt. I know you've come a long way, and I'm sorry for that. I didn't tell you I was coming, and I certainly don't remember inviting you. I know I mentioned our sham of an engagement was off. So, I have no idea why you're here or what you want but I can't give it to you and you can't follow me around expecting me to change my mind. If that's your plan, then you should go home now and save yourself a huge headache." I was proud of myself. I was keeping calm and being mature. Not usually my first reaction when he was around.

"No. If you wanted to be away from Luciana before, then you could've said something. I could've helped you. Whatever's going on with you, you're acting irrationally, and I'm not leaving you unwatched."

*Unwatched?* How had I ever thought this guy was nice?

I kept walking in what I hoped was the opposite direction of my room. Leading him right to it would be a mistake I couldn't afford. "Good-bye, Matt. I hope I don't ever see you again." I was exhausted and under so much pressure that I didn't have the patience to placate him. And for once, I didn't really care.

I started walking again, but he grabbed my arm and spun me toward him. "I didn't travel all this way to get blown off."

"And again, I didn't ask you to come." I gripped my hands into fists as I tried to get control of my frustration with the douche bag. Time had taught me that reacting in anger did no good. Especially with him.

He narrowed his gaze as he jerked me toward him. The weight of my backpack threw me off balance and I collapsed against him. "You're mine. If you think you're traipsing off to God only knows where, doing God only knows what, without someone to make sure you don't do anything stupid, then you're not as smart as I thought you were. From here on out, I'll be your shadow."

He'd lost his mind. He'd been overbearing before, but this was controlling to an extreme. I pushed him away, freeing myself from his grasp. I stumbled a few steps as I tried to balance the backpack. "What I'm doing here has nothing to do with you."

"Everything you do includes me."

He was insane. Had I not been clear enough with him? "We're not married. Not bound to each other. You don't get to—"

"Not yet. But we will be married. You'd better think how you want the rest of your life to go." He spat the last.

*Toe the line, and you'll have a future with me. Or don't and see what happens.* He hadn't said the words, but they hung there in the silence between us all the same.

I clunked into the wall behind me. Without my realizing it, he'd cornered me.

"*¿Está bien, señorita?*" A voice called from down the hall. I peeked over at the janitor, and he started for us, ready to rescue a lady. He spoke quietly into his walkie-talkie.

"That man is coming over here, and he's bringing help. If you don't let me go, you're going to cause a scene." Thank goodness. If there was one thing that Matt hated, it was being caught doing something "improper."

Matt's face turned red with barely contained anger. His hands shook as he took a step back. "I'll see you in the morning." With that lingering threat, he started back down the hall.

I slouched against the wall in relief as he finally disappeared around the corner.

"*¿Señorita?*" the man said, coming closer.

I took a few deep breaths and nodded at the janitor. "*Estoy bien. Gracias por su ayuda.*"

"*De nada.*" The man left, and I was alone in the hall. At last.

I opened the envelope to actually look at the room number. I had to get to my room and call Teresa. Warn them about the spy. I wished I could be there to help. If I'd brought someone into St. Ailbe's who could harm her... I'd done enough to her already.

I rushed down the corridor, hoping it wasn't too late to get word to her before real damage was done.

IT TOOK me way too long to figure out how to call internationally. I felt a little dumb by the end of it, but a quick question to the lovely lady at the front desk, and the phone was ringing.

"Hello?" Teresa's voice was clear.

"It's Claudia."

"Is everything okay?"

"Yeah. I'm fine. I think." I shook my head. "That's not why I'm calling. You remember the guy I'm engaged to?"

She snickered. "The douche bag you told off the other night. Yeah, I remember. Why?"

Why she thought it was so funny when I said those words, I'll never know. "He's here."

"He's what?" Her voice shifted from calm and relaxed to stressed in a split second. "Please, tell me that's a coincidence."

"I'm sorry. Luciana told him I was coming, and he managed to beat me all the way from New York."

"More direct flights," Teresa muttered. "Okay. So, what do you think? Is it a wash? Should you come home? We can figure out something else. Do some more digging in the library. I'm sure if we put our heads together we'll find something that can save Raphael. Maybe we should've tried harder before shipping you off, but it seemed like the easiest way to save him..."

*This was the easy way?* "No. Muraco's right. I've never

learned a thing about fighting demons and I grew up with *La Aquelarre.* It's been my life forever. Maybe Luciana has something in her spell room, but—"

"No one is going in there. Never ever."

It wasn't safe, which was why I hadn't suggested it. Teresa was the last person who'd snooped in there, and she'd ended up stripped of her powers and almost killed. "I'd never ask that of you. But I could—"

"No. We both know she's after your powers. She managed to strip me of mine, and now that you've left she wants yours just as bad. You can't go anywhere near her." She was quiet for a second. "I don't like the sound of this douche bag being in Peru with you."

"I know. But we all agreed. This is the best chance we have to save Raphael and stop Luciana."

"Right. Well, stay away from him."

"Thanks. I'll be okay. I've protected myself from Matt for years, but his being here isn't a good sign. I wanted to warn you. I'm not sure who is spying on us, but..." I hated to admit it was a possibility, but Teresa needed to know. "Maybe look into Beth, Tiffany, and Yvonne."

"Yeah, I had the same thought. But Dastien and Mr. Dawson talked to them when they showed up. If they were anything but genuine, one of them would've smelled a lie."

That both made sense and was a huge relief.

"There are a few wolves who aren't acting right. They should be following Mr. Dawson's orders, but they're being shifty."

I laughed. "They are shifters."

"Yeah. Yeah. Bad use of the word." The sound of her sigh came through the receiver. "I don't want you to worry, but Raphael—"

"He didn't... He's not..." My heart stopped as I waited for her to answer the question that I couldn't ask.

"No. He's still alive."

I let out a heavy breath. "Thank God."

"He's hanging in, but he's looking a lot worse tonight than he did this morning. You just do your best, and then come home fast. I've got a feeling if you're not back soon, well... I'm not sure what you'll come back to."

I leaned back against the pillows. "I know. I'm going to move as fast as I can."

"The thing is... He's fading faster than Dr. Gonzales expected. I'm wondering if it might make sense to get him to you. That way, by the time you find his cure, he's there. She says we can't put him on a plane—he's not stable enough for that—but I can get a few wolves and maybe a couple of your *brujos* to drive him down to Peru. It'll take a few days but could work out timewise. Then, once he's okay, you all fly back together."

That made sense. "Who would drive him down?"

"Adrian and Shane for sure. And then I was thinking maybe Beth, and one or two more wolves. I have to see who else might be up for it. Who we can spare right now."

"Okay. I agree. Drive him down and I'll move as quickly as I can."

"Just stay safe, Claudia. You can do this. I know you can. Call me if you need anything."

"Same to you. I'll be in touch as soon as I have more information. Call me if anything changes with Raphael."

"Of course."

"'Bye."

I relaxed back onto the bed made up with a mix of colorfully patterned pillows and blankets. The air in here was better —not so thin. I flipped on the TV, and as I lay there with my head throbbing, I thought of everything I wanted to change in my life. I was taking steps. And yet, my past always managed to catch up with me.

Matt being here meant that I had to be careful. I was pretty sure he wasn't here to spy for Luciana. They weren't close enough for that. Still, he might tell her what I was doing if she checked in with him. So, I had to watch what I said or else I'd fail this mission before it started. And, on a more personal level, I had to make sure he didn't think that I was in any way open to being with him. I wasn't with Luciana or her coven anymore. I didn't have to honor the agreement that she'd made, and I wasn't going to let him suck me in with his games. I didn't have to listen to him. Ignoring him was my best plan.

Okay. So, it was a passive-aggressive plan, but things changed. I had changed, and now he needed to change, too.

I called in an order for food, and then grudgingly switched it for the broth and tea Lucas had recommended. My head was pounding. The altitude was definitely affecting me. Broth then straight to bed. Something told me I'd need every ounce of energy I could muster to keep up with Lucas.

*Lucas.* Every time my mind wandered back to him, my heart raced. I needed to admit that I wanted him, and then move on. I couldn't have him. He was a wolf. He lived in Peru. I had a whole heap of problems—including one douche bag ex-fiancé.

But none of that kept me from wanting him.

God. I was twenty years old. Too old for a stupid crush.

My cheeks heated at that thought. He was probably annoyed he'd have to babysit me these next few days, but I'd done something to make him suspicious or he would've left me to Andrés.

Well, I just had to figure out where these mages were, get what I needed from them, save my brother, and stop Luciana from destroying the world. No time for romance. Especially since it was most definitely one-sided.

The knock on my door pulled me from my reverie. One step at a time. I'd get this done. Broth. Then bed. I'd deal with tomorrow, and all of its challenges, in the morning.

# CHAPTER TEN

I DIDN'T FEEL SO dizzy or lightheaded when I woke up. The broth had been good. The full night's sleep...that had been infinitely better.

Well, not totally full. But only a little nightmare. Faint. Distant. I hadn't woken up sweating. That was a first for me since I'd left the coven's grounds.

I took all of that as a sign that I was on the right track. I'd fix this. Teresa had texted an hour ago that the boys were already on the road, and I was determined I'd find an answer by the time they arrived.

I could do this. I had no other choice.

After a shower, I felt re-energized. I put on a pair of my khaki hiking pants, a black tank top, and hoodie. As I laced up my running shoes, I felt like a new me. A fresh start. The day was filled with possibilities. I grabbed my little crossbody purse. Mom had sent it to me from Mexico. It was handmade and covered with embroidered flowers. I dumped out the contents and put almost everything back in—my wallet, passport, Purell, tissues, lip gloss, aspirin, and Band-Aids. Just a little bit of everything. I wasn't sure what I'd come across and wanted to be prepared.

Now all I needed was a good meal to start the day off right. The menu book said that a complimentary breakfast was served in the lobby, but I could order in, too, for a price. I chewed on my lip for a moment. Avoiding the lobby was my first instinct. Matt could be there. But I didn't want to spend too much of Mr. Reyes' money—whoever he was.

The thing was that Matt already knew that I was here. So the damage was done. Just because I went to the lobby to eat breakfast didn't mean that I couldn't still ignore him.

I braided my semidry hair and tied off the end.

Time to face the day.

It was nice to feel confident. I didn't usually. Luciana had taken that away from me. I knew that now, but it had taken time for me to realize it.

I strolled into the lobby where a buffet was laid out on the marble-topped table. The flower arrangement had been moved to the side of the front desk to be replaced by a selection of hot and cold items. People milled around the table, while others sat in small groups around the lobby. A few sat alone, reading newspapers.

But no Matt. That gray and pink aura was nowhere to be seen.

*Good. Now I can enjoy my breakfast in peace.* I grabbed a plate and started picking through the offerings.

Cold cuts? For breakfast? No. Staying at St. Ailbe's had definitely spoiled me. Those omelets... I'd be back there soon enough.

Someone came down the hallway toward the table, and I caught his aura out of the corner of my eye. Matt.

*Fantastic. I made it a whole five minutes in the lobby before he showed up.* I barely suppressed the groan that was dying to break free. It was too early to deal with him. I did my best to avoid him as I rounded the table again, but I felt his presence like a tangible weight on my shoulders. He approached me and I did my very best to ignore him.

"Did you come to your senses?" he asked as he fell in behind me.

I pressed my lips together as I fought the urge to tell him off. Letting his arrogance grate on me wouldn't do me any good. "My senses? If you mean leaving with you, then no."

*One point to me.*

"What are your plans today?" His tone was haughty—which annoyed me—but I didn't dare turn around. I'd already given enough by responding to his first question.

"That's absolutely none of your business," I said in my most confident voice as I moved around the table.

"Look. If you need help with something, I'm happy to help."

Oh, so now he was going to play nice? I just bet he was happy to help. He wanted control over my ability to enhance magical powers, and even if he acknowledged that Luciana no longer held sway over me, he wasn't above making a new deal to get what he wanted. But there was no way I was taking his bait. "I already have a plan."

He leaned in close to whisper. "I know the local coven. I can get you in to see them. That's why you're here, right? To find some sort of magic?"

I tried to stay calm as I looked around the lobby. Everyone else was happily enjoying breakfast. Not paying attention to our conversation or seeing the horror that must've been plain on my face.

There really was a spy. For a moment, my vision swam. Only Teresa's friends and the Seven knew my reasons for coming here.

I looked back at Matt and then focused on the food again. "What do you know about it?"

"Only that you're mad at Luciana and here to find something to break your oath. Just take an oath to me, and yours will be overridden."

What a joke. "You think you're stronger than her?" I wasn't sure if he was arrogant or just stupid.

"Of course I am. I'm a man."

Oh, that was rich. Typical arrogant douche-bag talk. But I wasn't here just because of the oath. I was here for Raphael. There was nothing Matt could offer me that would help me save my brother.

"Look. I save you from an oath you don't want and you come to my coven and help me. I say it's a fair deal." When I didn't answer him, he kept on with his yammering. "Whatever the wolves have been telling you, you're misinformed. What do they know about magic? Nothing."

The thing about Matt was that he had the uncanny ability to see a person's biggest fear and bring it to light. That was the very thing I'd been worried about, but Muraco had been so confident that I'd listened to him. But what did he really know about magic?

He'd had such a good story about witches and wolves living together... But even if he remembered a different way, he wasn't a mage. He didn't practice. Did he really know what he was saying?

I resisted the temptation to fall into Matt's trap. I wouldn't let him take my confidence. I couldn't let him win. "As I said before, you shouldn't have come. And no, I don't need your help." My voice was clear and steady.

"Well, I'll be here when you change your mind." He grabbed a cup of coffee and went to sit at a table.

*Did that actually work?*

I thought on what he'd said for a second. *When* I changed my mind. Not *if* I changed my mind. He had no idea what I was up to, but he already assumed I'd fail. I wanted to walk over and bash my tray on his pompous head. Instead, I carefully placed a pastry on my plate. Then I thought about the calories and put it back.

*What I wouldn't give for the metabolism of a Were...*

I found hard-boiled eggs, some sort of potato pancake, and half a grapefruit. Good enough. I searched for a place to sit. The only open spot was across from Matt.

*Why is this my life?*

I circled the buffet as I searched the room again. *Please. Someone get up.* Finally, a couple left their spots. It was right next to Matt's table, but I didn't care.

I pushed their dirty dishes aside and sat down with my back to him.

"You're being a child."

Ignoring him. That had been my plan last night. I'd faltered just now, but I wouldn't keep doing it.

I carefully shelled my eggs. Cut them up. Put salt and pepper on them. All the while ignoring Matt. Only it wasn't helping. He wasn't stopping. He just got louder.

"This is stupid. You're being ridiculous. Whatever Luciana did, I'm sure it's gotten blown way out of proportion."

I took a sip of my orange juice and he somehow took that as a signal to get up and sit across from me.

"You're acting like a child." His tone was loud and harsh as if I hadn't heard him the first time.

It was really rich coming from him. He was the one throwing a temper tantrum.

"Your behavior today has been incredibly rude. And I'm your fiancé. I think that should afford me a measure of respect."

A measure of respect?

A *measure* of *respect?!*

What about respect for me? He was older than me by ten years, but sometimes he acted so immature. So selfish.

The more I thought about him and how I'd been cornered into agreeing to our engagement, the sicker I got. I was just a kid at the time, but he—*he* was an adult. At least, he was supposed to be.

"Say something," he shouted, and a drop of spittle hit my face.

Disgusting.

I picked up my napkin and wiped off my cheek. "You're the one who's yelling and causing a scene. When you calm down, maybe I'll talk to you." I was doing okay, but this whole situation was miserable. My hands shook with anger and frustration, but I was sticking to my plan. God had made me stubborn, if nothing else.

*Reacting to him won't help me at all.*

The sound of a chair being dragged across the room finally shut him up. I looked up to see Lucas' light golden aura. It was so nice and refreshing, like standing in warm sunlight.

"Good morning." Lucas sat down in the chair, his eyes only on me. "How are you feeling today? Altitude still getting to you?"

Suddenly the confidence was back. A smile spread across my face. *God. How did two little sentences just restore every-thing I wanted to feel about myself?* "No, the altitude isn't so bad today. I followed your advice and had some broth last night, and I slept—really slept—and it was great. I don't even have a headache now."

Lucas answered my grin with one of his own. "Good. They pump extra oxygen into the rooms here. That's why I booked it for you."

I took him in then. His hair, perfectly mussed. He wore a

long-sleeved T-shirt, with the sleeves scrunched to his elbows and a pair of black athletic pants that had white stripes down the sides.

I was staring. This was bad. I toyed with my food for a second as I looked for something to say. "You want to have some breakfast?"

He grinned big, and my heart did a double bump. "I already ate."

"Excuse me, we were having a conversation," Matt cut in.

Lucas raised his eyebrows, making a face at me before turning to Matt. "Looked to me like you were harassing her. That's no way to get her attention. Clearly." He winked at me.

"She's my fiancée. I'll talk to her however I like."

*God. Had I ever found him attractive?* I would've sworn he wasn't like this before. Now it seemed like every time I saw him, he got meaner.

"Fiancée?" Lucas mouthed to me.

I shrugged. Explaining right now would take too long. Plus, it wasn't like Lucas really cared if I was engaged or not.

"From the way you two were just acting, I wouldn't bet on seeing her in a white dress any time soon." Lucas stood, his eyes on me. "You ready?"

The half-eaten food on my plate wasn't worth sticking around to finish. "Sure." I brushed my hands off on a napkin and placed a tip on the table. No one else was doing it, but that didn't mean the staff didn't deserve at least a little tip for their hospitality. "I'm going to go see if they have some water bottles I can take. I'll just be a second." I started off for the front desk, but Lucas' voice stopped me.

"Don't worry about that. I'll take care of you."

I whipped around. The way he said it, so seriously, it sounded like he meant that he'd take care of more than just water. But by the time I turned, he was already walking out the door.

*I sighed. Just because you have a crush on a guy, doesn't mean he likes you, too.*

"You can't go with him." Matt pointed at Lucas. His face contorted with anger, making him look more than a little crazy. "He's a wolf." Disgust was thick in his voice.

*Sure, I can.* "Have a safe flight home, Matt," I said as I started after Lucas.

Today I was going to find a way to save my brother. That was the only thing that mattered.

# CHAPTER ELEVEN

I HOPPED into the van with Lucas and buckled my seat belt.

"So, we're looking for the old mages?" Lucas asked as he started the car.

"Yeah. Did Muraco tell you where to start?"

"He did. I'm heading to one of the smaller villages." He pulled into the street and started in the direction we'd come from last night. "It's closest to where the old temple was, but I've been all over those mountains and never seen a thing."

Perfect.

"I know that's not what you want to hear, but I want you to be realistic."

"Good. Realistic is good. But this is my best shot at saving my brother, breaking the oath that's binding me to maybe one of the worst people in the world, and finding a way to stop said person from raising demons that will destroy us all. So, no pressure."

He muttered a string of curses. "Muraco said that it was bad, but he didn't say it was that bad." He gave me a long look before focusing on the road again. "Your brother?"

"Twin brother."

"Somehow that makes it worse."

I shrugged. "It's bad either way. But, yes, he's my twin. And the only family I really have left. Besides my cousin, Teresa."

"She's Dastien's new mate, right?"

"Yes," I said, a little surprised that he knew about the happenings of small-town Texas.

He rubbed his forehead. "Muraco is always tight-lipped, but I feel like he's left out some need-to-know details this time. Fill me in. What are you up against?"

This wasn't the time to be shy. I wasn't sure why I felt comfortable spilling my guts to him, but it felt like if I left out anything, something bad would happen. I hadn't told everyone all of it. Not ever. But I told Lucas. About my family. About how my parents left. How things got bad with Luciana and she started draining my power. And, finally, how I manipulated Teresa and then left the coven. I even spilled about Matt.

Lucas was kind as I spoke. He was a total stranger, but he was outraged at all the right parts. He stayed quiet during the hard parts, and in the end I didn't think he judged me as anything less.

"You've been through a lot for someone so young."

I sighed. "I'm twenty now, but I feel older. I'm exhausted, and I feel like this fight is only just beginning. Sometimes it's difficult to see the light at the end, you know?"

"It's there. I promise."

"Hmm." I wasn't sure I believed him.

"Thank you for being so honest with me. I know that can't have been easy."

I gave him my best semblance of a smile. "Thanks for listening." I held my breath for a moment before asking the question that was burning at the back of my mind. "So, now that you know everything, what do you think my chances are? Am I on a wild-goose chase? Should I go home?"

"I don't think I can answer that. Just because these mages haven't been around for a while doesn't mean that they're not there. Or that something of their magic isn't in these forests. I can guide you to places that used to have spiritual meaning—that still do, just not as much as they used to—and maybe your abilities will lead you to what you need."

I sighed. "That's not very reassuring."

"Nothing about what you have going on is good. Let me at least try to help with the search. If we come up empty, I'll take you to the village elders. Muraco wasn't lying there. Wolves and witches have mixed a lot over the years, and some of ours are so old they have a unique magic all their own." He reached over and squeezed my hand. A shiver ran through my body at the contact. His fingers were rough and calloused, and the feel of them against my skin heated me through. "Don't give up before we've even started. We'll find something." The road started getting a bit treacherous, and he let go to hold on to the wheel with both hands.

An hour later and I had a death grip on the "oh-shit" bar in the van. My jaw was clenched so tightly that my face was starting to hurt. Relaxing would be good, but that was impossible. The "road" we were on—and I used that term loosely because this was so not a road—dropped off on my side. Straight down. The ground had to be a million miles below us. Half the tire wasn't even on the path as we bounced over potholes so deep someone could practically live there.

"You okay over there, princess?" Lucas' gravelly voice drew my attention away from the steep edge.

"No. We're going to die." I let go of the bar for a second and we hit another bump. I reached right back up and held on for dear life.

Lucas chuckled. "We're not going to die."

He was nuts. This path clearly wasn't meant for vehicles.

Not that he had much to worry about regardless of the drop-off. "You might survive the fall. You're a wolf. You heal fast. But I won't. I'm essentially human. I'll be worm food."

"Don't worry. I've done this drive a million times. I'm not going over the edge."

I glanced down again, against my better judgment. "Looks like you already are from here," I said softly, but he heard me anyhow.

"I promise. You're not going to die. I won't let you. Not today. Not for a long while. So you can loosen your death grip on that handle."

I tore my gaze away from the edge and took him in as he concentrated on the road ahead. "I don't like heights."

"I can tell. But don't worry. I've lived in this part of the country off and on most of my life." Lucas paused as he went over another hole in the ground and the van bottomed out. "Believe it or not, the road used to be much worse."

"Worse than this?" Not possible. Not in a million years.

"Yup." He nodded with certainty.

I couldn't imagine worse conditions. "It's a miracle you're still alive then."

"Eh. Back then we walked."

"What? You didn't have cars?"

"There were no cars."

That made me pause. Man. I was so dense sometimes.

The wolves all looked much younger than they were. He probably wasn't anywhere near as young as I thought he was. I'd figured he was a few years older than me, but not thirty yet. "How old are you?"

"How old do you think I am?" he asked with a wink.

Was that flirting?

No. Impossible. No way would he be flirting with me. He was far too good-looking, and a wolf to boot. "I don't know. I thought you were maybe twenty-seven, but I have a feeling I'm way off if you were around before cars made it to Peru." He was grinning big time. It felt like the joke was on me. "Yeah. I'm definitely wrong. You're way older than that. So how off am I?"

He laughed.

"Seriously. How old are you?"

"Old enough, princess. Old enough."

I sighed. "I wish you'd stop calling me that."

"What? Princess?"

"Yeah. It's demeaning." I turned away from him, taking in the horizon. "I've had enough of that in my life."

"Hey," he said as he gripped my hand for a second.

That one touch and I felt his aura warming me to the core. It was so clear and bright. So strong. I could see a supernatural's aura all the time, but feeling it, that was something infinitely more personal and unique. It didn't happen that often. Only when the person was being very open with me and letting me in.

Almost as soon as the touch was there, it was gone.

And I missed it.

What was going on with my feelings for him? I was attracted to him, sure. But then I spilled my guts to him, and now...

"I'm not using the word to be demeaning," he said, bringing me back to the conversation. I hoped I hadn't zoned out too much. "I was using it in a very literal way. But if you don't like it, I'll stop."

Literal way? Someone had grossly misinformed him. "Me? Princess? Of what? The coven?" I nearly laughed. It was a completely ludicrous notion. "That couldn't be farther from the truth and there's no way I'm going back there. Even once this whole mess is done with. I can't. So, yeah. No."

He frowned. "That wasn't what I was referring to."

What was he talking about? "Then..." I was so confused. Or he was confused.

"Don't worry about it. I won't call you that anymore if you don't like it."

"Okay." I laughed, feeling like I was missing something.

We rounded a corner and the cutest little village spread out before us. A church stood off to the left, with little shops and restaurants dotting the road. Homes were practically carved into the side of the mountain. "We're here?"

"You got it. We walk the rest of the way. The streets in the village are too small for cars." He grinned at me, and my heart did an embarrassing little flip-flop. "This way. We'll hit the market first. A lot of people who are indigenous to this area bring their goods to sell. Luckily, you're here on market day."

My first thought was that I wished Raphael were here. He loved markets. He would so get a kick out of this. I pushed away all the scary thoughts of what might happen and thought only of good things. It was hard, but I had to do it. One day, if this market was cool, I'd come back with him.

"You okay?" Lucas asked.

I hopped out of the car and started to follow him. "No. But I'm hoping I will be soon."

"You will be."

We turned a corner and a wide-open field spread out in front of us. People in traditional Peruvian dress stood behind tables filled with all kinds of things. Some had fruits and vegetables. Some had clothes. Others had baked goods. But what hit me the most were all of the colors. Everything was so vibrant and alive.

"Do you see any auras here?"

I scanned the people standing around, looking deeper than with just my normal eyesight, but all I picked up were the energies of normal humans. Nothing supernatural or at all magical. "No." I couldn't keep the disappointment from my voice.

"Come on. Let's take a closer look. Maybe it's faint."

I nodded. "Okay." We'd come all this way. Might as well really look at these people.

As we moved from stall to stall, I thought it odd how Lucas paid each person special attention. One lady was selling cheese. Her colorful skirt and blouse were hand embroidered. A pristine white hat with a small brim sat atop her head. She grinned as Lucas approached and waved him over.

She had her baby playing in a box next to her. Lucas leaned down and gave the baby a kiss. "How are you doing today?" he asked her in Spanish.

"We're doing same as always. You don't have to stop by every time."

"Would I miss a chance to see this little one?"

The lady's cheeks heated, and she swatted him away before Lucas went on to the next stand. A lady with coca leaves. He negotiated for a bag and took out a handful. "Here you go," he said as he held out a bunch for me. "Your breathing is a little tight."

"You can hear my breathing?" I hadn't even realized I wasn't breathing right.

"I'm a Were. I can hear a lot of things. Just try them."

Flustered, I grabbed a few and put them in my mouth. They didn't taste great, but I'd drunk down my mother's wellness potions for the early part of my life. I was well used to earthy flavors.

A few stalls down, I found little flat sugar cookies decorated with chocolate and rainbow sprinkles. It was the first time I engaged with one of the people manning the stalls, but the woman there looked behind me and nodded to Lucas before talking to me.

What was with that? Why were they treating him like he was special?

Maybe he spent a lot of time at this market?

The portly woman reached into her jar, grabbing out three cookies for me as I reached into my coin purse for change. I noticed the crystal hanging between her collarbones. It was small and white, but it had a tiny glow of power.

Interesting.

"Thank you," I said as I handed her the change for the cookies. Just as our skins touched I saw a flicker. Barely there, but enough. It was white and pure.

The lady smiled, and I felt like a weight had been lifted.

She handed me the cookies and the contact was gone. I couldn't see it anymore.

"Lucas!" I shouted before I could stop myself.

"What? What is it?"

I spun around, grabbing Lucas' arms with my hands, nearly dropping my bag of cookies. "I saw it. I saw it. Her aura. It was white. So pure. I've never seen an aura so white. And I don't usually see anything at all from humans. You know what that means?" I jumped up and down before rambling on. "She has to be a descendant of the mages. Which means they're here. Muraco was right." I squealed like a mad person.

He laughed, and a stupid grin spread across my face. Being here—laughing with him—filled my heart in an indescribable way. He reached up and ran his thumb down my cheek, and I stilled. His eyes were bright and clear. I could see the joy in them, and something else that I couldn't identify. "That's so good, Claudia."

"It's not a lot, but it's something. It means that this isn't a lost cause." Hope filled me to the point of bursting. "I really can save him."

"Of course you can."

I let out the biggest sigh. "Thank you."

"You're welcome." He turned toward the aisle and grasped my hand in his. "Come on. Let's see what more you can see. I bet we can find a lead before lunch."

Tears started to fill my eyes, but I held them open. I'd already made one scene, so I wasn't going to let myself cry in the middle of the market. "That would be really good."

I stumbled to keep up with Lucas. His hand felt hot in mine as he twined our fingers together. This was going so much better than I'd expected.

When he stopped to talk to the butcher at the next stall, Lucas didn't let go of my hand. He spoke, and I wasn't paying attention to the words, but the deep rumble of his voice gave me goose bumps.

He glanced my way with a grin, not pausing in his conversation, and all of a sudden I could see it.

Holy moly. I liked him. More than liked him, I was attracted to him. This guy was drawing me in. Both Cosette and Teresa had mentioned me finding someone...

Suddenly nervous, I tugged my hand away and busied myself getting out a cookie.

I didn't have time for a romance. Not now. But maybe I could come back once this was over and see if Lucas wanted to go out on a date. It was the twenty-first century. I could ask him. Couldn't I?

It would be the light at the end of the very long tunnel that my life had been so far. He would be my light.

# CHAPTER TWELVE

"I THINK we should go for a hike after this," Lucas said.

We'd stopped for lunch at a cafe next to the market. The food was fresh and delicious. I ordered grilled trout with vegetable quinoa and I'd practically been shoveling it in since I took the first bite. "A hike? I was hoping to talk to more people."

"Were you getting anywhere?"

"No."

That was the problem and we both knew it. The locals all flared with a bit of aura when I touched them, but when asked about mages they had no idea what we were talking about. A few of them wore glowing crystals, but other than being handed down for many generations to keep away evil spirits, they knew nothing about where they came from. Some of them were afraid of me after I asked about the mages—which was disheartening—and it made me wonder if all humans in this region flared a little. Maybe all humans did. I'd only ever been around witches and supernaturals, and now that seemed like a terrible gap in my knowledge of the world. I was second-guessing myself that much.

"But how is a hike going to solve anything?"

He set down his fork. I'd momentarily wondered why the locals hadn't flinched when he ordered enough food for four people, but I'd forgotten to think about it after tasting the food. Now I was back to thinking about it. How much did the locals know about the pack? And if they knew about the pack then why didn't they know anything about the mages?

I didn't expect anyone to point me straight to ancient magic, but surely someone should have heard about the local covens or maybe some old shrine where locals went to pray. I'd take any lead I could get right now.

"A hike might solve nothing," he said. I started to speak, but he kept on talking. "But it might give us some clues. You'll get a better view from up high. If you look down and sense energy somewhere, then I can lead you there."

I sighed. I'd liked the idea of staying in the village. The people were nice and exploring was more fun on flat ground. But Lucas had a point. "Okay. A hike sounds doable."

"Good." He started in on his second plate of food.

"So how much do they know?"

He raised an eyebrow. "Does who know?"

"These people." I gestured around the room. Most of the round tables were empty, but the people at the few occupied ones all stared at us. Some were more subtle than others, but most kept glancing our way. I fiddled with the edge of the colorful tablecloth.

Combine the looks with the way everyone in the market treated Lucas, and something was obviously up. These people knew him. If not because he was a wolf then for some other reason.

He didn't answer me, but I wasn't giving up that easily. "Who are you to them? A wolf? Or something else? Because I feel like you're getting special treatment everywhere we go, and it's not just because of your looks."

His grin transformed his face from handsome to godlike. It was breathtaking. "How do you think I look?"

I laughed. He was just like every other guy I knew. "Come on. You're a wolf. It comes with the territory, right?"

He shrugged. "I guess so. I never really thought about it."

"So?"

"So, what?"

He was starting to frustrate me. "Don't be so obtuse. Answer the question."

"They don't know about the pack exactly. What they do know is that some of us in the area live a very long time and work hard to protect them from anything bad. There are a lot of predators in these mountains—both supernatural and not—and we make sure the locals get to live without the drama that people face elsewhere in the country."

"So why this one? Why not one of those other villages?"

"Mostly because of proximity to our own stronghold. Also, because of legacy. These are the supposed descendants of the old mages and that's why we're here in the first place."

I guessed that made sense. They couldn't exactly protect all of Peru. No pack could handle so much territory with so many mountains. So the village closest to their home would reap the benefits of being close to the pack.

"Then why don't any of them know about the mages?"

"Because they don't exist to modern humans. These people might know their fairytales and legends, but their knowledge is just a memory from a dream. That's why I said this wouldn't be easy."

"Right." I took another bite of my quinoa before asking the next question. "So, they know how much you eat?"

"They know enough to not question when we ask for something. I won't waste their food. There's a trust there that goes both ways." He paused, watching me as if he waited for some-thing. "No more questions?"

My face heated and I fought it as best as I could. "Not at the moment."

"Good." He started eating again, and we settled into a comfortable silence.

It was always a measure to me if I could just sit and be with someone in silence. If I felt the need to talk or sensed awkward-ness from the silence then it was a sure sign that the friendship wasn't meant to be. But I felt neither of those things with him. Just being next to him was comforting.

It was odd. The only people I'd felt this way with were Raphael and Daniel.

One of them was gone forever.

And my brother... I focused on my plate of food, blinking away the tears that formed.

"Hey. You okay?" Lucas said.

"Fine." I lifted my fork but couldn't bring myself to take a bite.

Lucas reached under the table, and his hand squeezed my knee. Heat rushed through my body and it was almost enough to distract me from the thought that Raphael might not make it. "It's going to be okay," Lucas said.

"Yeah," I said the word, but without much faith behind it.

"I mean it."

When I met his gaze, his aura had brightened a little. Gotten more intense. For whatever reason, I could pick up on that subtle difference. "I know you do." I just wished I fully believed it.

"Don't get down. Not yet. We'll find the answer."

I nodded, and he removed his hand. I instantly missed the feel of it there. His touch soothed my soul and made me feel like I wasn't alone.

If I made it through this without embarrassing myself in front of him, it would be a miracle.

LUCAS CLAIMED we were on a hiking trail but that seemed dubious at best. Nature had encroached on almost every inch of the essentially nonexistent path. Branches scraped against my arms and legs as we pushed forward, and I was glad that Meredith and Teresa had made me go shopping. My beloved flip-flops wouldn't have cut it for a second. The hiking pants and thick fleece jacket were much better suited to Peru. I probably should've bought the hiking shoes that Dastien had picked, but they were so ugly I'd gone with the less sturdy pink and purple running shoes. Hopefully that choice wouldn't earn me a twisted ankle.

The air was getting thinner and cooler. I zipped up my fleece and hooked my thumbs in the little holes at the end of the sleeve so that my hands were nearly covered. It felt like I'd walked miles since we left the van. "Have you been up this way before?"

"Once or twice." Lucas held some branches out of my way. "Don't worry, I know these mountains well. I've spent most of my life here. Although I usually travel this area as a wolf. It's much faster that way."

"But you haven't lived here *all* your life? You don't have an accent." Now that he'd revealed one little piece of himself, I wanted more.

"No. I've traveled quite a bit. Most of us roam a few decades once we're in our thirties. I lived in the US for a while, but the mountains called me home in the end."

"And you don't miss it?"

"America? Nah. We've got a McDonald's in Cusco's town square. Good enough for me." He winked at me.

He had to be joking. "McDonald's is all you miss?"

"Doesn't everyone? It's the epitome of America, right?"

I scrunched up my nose. "I don't know about that. After the truth about the pink slime came out..." I teased him.

"Pink slime?" he asked.

He didn't know about the pink slime? It had been all over the news, but if his village was this remote, he probably wasn't that in touch with the rest of the world. "It's this meat-like substance they use in their burgers. It's basically dog food."

He stopped walking for a second. "I ate there last night."

I shrugged. "Maybe they use real meat here. But, yeah, in America, it's pretty disturbing. I wouldn't touch the stuff. And that's what you miss?"

"Not anymore." He shook his head as he walked. "You've ruined it."

I grinned at him to lighten the blow. "Sorry."

"You should be. I used to sit up here and dream of their burgers." He sighed wistfully.

"Now, Whataburger. Those are something you can dream about."

"Whataburger?"

"Haven't you ever visited the pack in Texas?"

"Eh. It's been a while."

"It's been around for decades." *Oh my God. How old was he?*

"Yeah," he said slowly. "It's been a really long while."

Oh man. I was really losing it. There were so many reasons he was off limits, and age just added to the list. If only he didn't look like he belonged on a Calvin Klein billboard.

"Almost to the top," he said, and I was grateful for the

change in subject. "See that tree up there with that big branch on the right that arches down?"

I tried to follow where he was pointing and saw a massive tree. The bottom right branch arced down, and from here it looked like it almost touched the ground. "Sure."

"There's a really good lookout there. You should be able to see the surrounding valleys. There are a few villages we could check out, or maybe you can find an old ruin or two."

I took his word for it on the lookout. There didn't even seem to be a break in the forest. I stepped forward to look closer and almost ate it. Lucas caught me just before my face planted into the ground. My breath caught as he held me.

The way he looked at me, with his aura shining down, I sensed that he wanted to say something important. The feeling was slight. If I hadn't been able to feel his aura, then I might not have noticed the yearning in his eyes. But I did notice it.

And it took my breath away.

He gently set me on my feet in front of him. "You okay?"

I brushed myself off as I tried to pretend that nothing had happened. That I hadn't seen the desire for something more in his eyes. But my hands were shaking. "Yeah. Fine. Sorry."

"Do you need a break?"

"No. I'm just clumsy sometimes." I wiped my hands on my pants one more time to get the last of the dirt off and then motioned for him to keep going.

"Okay." He started walking again and I followed. This time I made sure I didn't trip over fallen branches.

*Get yourself together, Claudia. You need to work with this man. Not drool over him.*

Wanting things to be different wouldn't change them. Even if Lucas wanted to be with me, there were so many obstacles to overcome—the least of which was that he was a wolf and I was a witch. Whatever happened in these mountains, those two things didn't mix in my world. The only reason I was getting any help from him was because Teresa was my cousin. She was the tie that bound our two groups together. And then there was that little battle we had coming...

Not to mention Matt. I had enough on my plate just trying to get rid of him. I'd thought telling him straight out that we were over would be enough to put him off, but apparently it wasn't.

I focused on Lucas, but it was hard to follow him without watching his back muscles moving against his shirt. Or his butt. Because that wasn't a good idea. Not at all.

He made me forget all those reasons why it wouldn't work. In either case, I was getting ahead of myself.

Did he like me? Was that what the yearning was all about? Or was I just projecting that onto him? I didn't think so, but it wasn't like my judgment had been completely reliable in the past.

For a moment, I decided to let go of all those reasons. To throw them out the window.

For just this little while, what was the harm in appreciating the scenery?

A few more minutes, and we reached the spot he'd mentioned. "Here you go." He moved the branches out of the way, and all of a sudden it was like I could see Peru spread out in front of me. It was just a small piece of the country, but it felt huge.

Then I looked down and all the air left my lungs. I grabbed Lucas' arm as my stomach flip-flopped. "Oh God. We're so high up..." And the edge was right there. One misstep, some loose dirt underfoot, and that would be it. I'd fall down the side of the mountain.

Lucas pulled me close, until my back was pressed to his

front. His arms wrapped around my waist, and I leaned back into him. "Don't worry. I got you. You won't fall."

I tried to get my breathing under control.

"Close your eyes."

He didn't have to ask me twice. The view was breathtaking, but terrifying.

"Now, take a deep breath and feel my arms around you. Trust me to keep you safe."

I let out the breath slowly.

"You feeling better?"

I was. Lucas made me feel safe. Taken care of. No one had ever made me feel that way before. "Yes."

"Now, instead of looking down when you open your eyes, look out. Okay?"

"Okay."

"Remember. I'm right here. I'm not going to let you fall."

"Okay."

"Open your eyes."

I followed his command. This time, when I looked out, I felt a sense of calm and peace. I could enjoy the beauty of the area. There was so much green. The peaks of the Andes touched the clouds as far as I could see.

"When you're ready, look down. Maybe you can sense something no one else can." Lucas' deep voice rumbled against my back.

I prepared myself to lose it before I looked down, but when I did, I was surprisingly okay. I could see a long, winding road that cut down the side of the mountain we were on. Other roads intersected in the valley below. The village we'd been in this morning was just down the way.

My sight wasn't something that I had to turn on. It was always there. I chose to ignore it sometimes, but it never went away. I focused on the hints of color around me. This land was so spiritual. Full of life. It was like everything had an aura, but none of the white notes I spotted were as pure as what I'd expect from the mages. The energies weren't even shadows of the flashes I'd gotten from the villagers.

I turned to say as much, but a flare of white aura caught the corner of my eye and I froze. It was far away and dim, but it was there. I stepped out of Lucas' arms, and he let me go. It was pure and white, just like the flash I'd gotten from the villagers. I took a couple steps before he grabbed the back of my fleece.

"Whoa. Watch your step."

I looked down and my vision swam. Before I could faint, Lucas pulled me back against his chest and covered my eyes with his hand. "You got a little ahead of yourself there, huh?"

"Yeah," I said as my breathing stabilized once again. "But I feel... There was an aura. It was faint but it was there." I pushed his hand down and turned to look at him. "Can we go? Now?"

He frowned. "Where exactly did you see it?"

I pointed at the spot, just around the side of the mountain. It was barely visible from where we were standing, but if he knew the area as well as he said he did then he should be able to get us there.

"Are you sure?"

I nodded. "Absolutely."

He looked back to where I pointed and sucked in a sharp breath. "It's impossible. Not there. I just..."

"What's impossible? Why is it impossible?"

He closed his eyes for a second, and when he opened them again his dark eyes had warmed to a glowing chocolate color. "A sect of *brujos* is based in that area. They live like monks—"

"That's them! Those are the ones we're looking for." Hope filled my heart. The answer to all of my problems was right there. So close.

He shook his head. "They're evil, Claudia. Pure evil."

My jaw dropped open before I could stop it. The hope I'd been feeling smashed into a million pieces. "No. They can't be." I looked back at the spot. The pure white aura was there. A bit of darkness surrounded it if I really squinted, but the center of the aura looked like freshly fallen snow. "It's white. What I see is white. White magic always means good magic."

"I can't explain why you're seeing what you're seeing, but I know those mages. They're beyond bad. We've had a few run-ins with the foul things they've summoned, and they weren't pretty. I can't take you there."

I chewed on my lip as I thought it through. There was only one possibility that made sense. "Regardless of whether they're evil, they must have something that belongs to the white mages we're looking for. I have to go check."

Lucas grasped my arms. "I meant that literally. I can't take you. The second I step on their land, they'll know I'm there. Even if I could bring you there, they won't help you or give you what you want. There has to be something else. Take another look." He spun me around. "Please."

I looked, methodically scanning the view and hoping for once there was a solution that didn't involve me reaching out to dark mages, but none of the energies out there came close to pure white. Except that one spot. "No. If we had a better lead, I'd take your advice, but I don't have that luxury. There's nothing else." Someday, I'd be allowed to make a choice that wasn't a last resort, but until then...

If had to go through more dark magic to save Raphael then I'd do it.

Regardless of the cost.

"I can't take you." He let go of me, and ran his hands through his hair, pulling it for a second before letting go. He looked down at me with resignation. "Nothing will change that."

Then I remembered something that made everything that much more awful.

Boy did I not want to do this. But if Lucas wouldn't—couldn't—help me then I had to find someone who would. "There's another way I can get in."

His expression changed from resignation to anger. "Please tell me you're not talking about that asshole from this morning."

I winced. "He's the next in line to his coven in upstate New York. He knows all the other coven leaders. They have meetings over winter solstice. He can get me in for sure."

"No. No. Just no," he said the word fiercely. "I don't like you spending any time with him. At all."

I wasn't sure if he was jealous or just plain didn't like Matt. I was probably imagining the former, but he did seem a little jealous. "Me neither, but I don't have a lot of options."

Lucas grabbed my hand before starting back down the path. He didn't say anything the whole hike back, but he never once let go of my hand. Not until after he'd helped me into the van.

When we got in and started back toward Cusco, he finally broke the silence. "Fine. You go with that asshole to see the *brujos*, but I'll be watching you. I'll get as close as I can without setting off their wards. If something goes wrong—if you feel for one second like they're trying something on you—you shout. I'll be there in minutes. You just hang in there for me. You got it?"

I nodded. He seemed too upset for me to answer in actual words.

"I need verbal confirmation that you understand."

I raised a brow at him. *Verbal confirmation?* "I understand. I'll yell if I get into any trouble." I wasn't sure why he was getting so agitated. "Don't worry so much. Matt isn't going to let anything happen to me. I'm too valuable to him."

"He's not the only one you're valuable to."

I shifted in my seat so that I could see him better, but he

didn't say anything. Just stared at the road as he drove. He gripped the steering wheel tightly, twisting his hands every few seconds.

For the longest time, I'd been protecting everyone else. No one thought about me. Not until this moment. It felt really good. Like I might actually be safe here. Even when I go on the evil *brujos'* land, I'd be okay as long as I had Lucas watching out for me.

I was sure I could handle them myself. No matter how evil the sect was, they didn't have a family member of mine to hold hostage. I was free to defend myself however I wanted.

But still, it was nice that someone cared.

After a few minutes, I sat straight in my seat. "I'll be okay. Promise. No need to worry about me."

He grunted, and I had no idea what that meant.

Just when I thought I understood Lucas, he went and changed the game.

# CHAPTER THIRTEEN

FROM THE WAY Lucas white-knuckled the steering wheel the whole drive back, it was easy to assume he was pissed. He didn't like my plan. It was too dangerous and I'd be with "that asshole." The problem was that I didn't see any other way around it. Those *brujos* held my one clue. The only thing that could save my brother.

So, I had to do this. Pretend to go along with whatever Matt said so that he'd take me where I needed to go.

Still, Lucas' reaction was freaking me out. It was like I was missing something. It took me a bit, but I finally worked up the courage to ask. "Why are you so upset? You don't even know me. Not really."

"That's not true. You told me all about your life. I think I know a lot about you, especially now."

No. I wasn't buying that. He was upset. And then all the touching. And the way he'd acted when I first met him. Something was up, but I didn't want to assume anything that wasn't right. I wanted to know that I wasn't imagining things.

"That could be right, but you're not telling me what's really bothering you. Why not?"

When he turned his head, I saw the glow in his eyes. His wolf was close. I knew enough to know that that was dangerous. "You don't want me to answer that. Not yet. You're not ready."

If I didn't want the answer, I wouldn't have asked the question. "Ready for what?"

He gave me a small smile that had a hint of sadness. It wasn't his big one that made my heart stop. This one made it ache instead. "Me."

"You?"

He nodded.

I licked my lips as I searched for what to say. Honestly, I was feeling so many things—fear, longing, hope, to name a few— that I wasn't sure how to articulate anything. "I... I..."

"Don't worry about it, princess. I know you're not ready. We'll get you through this, and then we'll deal with what's next."

I swallowed, suddenly feeling short of breath in a way that had nothing to do with the altitude. "Okay."

He reached over and grabbed my hand. "It's going to be okay."

I nodded. "Okay." A hint of panic hit me.

He liked me. Like, *liked me* liked me.

*Oh boy. Why is everything so complicated?*

He ran his thumb up and down my hand, and I glanced at him.

He winked, giving me a different small smile. This one had hope.

I relaxed back against the seat. "Holy moly."

He laughed. "I told you, you weren't ready."

"No kidding."

Me? With Mr. July?

Oh boy...

BY THE TIME we pulled up to the hotel, the silence had become tense. It wasn't the easy silence that we'd had moments —or what felt like moments—before. No. That was gone. Lucas was growing more agitated the closer we got to the hotel.

He put the van in Park. "Are you sure there isn't another way?"

I undid my seat belt and faced him. "Maybe. But *this* is a real option and it's all I have right now. A real chance to save my brother. I have to try." I almost laughed. It seemed that no matter what I did, I was faced with impossible choices. Every time I tried to do what was best without thinking of myself. One day I'd put what I wanted first, but not today.

"If you change your mind, we can figure out something else."

I shook my head. "There isn't any time for figuring out something else. Tomorrow I need to get whatever it is that the mages have. Then we'll go from there."

"I don't like it, but..." He looked out through the windshield, effectively ending the conversation.

I stared at him for a moment. At the strong lines of his face. The curve of his shoulder. The muscle that stretched his long-sleeved T-shirt. "I'll be okay."

"I know. I just don't like you being with *him* and going to see those *brujos*. It's dangerous."

I took a breath. "I've been around a very dangerous witch my whole life. So far, I'm still alive, despite it all. I plan to stay that way." *Back to reality.* I hopped down from the van and slammed the door, not looking back as I stepped toward the lobby. I didn't dare glance back and see whatever expression he was wearing now.

I checked my watch. It wasn't quite dinnertime, and I didn't really want to mope in my bedroom all evening. I could find Matt, but chances were we couldn't visit the mages today anyhow.

It'd have to wait for morning like Lucas had planned.

So, what now?

I needed to check on Raphael. I felt so far away from him. We'd never been apart like this. And with everything... It was like he was gone.

I'd take an oath with Luciana a million times over if I thought it'd do any good, but I guess I'd learned that lesson. We'd always end up here, with someone I loved in danger. That was how Luciana built her power.

I had to save him. Then I'd break the oath and get rid of her one way or another.

Breaking the oath...

I walked through hotel in a half-daze, thinking about what Lucas had said. If he meant what I was pretty sure he meant, then I could bond with him and it would all be over.

But did I want that? I always thought I'd marry another witch. Even though I was a little jealous of what Teresa had, I didn't want to be a wolf. I couldn't imagine fitting into that life-style with Lucas or anyone else.

I slid the key into my hotel room door, and my twindar went crazy, stopping me in my tracks.

Raphael. Something was wrong with Raphael.

I rushed inside and dumped out the contents of my purse, looking for Raphael's stupid flip phone.

*Damn it. Why do I keep so much junk in my purse?*

I spotted the black square and grabbed it with shaking hands. It took me two tries to dial Adrian's number correctly.

As soon as Adrian picked up, I could hear yelling.

"What's going on?"

"Your brother is losing it, that's what's going on! He nearly bit Beth. We're trying to tie him down. Hang on." The phone clattered as it dropped.

A bunch of shouting and screaming that I couldn't make out echoed through the line before it went quiet.

*Please let everything be okay.*

I paced the room with the phone glued to my ear. Maybe I wouldn't mind being a wolf. At least then I could hear what was going on.

It felt like a million years passed before Adrian picked up the phone again. "You still there?"

"Yeah," I said. "Is he okay?"

"He's alive."

"That's not the same thing, and you know it."

He let out a breath. "How close are you to finding something to fix him?"

"I don't know. I have a lead, but I'm not sure what I'll find. It could be a day. It could be five. I need time." My anxiety level shot through the roof. What if I took too long? What if after all this, I found what I needed and I was too late to save him?

He had to hang on.

"Claudia... I just... I don't know if he's got that kind of time."

I thought hard and fast. There had to be something I could do. "Is he sedated?"

"Yeah. But the drugs are wearing off faster and faster. He was only knocked out for an hour and a half before he ripped apart our RV and I gave him enough to put out an Alpha. We nearly wrecked... I don't think we can stay on the road much longer."

I let out a breath. Last I knew they were in Mexico City. "Where are you now?"

"We're almost to Guatemala. We've been taking turns driving, so we're going as fast as we can."

If they couldn't make it all the way here, then I'd have to

find a way to get to them. I'd had a few hours between flights at the Lima airport, so I'd scanned the flight boards. There'd been a lot of people traveling to Central and South America, but I'd seen a lot of flights headed to Costa Rica. "Okay. San Jose is in-between here and there. And I think there are regular flights from Peru. Can you get there?"

"Yeah. We can make it that far."

"Good. I'll meet you there." I took a steadying breath. "Four days." I could do it in four. I just had to hurry. "Just give me four days."

"I'll do my best. But I'm not God. There's nothing more we can do for him until you get here."

Maybe I could do something for him. "Put me on speaker. I'm going to do a healing chant."

"Does that work over the phone?"

God. I hoped so. "I've never tried it, but it can't hurt."

The phone clicked and I could hear the background noise in the room. "Beth? Shane?"

"Yeah?" they said.

"I'm doing a healing chant. Join in if you want."

"Okay," Shane said. "We're ready. You lead. We'll follow."

I started singing an old song that talked of healing the soul and body. The tone was repetitive, which was supposed to be soothing. As a kid, I'd hated this chant, but now I was glad my mother had forced me to learn it.

The words slid off my tongue, and with them magic sparked. My voice twined with Beth and Shane's. I focused my power, melding with theirs, strengthening their magic. As the power grew, I felt myself growing tired, and I reveled in it.

It was working.

When the spell ended, I held my breath, waiting to hear how Raphael was.

"His color is better," Adrian said. "Much better."

I let out a long breath. It wasn't a fix by any means, but I was so thankful it had helped at all. "Good." I wiped my now-sweating face. "Good." I checked my watch. It was just about dinnertime now. I still had time to eat and rest before the morning. Hopefully a good night's sleep would help gain back some of my magic before I went to see the evil *brujos*. "Will you take me off speaker and put the phone to Raphael's ear?"

"Sure." All the ambient sounds from the RV quieted. "Putting it against his ear now."

I cleared my throat. "Raphael de Santos. You listen to me! You hang on. Don't give up. Don't give in to Luciana's magic. Not ever. You wait for me. Whatever it takes. You wait for me to come to you." I heard a grunt, and I took that as him agreeing. "Good. I love you. So much."

"Are you okay?" Adrian asked.

I took about a second to be embarrassed that he probably heard all of that before letting it go. "No. I'm not even remotely okay."

"Is there anything I can do?"

"No. Just... Keep him alive for me, okay. He's really all I've got left."

"That's not true. You've got Tessa and Dastien and me and all of the rest of the pack. You've got the coven members who left Luciana. You've got Axel and your aunt and uncle. You've got Tía Rosa. You're not alone. Even if the worst happens, you won't be alone. Never."

A tear fell down my cheek, and I brushed it away. "Thank you. That means a lot to me."

"Nothing to thank me for. Just the truth." He paused. "Get what you're looking for. Fast. I'll text you where to find us when we're settled in San Jose."

"Okay." Because of Luciana, I often found it hard to trust people. I'd been suspicious of Adrian because he seemed too eager to learn magic, but I'd misjudged him. I was trusting him with my brother, and I didn't think that trust was misplaced. When I got back, I'd teach him whatever he wanted to know. I owed him at least that much. "Thanks for taking care of him."

"You got it. Talk to you soon."

"'Bye." I hung up and threw the phone on my bed, willing the morning to come sooner. There wasn't a second to spare.

# CHAPTER FOURTEEN

WHEN I WOKE UP, I was still feeling a little tired from the long-distance magic. The good thing was that I knew what I had to do, no matter how much I didn't want to do it.

Matt would be at breakfast, waiting for me. He wasn't one to give up when he wanted something, and since I'd been there yesterday morning, he'd be there today ready for round two. There was no time to stall. I had to get this done.

I put on the new pair of black pants I'd gotten for the trip. They were hiking pants, but way nicer. They made my butt look really good. I paired them with a magenta tank, and a peasant top. Trading the fleece I wore yesterday for a cardigan, I felt confident. I carefully put on my makeup, feeling like it was war paint. I thought about casting some protection spells—arming myself with a knot or two—but I was already feeling sapped. I'd only been gone from Texas for forty-eight hours. I still hadn't recovered from Luciana's heavy draining when I used that big chunk of magic last night. And if these *brujos* were evil, I was going to need every last scrap of magic I had. Lucas said he'd be watching out for me, but I couldn't count on that. I had to take care of myself and be ready to fight Matt and whatever these *brujos* could throw at me.

When I was ready, I grabbed my purse and headed out to the lobby. Sure enough, Matt was sitting at a table, reading a newspaper. He wore a white button-down, with a brightly colored plaid sweater over it, and navy slacks. The sweater was loud and obnoxious, but it made a statement. I wasn't sure what that statement was...but it was there.

He noticed me and grinned. Something about the grin was off. He looked a little too triumphant, considering he didn't know what I planned to say.

*You can do this. You* have *to do this.* I blindly grabbed some food and then approached his table—not wanting to waste any time. Might as well get this over with.

He put down the newspaper, folding it carefully as he looked up at me.

"Can I sit here?"

He sat up straighter, waving a hand at the chair across from him. "Of course." He took a sip of his coffee, trying to hide the smug look on his face. His grin had to mean he was pleased I'd come to him, and for a second I thought he wouldn't give me any grief for being rude to him yesterday.

Maybe this wasn't going to be so hard after all.

"The wolf get tired of you already?" he said right as I took my first bite of grapefruit.

I'd known the dig was coming—had even been waiting for it—and still he managed to catch me off guard. Had Matt picked up on my crush? I hoped not, or I'd never hear the end of it.

*He couldn't know. Only I knew. Unless I'd made a complete idiot of myself at breakfast yesterday.*

I slowly chewed and swallowed, as I thought about what to say. The best I could come up with was not to dignify it with a response. Instead, I changed the subject. "You said you knew the local coven?"

He relaxed back against the chair. "Yes, I do."

I took another bite of my grapefruit. He was going to make me pry it out of him, but I would do my parents proud and not lose my temper. "And what do you know of them?"

"They're an all-male sect. They live like monks in a small town an hour south of here."

I was trying not to just jump into the favor. If I asked the right question, maybe he'd offer to take me there and save me from asking. It might be a long shot, but it was worth a try. "Do you know anything about the kind of magic they practice?"

He scrunched up his brows as he leaned forward. "What kind of a question is that?"

I nearly sighed. Could he really be that dense? "A valid one." Although if he said anything other than black magic, I was going to be suspicious.

"All magic is the same."

Now that I hadn't been expecting. "Come on, Matt. You don't really believe that, do you?" I'd thought he knew what Luciana was like—and what she'd put me and the rest of us through—but maybe I was wrong.

What if he was just a jerk? Not an evil, black magic-practicing jerk, but just an everyday type of controlling, misogynistic man?

When he didn't say anything, I leaned against the table, my elbows just resting on the edge. "We both know that there are all sorts of magic. Elemental. Blood. White. Black... And covens can lean more one way than the other. Some extremely so." I took a breath. "What kind of sect are they?"

Matt shook his head slowly. "The only kind that I know. Somewhere in the gray area between white and black." He studied me for a second and I itched to move, but didn't. I couldn't show him any weakness. "If you really think that there are covens that practice only one kind of magic then you're even more naive than I thought."

I took the insult with a grain of salt. If he wanted to lash out at me because I'd ignored him yesterday, I could deal. I'd surely dealt with worse. "Maybe so."

"Well, this all-male sect is the only one practicing any sort of magic in this part of South America. Period. So, if you're looking for a coven, this would be them."

I took a moment to brace myself. *I hate that I have to do this...* "If your offer is still on the table, I'd like your help. I need to talk to them about something."

His answering grin definitely made me suspicious. Whatever he was going to say, I probably wasn't going to like it. "What am I getting out of this?"

He was such a douche bag. "Do you only think in terms of what's good for you?"

"Yes. I'm the most important person to me. No one else will put me first if I don't."

Even though I wasn't surprised by that statement, it made me want to hit him. "That comes off as pretty self-centered."

He crossed his arms as he glared at me. "Call it what you like. If you were honest with yourself, you'd realize you're the same way. You're here asking me to do you a favor without thinking about me at all. So, my point is proven. If I'm not getting something out of this then why would I do it? You'll blow me off as soon as I give you what you want."

He had a point. I was going to blow him off the second I had what I wanted. But the key difference was that I wasn't doing this for myself. I was doing this for my brother. For what was left of my coven.

But we'd gone way off topic, and I was officially wasting time. "Fine. What do you want?"

"For you to finally stop fighting what's already been agreed upon. You should've come to New York last year."

Even if I'd wanted to, which I didn't, Luciana never would've let me go last year. "How was I supposed to know that you wanted me there? I haven't heard from you in months."

"I told Luciana," he said it like it should mean something to me.

I nearly smiled. He was giving me a piece of information that could carve a wedge between Luciana and the New York coven. "You'll have to take your complaints to her, because she didn't say a thing to me."

His mouth dropped open. "Really?"

I studied him for a minute. All this time truly I'd thought Matt was working with Luciana, but maybe he wasn't. If Luciana had lied to him about one thing, it stood to reason that she'd lied to him about other things as well. "Honestly. Do I look like I'm lying?"

He narrowed his gaze at me. "I don't know."

I shrugged. "Here's the thing. Luciana wants to keep me around. I know you know what I specialize in—"

"Enhancing others' energies."

I nodded. "Right. Well, I do that for Luciana. And—as far as I know—the only thing Luciana wants is more power. By losing me, she loses power. So, why would she ever follow through with whatever bargain you two concocted?"

He leaned back in his chair, not saying a word.

"Why do you want me? Really?"

He looked at the ceiling before apparently coming to some decision. "The same reason Luciana wants you."

My jaw clenched as I took in his words. This was infuriating. Did everyone just want me for what I could do for them? "Well, I'm not marrying you. Even if you decide to help me today, I can't promise that. Luciana has been controlling me for long enough. I really don't think I can go back to coven life. Anywhere." While I had him opening it up, I figured now was a great time to find out what Luciana was getting out of pretending to marry me off. Knowing that could mean the difference between defeating her or dying.

I leaned in, trying to make it seem like I was conspiring with him. "So, what did she get out of the deal? Did she just want your coven as allies?" That was my best guess so far, but my instincts said there was more to it than that.

He scoffed. "No. She couldn't care less about being allies. We had an item she wanted. I didn't think too much about it. My coven... Things aren't easy over there. I needed your help, so I traded. You for it. And, one way or another, I need you there."

*One way or another?* My nails dug into my palms as I fisted my hands. I wasn't an object to be traded. I was a human being. "At least tell me what you traded for me."

"Doesn't matter. She can't use it."

He was so unbelievably wrong. When she wanted something that badly, she'd find a way to make it work. "If you really believe that then *you're* more naive than *I* thought."

"You're really not going back with me?"

Should I lie? Maybe. But I couldn't. "No. I'm not."

Matt stood and started for the door.

Where was he going? Panic tightened my chest.

No. I needed his help.

Damn it. Why had I pushed him so much?

I sat there watching him leave, wondering what I could say to get him back. What was I willing to agree to?

He paused in the exit. "You coming?"

That had been so much easier than I'd expected. And I hadn't actually agreed to do anything for him. Why would he take me there?

I knew he'd ask for something later. He wasn't the type to let me forget a favor, but I'd deal with that when the time came. I scrambled to put a tip on the table, and caught up with him. "We're going now?"

"The sooner we get this taken care of, the sooner I can get home. I have to get back to New York. My coven is falling apart."

I almost felt bad for him. Then I remembered that he'd tried to trade some magical object for me. He was going to push me to marry him just so I could fix whatever messed-up situation his coven was in.

*Not your problem, Claudia. You can't fix everything that's wrong in this world. You can barely protect your own family.*

I followed him out of the hotel, trailing behind as he walked down the narrow street to a parked car. He opened the driver's side door for himself. "Get in."

I didn't wait for him to ask twice. I opened the door to his little blue Honda rental and slid into the passenger seat. "You know where you're going? We don't need directions?"

"No." He started the engine and drove down the street. I buckled my seat belt as he nearly sideswiped a car.

Lucas had made driving down the tiny roads look easy. I'd never felt anything but safe with him, except for being terrified when we went up that mountain road. Even then, he'd reassured me. But a few seconds into the drive with Matt I knew I was really putting my life in his hands.

"My cousin joined up with this sect a while back," Matt said as he cut off a truck. "We all thought he was nuts, but he was always a little on the odd side. I've visited a few times over the years. Luciana has been known to stop in, too."

I didn't like that Luciana had been there. It definitely supported what Lucas said about those *brujos* being evil. I cracked my knuckles as I contemplated asking Matt to turn around, but kept my mouth shut. If there was another way, I'd take it. But there wasn't.

As I sat there, I wondered if there was any way I could get Matt on our side. I knew I couldn't trust him, but while we were stuck in the car together, I figured I might as well try to convince him to support us against Luciana. He'd definitely pass along anything I said to his mother—the leader of his coven. And she might pass that information along to Luciana. But she might not.

Worst he could do was say no and tell Luciana I'd asked. It wasn't like she didn't know I'd left the coven.

I blew out a breath as I thought about what to say. Keeping it simple was probably the best way to go. "I know it's asking a lot, but it would be amazing if I could get your support against Luciana. You said your coven was in trouble. Forming a little alliance right now could do both of us some good."

"Why are you so set against her? What's she done to you?"

That question was so absurd to me, I wanted to laugh. Or cry. What hadn't she done? "She's gone solid black. A few weeks ago, she attacked the pack and tried to raise demons. She only stopped because Daniel was killed."

"Demons?" The car swerved as he looked at me.

"Watch it!" I waved my hands at the road.

He jerked the steering wheel, bringing the car back onto the road. "Sorry. But demons?" He shouted. "I knew we shouldn't have..." He paused, but I really wanted him to finish that thought.

They shouldn't have *what?*

"Daniel's dead? That's a shame. He was always nice to me."

A shame? That was much too tame a word for how I felt about it, but I merely nodded as I tried not to let the sadness take hold. "He was a nice guy," I finally managed to say. "I miss him a lot."

We were quiet for a little bit, before Matt spoke up. "Are you sure you know what you're talking about?"

Could he be any more patronizing? I willed myself not to lose my temper. *Allies. We need allies.* We'd have a better chance against Luciana and the others if we had more witches on our side. "I'm certain. And not only that, she called up a demon to raise Daniel from the dead. He... It wasn't right. His skin was gray and starting to rot. She turned her own son into a monster. She has to be stopped."

He scanned my face, most likely looking to see if I was lying.

"Watch the road!" I yelled as the tires skidded on gravel again. He faced forward in time to swerve away from the oncoming traffic.

God. He was going to kill us. "Just watch the road." I said it much softer the second time.

"Raising demons is really bad. That's not gray magic, that's black. Why isn't your coven standing up to her?"

Where did I start? "The thing about Luciana is that she's a good speaker. She's convinced everyone that what she's doing is what's best for the coven and now they follow her like lemmings. And she's got a massive hatred for the wolves. Any complaints that the coven had, she found a way to blame them on the pack."

"Come on, Claudia."

I ground my teeth together as he said my name. *Clod*-ia. With that one word, I knew douche bag Matt was back. All the hope that he might help us fled.

"You have to realize that the wolves aren't our friends."

No. I didn't realize that. So far, they were the only ones willing to help. "Why not?"

"Because of a centuries-old feud. That friction isn't going to end just because you made a few friends."

"I know all about the feud. And I know it's not going to end

147

just because *I* want it to, but she's evil. She's willing to start a war with the Weres just because my cousin was bitten—"

"Sounds like reason enough—"

"But," I spoke over him, "it's just an excuse. She was even working with one of the wolves. She has a bigger plan to expose all supernaturals to humans. This affects everyone—even you. I know they're going to find out about us. It's only a matter of time. But if she does it her way, she's going to make enemies not just of the pack, but of the humans, too." He started to speak, but I kept on talking. I had to get this out. "And all this fighting with the pack isn't necessary. They weren't out to get us. All we had to do was reach out and they would've been friends. Allies. We'll need a lot more of those once the world finds out about us. I mean, am I the only one who's heard of the Salem Witch Trials? The humans have hunted us in the past, and they could again. So yeah, it'd be nice—for once—to have someone protect us—which is what the wolves have been doing all along. From vampires and fey gone bad and all other bad supers out there. Instead of thanking them, we try to kill them? Try to help an evil man get control of the pack? And," I drew the word out. "She stripped Tessa of her power—"

"She managed to do it? Was it successful?"

I narrowed my gaze at him. "Yes. It was. And it was horrible."

He grinned for a second and then a serious mask came over his face.

But that smile stuck with me. Chills broke over my skin.

He cleared his throat, as if nothing had happened. "That seems really far-fetched. I can't believe she could do that. I've never heard of a witch being able to."

I was quiet for a second, studying him. I didn't need my intuition to tell me not to trust him when all the signs he was giving off were screaming it. "You don't have to believe me, but

Luciana is raising demons she can't control. She'll destroy us all and then anyone who survives will be running from the humans. All it'll take is one photo leaking to the news and we'll have another rash of witch-hunts. Guaranteed." I took a breath. "It'd be good if you were willing to work with us and the pack."

"I think you're getting your wires crossed. Stripping witches? Conjuring demons? Black magic? It seems a little crazy..."

He yammered on, but I tuned him out. This was useless.

Good thing I didn't need him to do anything but get me on the *brujos'* land. Which he was doing. Once I was there, I'd get the magic I needed and leave.

It had been stupid to think that he'd want to be allies. Most witches hated the wolves. But those prejudices wouldn't get us anywhere. Just in the short time I'd been at St. Ailbe's I'd understood the truth. While we hid from the world behind our barriers, learning cleansing rituals and brewing potions, the wolves started training to fight from childhood. Their hunters had been clearing the world of evil for years, giving us the freedom to thrive.

If it got back to Luciana that I was trying to make allies then so be it. She'd lost her leverage over me and I wasn't letting her or anyone else push me around anymore.

I closed my eyes and tried to calm down. I hadn't meant to get so riled up. I had to think clearly. Calmly.

*Picture what you want and believe it will be so.*

I was going to find a cure for my brother. I wasn't leaving this evil sect's lands until I had what I was looking for.

# CHAPTER FIFTEEN

IT FELT like ages before we stopped, but it only took an hour. The closer we got, the more I had the urge to turn around. My gut was sending me all kinds of warning signals. The black aura ahead of us that grew bigger with every passing second only made that feeling worse.

*Had I really seen that bright white aura in all this darkness?*

The sect's compound was small, with only one narrow, dead-end dirt road that ran among a cluster of old stone buildings. The only thing that identified it was the sign on the side of the road. It was a tiny rectangle, almost completely covered by moss and dirt, but I could just make out the name. Not that it helped me identify the place. The word was long and unpronounceable, with way too many consonants.

From what I could see, there were four bigger structures, although the word "big" was a bit much for what was there. They were small, one story, and probably one room inside. The two smaller buildings looked like little more than huts.

Matt got out of the car and I followed suit. As soon as I did, chills ran down my arms. This place had a deadened feeling, and I didn't think I was sensing that because the compound was warded. Peru was so vibrant. So full of life. It was like there was magic in every piece of grass. But not here. The quiet felt empty.

An old man stepped from one of the bigger buildings. He took careful steps toward us, his back hunched over from his age. But his aura...

Black as pitch, shot through with blood-red ribbons.

The sight of it had my legs tensing, urging me to run in the other direction. I fought my instincts, hoping that Lucas hadn't changed his mind. That he really was out there somewhere. Listening, in case I needed him.

Because I had a feeling I might need him very soon.

Another man came out of the building wearing the same outfit—black pants with a long black tunic. Coordinated clothes seemed normal for a secluded sect like this, but not coordinated auras.

The evil was there, like Lucas had warned me. I'd expected that. But identical auras?

Auras were usually unique. Even the wolves, who had lots of similarities within their pack, varied in gold tones from white to orange to amber. Lucas' was a very light yellow, almost white, while Dastien's was a dark amber color. I couldn't read my own aura but I doubted mine was that close to Raphael's, and these two men weren't twins by any means.

Matt stepped forward and talked quietly with the older man for a minute. The man nodded and turned to me, waving me over.

Swallowing my apprehension, I forced my feet to move. I had to do this. It was the only option. I repeated that in my head as a drop of sweat rolled between my shoulder blades.

"Hello, I'm Father Valentine. This is Father Alfred," the old man said as I stood there, studying him. His tone was friendly enough, but I could see so much more. No matter how nice he pretended to be, this man wasn't someone I should trust. "Don't be shy. Come this way."

I pushed all my fear aside and gave him by best grin. "I'm Claudia de Santos." My plan was to kill them with kindness, as my father always said. People usually underestimated what a kind person could do. "I'm sorry to come without calling first. I hope we're not intruding on your day too much."

He scoffed at that. "Not to worry, my dear. There's no way to reach us without stopping by. We lack many of the amenities of the modern world—like running water and electricity. It's nice to get an unexpected visitor or two." He turned back toward the building. "Come to my house. We'll have tea and see why you've traveled all this way."

Father Alfred nodded and led the way. From what I could tell, the older man, Father Valentine, ran the show around here.

As we walked into the compound, I tried to search for a glimmer of the white aura I'd seen yesterday. If I could narrow down where it was then maybe I could sneak away to investigate.

A bright light caught my eye and I turned to find the source: a building in the back. It had no windows, only an open doorway, but something glowed inside.

That was where I needed to go. Somehow I had to convince them to take me into that building.

"In here," Father Valentine said, gesturing to one of the smaller buildings.

Caught already. So much for trying to be subtle. "What's over there?" I motioned to the last building, where the road ended.

"Oh, just another house. Nothing in there to interest a young girl like you."

I wiped my sweaty palms on my pants. He wasn't going to make this easy.

He disappeared into the smaller building on our right and Matt followed him.

"Go on," Father Alfred said from behind me.

I'd hesitated just long enough to arouse suspicion, but my body didn't want to obey the command to go inside.

Father Alfred touched my shoulder. "This way. Nothing will harm you here."

I managed not to cringe away from his touch. If I'd been a wolf, I knew his words would've stunk of lies.

*Just do it, Claudia.* I stepped through the doorway and immediately felt something brush past me. It felt slithery and slimy. I shuddered and looked down. A row of horseshoes was pressed into the dirt floor.

The small house was warded, but I couldn't tell against what.

As soon as my eyes adjusted, all I could see was the altar. Incense burned on the stone, and it was surrounded with...

I swallowed. The things hanging there looked like dried baby goats.

*What the...* I knew some evil *brujos* used ritual sacrifice in their magic, but I'd never heard of shrunken, dried carcasses being kept as decoration. At least, I hoped they were decoration. I didn't want to know what they did if they were still active. That idea more than creeped me out.

*You're here for Raphael.* Remembering that truth kept me from running out the door.

I took in the rest of the altar. The more I stared at it, the weirder it got. The little deity holding a burning cigarette and surrounded by fake dollar bills took the cake. I'd seen some weird things in my life, but this was just...

Something ran across my shoe and I squealed.

"Calm down," Matt said. "It's just a guinea pig."

"Oh. Right." Because it was normal to have guinea pigs running through the house.

I took in the rest of the room. A small table with four chairs was placed against the far wall. To my right—the altar. And to my left was a hearth, with grating above it for cooking. In between the oven and the table, a neatly made twin bed pressed against the wall. The only window in the house—if house was the right word—was above the bed, but dark curtains blocked any light from coming through.

The fire burning in the hearth was the only real source of light. There was a chimney, but it must be blocked, because a lot of the smoke wafted into the room, making it hazy and foggy. It added to the creep factor. I wanted to pull the curtain aside and throw open the window, but that would've been rude.

Another guinea pig sniffed at my ankle, drawing my attention to the floor.

"Here," said Father Alfred. "They'll come out if I feed them." He threw a bunch of greens on the floor, and seemingly out of nowhere, guinea pigs came running. There had to be at least fifty of them. Some big. Some little. All different colors.

It was so weird to think of these men taking care of animals. "You have a lot of pets, Father Valentine."

The men started laughing.

"What?" What was so funny?

"They're not pets, child," said Father Valentine. "They're dinner."

*What?* They had to be joking. No way would I ever eat one of those. I'd had a hamster way back when. Raphael had hated her, but I loved her. He eventually made such a stink that Daniel had to adopt Harriet the Hamster. I'd still gone to visit her every day at Daniel's house.

Just like that, a wave of grief hit me. It was so quick. The image of Daniel playing with Harriet filled my mind and tears welled.

"Don't cry after this lot," said Father Alfred, a British accent thick in his voice. "They're more varmint than anything else. We only eat them once a week."

That meant they killed them. And cut off their skin.

Oh God. I was going to be sick. If I thought about it anymore I was going to go vegetarian. I pushed all of that horror out of my mind. I needed something that these men had. Being polite was of the utmost importance.

Father Alfred moved around the room, grabbing the kettle from the fire and setting it on a trivet on the table. He placed four handleless cups on the table and went back to the hearth to grab a few jars that rested on the shelf above it. He sprinkled an assortment of herbs into the cups and then filled them with water to steep.

I watched every move and realized I couldn't possibly drink whatever was in that cup. Taking herbs from these men would be beyond stupid, but I wasn't sure how I could get out of drinking without being suspicious.

"Come sit," said Father Valentine as he settled into one of the chairs.

Matt took the seat next to him. "Where's my cousin?"

"Oh, the others are on a spirit quest in the mountains. They've been gone for a fortnight. I don't think they'll be back for another few days. But I like to stick around here." He chuckled to himself. "My bones are old. This young one stayed behind to make sure I didn't do anything foolish."

"That's not quite accurate," said Father Alfred. "I stayed back because last time we all left, you got yourself in a bit of trouble. Wolves." He said the last word like it was disgusting.

It was to be expected, but it still annoyed me.

"Don't talk too poorly of them in front of her. She seems to have grown fond of the wolves recently," Matt said.

Father Valentine leaned back in his chair. "Is that right? Why would you waste your time with those dogs?"

I'd been around the wolves enough to know that "dog" was a huge insult. "I ran into a problem with my coven. I needed a place to go, and my cousin who was bitten offered sanctuary." I didn't want to go into too much detail. If Luciana liked to come here then the old man definitely knew her. They might even be best friends.

Father Valentine grunted.

Well, this was going fantastically. How long did I need to give it before I politely segued into asking for access to the rest of their compound?

Matt motioned to me. "She thinks Luciana is raising demons."

*Matt! You idiot.*

"What gives you that impression?" Father Alfred set his cup on the table with a *thunk*.

I wanted to wring Matt's stupid neck. I had to play this carefully. If they really were the kind who dabbled in summoning then I couldn't come out and say I was looking for white magic. "She tried to raise some about a week ago, but she doesn't have enough power to hold them. She's playing a dangerous game." Father Alfred and Father Valentine shared a disbelieving look, and I barely contained a sigh. This wasn't going well. "I know it sounds far-fetched, but I've come a long way for help." I didn't say their help, because I didn't want their help.

Father Valentine's bushy white eyebrows nearly disappeared along his hairline. "You want our help? I see." He pushed the cup in front of me a little closer. "Well, let's have a think on how we might be able to do that."

None of the men made a move to sip their tea while they

stared at me, and I couldn't help feeling a twinge of suspicion. I really, really didn't want to take herbs from *brujos* I didn't know. Especially ones with auras like theirs.

I picked up the cup, blew off the steam, and pretended to take a small sip before setting it back down. "A little hot." I gave them my best smile.

Father Alfred smiled, but it wasn't a nice one. "I'm not sure we have much experience with demons. What type are you trying to raise?"

Of course they'd assume I wanted to raise demons. They were evil. They'd expect me to want to do evil things, too, but that didn't mean I wasn't horribly outraged by the suggestion. "There's been a misunderstanding. I don't want to raise any demons."

"Oh, well then." Father Valentine bristled. "I was going to say that it would be very difficult for someone like yourself to raise a demon. That means you want to fight them?"

I nodded.

"That's not wise," Father Valentine said. "If you see one, you should leave the area. Fast."

I wasn't going to take this personally. Nope. Not at all. "I understand that would be the best thing to do, but sometimes that's not an option. Sometimes you have to fight."

"I see." Father Valentine pressed his lips together firmly as he judged me.

This wasn't working. I needed to not do what I always did—follow where I was led. I needed to be like Teresa. If someone wasn't giving me what I wanted, I needed to get it myself.

I took a little sip of the tea and instantly regretted it. The brew was bitter and foul. I barely managed not to make a face as I set down the cup. "I'm sorry. It's been a long journey. I know you said you didn't have any facilities here, but is there an outhouse or...?"

"Oh. Yes, of course. Out the door to the left, behind the next building. You can't miss it." Father Valentine grinned, and it chilled me to the core. "Come back and finish your tea, and we can see what we can tell you about fighting demons."

I plastered on a grin. "Thank you. I'll be right back."

"Take your time, dear. It won't do to rush a lady."

I nodded, not sure what to say to that, and left the suffocating room. Another slithering wave hit me as I crossed the line of horseshoes and I gasped for breath in the fresh air.

The street outside was totally empty. If they were telling the truth then only the two of them were here. And if they thought I was "taking my time" in the outhouse then that gave me at least five minutes of safe snooping.

The only problem was the wards. Passing over them could sound some kind of silent alarm. Lucas had mentioned it, so I had to be very careful. If I set one off, there was no doubt in my mind the Fathers would be breathing down my neck in seconds.

The good news was, I knew exactly where I was going. I walked around the compound to get to the building in the back. It was slightly bigger than the others but had no windows. No chimney either. I peeked inside the open doorway, but didn't see any auras. Nothing white and glowing.

I closed my eyes and rubbed them. Again, nothing.

No. This was wrong. I knew it was in there. I'd seen the aura not fifteen minutes ago. It couldn't be gone.

I squinted inside, but it was too dark to see much. A mountain of books piled on the floor. I spotted some mixings for potions. But the altar...

Unlit candles crowded its surface. Even though I couldn't make out the surrounding shapes, I knew something was off about this one. Odd-shaped lumps covered its surface, and I wasn't sure I wanted to know what they were. Especially since it smelled like something had died in there.

I held my breath as I focused in on my magic, feeling it ignite within my soul. *"Fire hotter than the sun, give me light where there is none."*

The candles flared as my magic filled the room.

*Oh God.* It smelled like something had died because something had.

Many things.

What I'd hoped was a lumpy blanket was actually the remains of a few guinea pigs. A magic circle was carved into the ground, with a pentagram in the center. The remains of old candles were piled up on top of each other at each point of the star.

I held my hand over my mouth and tried not to throw up. Whatever these mages were up to, I wanted no part of it, but I couldn't turn back. No matter how grossed out I was, the thing I needed was here. It had to be.

I quickly warded myself to keep negative energy away, and stepped through the doorway. The slimy sensation was the same as crossing the threshold into Father Valentine's house. I only had a few moments before the Fathers came to find me.

I ran to the pile of books and scanned the titles. *Demon Casting. Spells of Light and Dark. Herbs of Witchery.* More than a few of the books sounded helpful, but my little purse wouldn't hold much of anything. I had to pick one book. Just one.

*"God above, give me luck. Help me out so I'm not stuck."*

I reached for a book and knocked over three more.

*Way to backfire, spell.*

I knelt down on the floor to pile up the dropped books and a flash of white caught my eye. A glow came from inside a book that had fallen under the bookcase. I never would've seen it, but now that I was down here, I knew without doubt that this was the key to finding exactly what I needed.

My fingers shook as I slid it out. The cover was blank. I

opened it to the first page. Writing was scrawled in a language I didn't understand, but the book itself wasn't what caught my attention.

A loose, folded piece of paper stuck out from the binding.

It gave off a pure white aura.

I slipped it out and set the book down. As I opened the folds, I got a case of the giggles.

I'd found a map. And if I was reading the symbols right, it led to a temple.

*Oh my God*. I'd found a map that led to the temple of the white mages.

I shoved the map into my purse. I needed to get out of here before the Fathers found me.

A throat cleared behind me. Father Alfred stood in the doorway, and behind him Father Valentine and Matt glared.

*Shit.* I fumbled with the books that I'd dropped, trying to conceal the fact that I'd taken something from their stash. "I'm sorry. I got lost and thought this might be the outhouse. The smell was... So, I lit the candles, and then I saw the books..." I piled all the fallen books in my hands and got up, trying not to drop them. "I do love a good magic book. I didn't mean to snoop."

"I'll take those," Father Alfred said, anger dripping from his words.

I swallowed. Should I scream now and hope Lucas got here in time, or see how it played out? Was Lucas even nearby? I couldn't count on that. It would be better to get myself out of this. If I still could. My hands shook as I handed Father Alfred the books. "Thank you. Sorry if I ruined your arrangement."

As Father Alfred took the books from me, he muttered something in Latin.

Before I could do anything—run, scream, anything at all— my body crumpled to the ground. I had no control over it.

Pure terror coursed through me and a drop of sweat rolled down my temple. I could feel it, but I couldn't move.

"Drag her to the center of the circle," Father Valentine said. "We'll get you her power, but then you'll owe a favor of our choosing. Do you agree to the terms?"

"Yes," Matt said.

Rage like I'd never felt burned hot inside me.

I hadn't liked Matt before, but now I hated him. Despised him.

He wanted to strip my power. He'd lied to my face yet again, and yet again I'd fallen for it. Stupid. *So, so stupid.*

I tried to call out, but I couldn't. It was like my voice was stuck. But my magic...

Now I knew what was in the tea. If I'd actually swallowed it down, chances were it would've blocked my power. Thank God I'd only tasted the tiniest drop.

I used rhymes to access my magic, because I felt like they gave me strength, but I didn't need to say the words aloud. I didn't need words at all. I just liked to use them.

That was the problem. I used them as a crutch.

The Fathers moved my body like I was a doll, and their dark auras seeped into me wherever their cold fingers touched. They dragged me into the middle of their circle.

A knife burned as it cut along my arms. The metallic scent of my blood filled the room.

I had to focus. They wouldn't steal my magic. Luciana hadn't managed it. And these three douches wouldn't either. I just had to get enough magic out so that I could scream.

Lucas would come. If he really was what he thought he was to me then he wouldn't be able to stop himself. I prayed I was right, because I'd only get one chance.

I closed my eyes and felt the tiny trickle of magic I had left.

*Release my voice. Release my voice. Release my voice.*

I said the simple spell over and over in my head, until I was sure—or as sure as I could be—that it had worked.

The two *brujos* started chanting as Matt watched over me with a smug look.

The scent of sulfur filled the room.

I sent a silent prayer that my spell worked, took a breath, and screamed as loud as I could.

The men froze in stunned silence for a second. The chanting was gone, and the smell of sulfur vanished.

I heard a howl in the distance.

*Lucas.* I wasn't safe yet. Not nearly, but a wave of relief washed over me. I wasn't alone this time.

"You stupid fucking bitch." Matt's kick landed in my side, knocking the breath from me.

I couldn't move to protect myself. All I could see was his foot as it came toward my face.

Then I saw nothing at all.

# CHAPTER SIXTEEN

I WOKE up swinging punches and screaming.

Someone grabbed my wrists and pressed them into the mattress above my head. It hurt. Everything hurt.

The room was too dark to see. I screamed again. "Let me go!"

"Stop, Claudia. You're okay."

I froze. *Lucas.* "Where am I?"

"Your hotel room. If you promise to hold still, I'll turn on the light. But you're hurt. So just... Please, don't move, okay?"

I nodded. "Okay." The terror was slowly fading, and the more it did the more I could feel the aches across my body. "What happened?"

Lucas flicked on the light, and his eyes glowed with a dark, intense energy. The bed dipped as he sat down beside me. "I've been alive for a long time. I've fought in wars—human and supernatural. I've lost friends and family and been helpless against it. But nothing—not ever in my years on this earth—terrified me more than the sound of that scream."

He grabbed his hair, pulling it as he looked away from me. "I got there before they were able to do too much damage, but..."

He brushed his thumb against my temple and I winced. "That douche bag ex-fiancé of yours got in a few good kicks."

I took a breath that turned into a wince. "Feels like it."

Lucas stood and paced away from the bed. His hands balled in tight fists and he kept his back to me. "I shouldn't have let you go. I knew better. You got hurt and it's my fault."

My jaw would've dropped, but some part of me sensed that that would hurt too much. How could he possibly blame himself? "First off, it's not your fault."

"It *is* my fault. I'm supposed to protect you." Lucas spun to face me, and it only took a moment before pain flashed in his eyes. "I cleaned your cuts and put some liquid stitch and bandages on them. I can't do anything for the ribs or the knot on your head that seems to be growing by the second, but I've got some pain pills."

The way he was behaving...

I wouldn't be ready to deal with that until I got some of those pain pills in me. I tried to sit up and winced again.

This was so bad. I didn't have time to be hurt. I needed to get to that temple.

Which reminded me... "Please tell me you got my purse."

"You're damned right I did. And I burned your blood and everything else in that evil torture room of theirs."

"How did you—"

"I'm the Alpha of the Peruvian pack."

*He was Alpha? Of the Peruvian pack?* Wasn't that Muraco's job? Or did being one of the Seven mean he wasn't involved in the local pack? Suddenly, I doubted everything I'd learned about the wolves.

And what did that mean for—

No. That wasn't important right now. He'd saved me, and I'd think about the rest when my whole body wasn't screaming.

"I can take on a couple of witches. If the whole sect had

been there, I might've needed reinforcements, but they weren't and the ritual already had them distracted, so we lucked out. They ran off when I came through the door, and I was too worried about you to go after them. But I will. When the time is right, they'll pay."

I swallowed. With his tone, I knew he wasn't joking. And I was glad it wasn't me he was angry with.

He put his hands under my shoulders and lifted me carefully until I was sitting up. He reached over to the nightstand. "Here you go."

He placed two white pills on my palm, and I swallowed them with the glass of water he handed me. "You should be feeling better in twenty minutes. At least that's what the doctor said."

Doctor? "How long was I out?"

"A few hours. I was worried about a head injury, but the doctor is also a witch and he said the magic needed to work its way out of your system." He grumbled something unintelligible. "But he didn't say it'd take so long."

I sighed. "It would've been faster if I wasn't already so worn out."

"From Luciana draining you."

"Yeah. And from the healing chant I did last night on Raphael."

"What?"

I filled him in on the phone call. "So, I was already depleted."

"I see."

"May I have my purse?"

"Sure." He got up and grabbed it.

I looked up at him. He'd saved me from something really, truly horrible. Teresa had survived it, but I wasn't sure that I could live without my magic. Luciana's way of draining me was

167

one thing, but I always knew my power would recover. If he hadn't stopped it this time...

My hands shook as I took the purse from him. I met his gaze "Thank you for getting me out of there. I'm terrified of what would've happened if you hadn't shown up."

"I'll always show up for you." He cupped my face in his hand. "You're not ready for all of this, but I've been waiting a long time for you. I'd rather die than let you down."

I didn't know what to say to that. Right now, he was right. I wasn't ready. I had so much to deal with, I didn't know where to start.

I reached inside my purse. "Going there was awful, but it was worth it. I found this before they caught me snooping." I pulled out the old map. The paper had yellowed and the edges were frayed, but the ink was still bright on the page. And for something so old, the paper didn't feel too fragile. It had to be the magic that preserved it so well.

Lucas grunted, telling me that he wasn't sure it was worth it. As I unfolded the map, he leaned down to take a look.

"What do you think? Do you know where any of this is?"

He ran his hand along the symbols.

I pointed to the central image. "I know this is a mountain, which doesn't really narrow it down. But this looks like some sort of tracks. A train?" I hoped he'd know where it was. The train should narrow down the options a lot.

"Not train tracks. A mine. I think I might know where this is. Vaguely. I know this right here." He pointed to an icon on the map. "That's a local waterfall." Then he traced the line of tracks with a fingertip. "This is the mine entrance, but it's not connected to this part over here. I'd know it if it was."

I followed his fingertip. I hadn't had time to look closely while I was in that awful room, but I'd seen the mountain and the tracks. What I hadn't noticed was that the map was broken into two parts. A trail led up the mountain, past a waterfall, and to the mine. Then nothing. The next picture showed the exit from the mine into some sort of valley. The temple stood in the center of that valley.

"There's the exit to the mine here." I pointed to the left side of the valley. "So they connect. It looks like it must be some sort of secret valley between the mountains. The map just doesn't show how to get to the part of the mine that exits to the valley."

"No. I know that area. There's no valley there," Lucas said.

"What do you think it means?" I had to figure this out. It was the key to everything. I knew it was.

"I haven't been inside the mine, so there's a chance there's a hidden exit, but however it connects to the other half... It has to be magic."

"Maybe it's just hidden. Using wards to keep outsiders away is common enough. My coven's compound uses spells like that to keep normal humans from coming near."

"That's possible." He sat back down on the bed. "The fey use similar concealments for their underhill. It would make sense if the old mages had sealed themselves off."

The only problem would be finding the right way out of the mine, but we could figure that out when we saw it for ourselves. "Okay. So we get to the mine and find our way through to the temple. Then we get whatever's there and head straight back." It seemed like everything was lining up. "We'll make it in time."

Lucas didn't say anything as he lifted me up, sliding me onto his lap and pulling me close. Warmth surrounded me as he wrapped his arms around my shoulders. I sighed and followed along, putting my arms around his waist.

I felt safe with him. Secure. It was like coming home.

I was starting to think that maybe Teresa wasn't so crazy. Not that I really had thought that, but I'd wondered how much choice she'd had in mating with Dastien. He'd bitten her and that was that.

I still wasn't sure if it was what I wanted. The thought of being a wolf definitely seemed crazy. But every passing second with Lucas made me want him more. No one in the coven, not even Shane or Elsa, would understand if I bonded with Lucas. Raphael would flip.

Then again, they might not care if it got them—all of us, really—out of our oaths. At least that part wasn't such a big hurry. The oath pulled on me the worst, and the others were probably safe outside of Luciana's range by now. Jumping into a mate bond wouldn't save Raphael from the poison, so I had a little time to think it over.

But I couldn't help thinking about it as Lucas held me in his arms.

What if?

What if I did become his mate?

He smoothed his hand along my hair a few times before speaking. "You're not alone. You've got me."

I wouldn't let myself cry again, but it was hard. "Thanks."

"And we're going to save your brother. We'll move fast." He pulled away just enough so I could see his face. "We'll get to San Jose in time."

"Thank you."

He brushed a kiss across my forehead before gently placing me back on the bed. He folded up the map. "Okay then. We know what we have to do. Now, I'm going to order you some food and then you need to rest."

What? I didn't have time to rest. The clock was ticking and I was running out of time. I'd already lost five hours being unconscious. "No. I thought we could leave soon. I told you. My brother is dying." I swung my legs over the edge of the bed, but Lucas stopped me. "I can be ready in five minutes. Maybe less."

He put his hands on my legs, pressing them into the bed so I couldn't move. "Wait. Slow down."

"Wait? I can't wait. Adrian said the sooner the better. We have to go now. I don't know how much longer he has, and I need to go."

He didn't understand. I'd given Luciana the power to hurt my brother and do all kinds of evil. Everything I did was bad. And wrong. When I'd tried to make it right, I'd only made everything that much worse for everyone around me. Now, I finally had a chance to fix that.

My chest heaved as I spoke. "I have to do this. I have to save my brother. And I have to save the pack. If one more person gets hurt because of me... I don't think I could survive that." Tears welled and fell. He couldn't give me hope and then snatch it away. "I'll rest later. It's not that bad."

"Not that bad? You were unconscious. For hours." His eyes glowed and I could almost see the wolf fighting to break free. "I didn't say we weren't going to go, but it's already dark and we have to trek through the forest again. I'd do fine as a wolf, but it's too dangerous when you don't have another form."

I took a breath to calm myself and realized by the ache that the pain pills were still percolating. I'd be useless if we left now. "I see your point." And I'd made an idiot of myself. Again.

Lucas gently cupped my face in his hand, lifting my chin until my gaze met his. "I can't pretend to understand what you've been through, but I know you've had to make hard choices and sacrifices. No one should ever blame you for trying to protect your family. You were just a child when it all started."

I swallowed. It was true. I had been a child. But I'd made so many mistakes. And yet, if I could go back in time, I wasn't sure how I could change things.

His thumb brushed against my jawline, and goose bumps

broke out over my skin. "You've done a good job," he said the words plainly, like he knew they were the truth.

I'd tried so hard to do good, but it always felt like I was wrong. Hearing him say I was doing a good job... It was the first time anyone had ever said that to me.

I couldn't help the embarrassing sob that broke through. I covered my face. God. I hadn't cried about any of this in so long. I couldn't start now.

"You've done a good job, Claudia." He pulled my hands from my face and brushed the tears away. "But this isn't your fault. What Luciana has done isn't your fault."

I wanted to believe him. So badly. "It is. At least partly."

"No," he said firmly. Without a hint of question to his voice. "It's not. You can only take responsibility for your own actions. You didn't make Luciana do all those horrible things." Our faces were so close that our noses were nearly touching. "You were taken advantage of. Abused. Scared. You were a child."

Abused? No. I'd handed over my power.

"Your parents should have protected you, but they didn't." He paused, and I stared into his eyes. Nearly losing myself in those dark pools. "Or maybe they couldn't protect you. Either way, *you* are *not* to blame. Now, you're doing everything you can to fight back. No one could possibly ask more of you."

With those words, it felt like a weight had been lifted. My parents had left without so much as a thank-you. I'd done my best, but that had never been good enough. And here was this guy. Telling me it was okay. That I'd done a good job.

"Come on." He lay on the bed and pulled me down with him. I rested my head on his chest as I cried. "It's going to be okay," he murmured as he ran his fingers up and down my arm.

I couldn't remember the last time I'd been held. Comforted. Raphael wasn't a huggy guy. Neither was anyone else in the coven.

But as I lay there, feeling so many different emotions, I wanted to hold on to Lucas forever. That feeling terrified me because now I had someone else in my life that I'd give up everything for. I'd already given so much. What would be left, if I kept giving pieces of myself away?

He hadn't asked for anything. Not yet. But I knew the other shoe would drop. Maybe not today or tomorrow. But sometime.

Even knowing that, I let myself enjoy this moment. The one time in my life that I truly felt loved. Cherished. Taken care of. By a man—a wolf—I barely knew yet felt so deeply connected with. For as long as this lasted, I gave myself permission to savor it.

This was what love felt like.

And boy, did I want it to last forever.

# CHAPTER SEVENTEEN

THE NEXT MORNING, I woke up sore. Lucas had been right. Leaving in the middle of the night would've been dumb, but now I was ready. The clock on my bedside table told me it was just after five in the morning.

After I settled down, Lucas had gotten me some food, tucked me into bed, and left. Exhaustion—emotional, physical, and magical—hit me like a ton of bricks. I'd barely managed to brush my teeth before climbing under the covers. I'd been so worn out that I hadn't even put on pajamas—I'd just slept in a pair of underwear and my white camisole.

I stretched in bed and, sure, I was achy and the knot on my head was tender, but I'd live. Now, I needed to make sure that my twin did.

I sent a quick text to Adrian confirming that everything was okay. He texted me back with a hotel address and the news that Raphael was still alive. Shane and Beth had done another healing chant, and he was hanging on.

I let myself relax, just a little. My brother was alive. The clock hadn't run out yet. Now, I needed to get packed before

Lucas showed up. We might not have time to come back to the hotel before we had to leave for San Jose.

I was trying to shove everything into my backpack when I heard the knock. I closed the distance and swung open the door without thinking twice about it.

"Good morn—" His voice cut off as his gaze slowly slid down my body.

I glanced down and promptly slammed the door in his face.

Holy moly. I was still in my underwear and camisole. He'd probably seen my nipples through my cami.

I pressed my hands to my heating face. I'd never been so embarrassed in my life.

"Don't be embarrassed," Lucas said through the door. "I liked the view."

My cheeks went from burning to totally on fire. "That's not helping." I raced across the room to find my pants from yesterday. I slipped them on, then grabbed a bra and fresh T-shirt. When I was presentable, I opened the door again. "Sorry. I was trying to get everything to fit into my backpack and I..." I took a breath and let it out slowly before starting again. This time with less rambling. "I'm sorry. I wasn't paying attention."

I motioned him into the room as I quickly braided my hair. I was sure if I looked into the mirror I would've been doubly embarrassed. *Messy hair and no clothes. Way to start the day off right, Claudia.* At least he seemed to not be bothered by it.

Oh no. Was I being awkward? We'd been getting close, now I wasn't sure what to do... Was I supposed to hug him? I mean, I wanted to hug him, but what if he didn't want to hug me?

Oh God. I wished Teresa or Cosette were here. I so desperately needed advice when it came to these kinds of things.

"Hang on," Lucas said as he pulled me in for a hug. He ran his hand up and down my back a few times before stepping back. "This still looks bad." He brushed a finger over the knot on my head. "How are you feeling today?"

I smiled. "Better. Thank you for taking such good care of me." And for making me feel exponentially less awkward.

"My pleasure." He grinned and I nearly melted. "Do you need help getting packed?"

"No. I'm almost finished. Just have to get it to zip." I motioned to the bed. "Give me one second and I'll be good to go."

"Let me help." He pressed everything down and got the zipper closed in one smooth move. I'd been fighting with it for the past ten minutes.

"Okay then." He swung up my pack like it weighed nothing.

Wolves were ridiculously strong. I always forgot that until one of them did something to remind me how very different they were. "You don't have to carry that. I can get it."

"I'll carry our stuff. Hiking the mountains is tiring enough. You've got a head injury, bruised ribs, and some nice gashes... This is easy for me. Let me help you."

Maybe he had a point. "Okay."

"Let's go."

As we left the hotel, I realized that just one little hug and some reassurance from Lucas had me feeling so much better. How had he done that? Was it some kind of pack magic? Or was it just him?

Either way, I didn't care. I felt stronger and more sure of myself. We were going to get to Raphael in time. There was no other option.

Failure wasn't a possibility. I wouldn't even entertain it.

As we loaded up the van, I let my fear go. It didn't help anything to be afraid.

Lucas handed me the map. "I'll drive us as far as I can and then we'll hike the rest of the way."

I nodded. "Okay."

"Better buckle up. The road there is pretty rough."

"Got it." I clicked my seat belt and then rested my hands on my thighs as he started driving. After about a minute on the road, his hand settled over mine.

I peeked over at him, and he grinned. I couldn't keep looking at him without breaking into a fit of embarrassing giggles, so I stared out the window while I laced our fingers together.

It was nearly unbelievable. I'd somehow found my match in the middle of all this craziness.

WHEN LUCAS finally stopped the van, all I could see was dense foliage. The ride up the mountain had been so bad that I'd squeezed my eyes shut. My heart had been pounding so hard for so long, I felt like I'd already had a workout.

I took a look around. What little bit of road was in front of us abruptly ended and a large tree with gnarled roots stood in the way of the van. We weren't at the top of the mountain, but we were close. To the right, I could see the valley below us. Off in the distance, a small town. But ahead of us and to the left was nothing but forest.

"Come on. We walk from here." Lucas grinned at me, and butterflies fluttered in my stomach. Lucas shoved his door into the dirt wall next to the van.

One smile and I was mush. This was pathetic.

Laughing at my own ridiculousness, I unbuckled my seat belt and opened my door. My foot was outside before I realized there was nothing below but air.

Lucas jerked me back into the van. "Whoa. Not that way. You have to climb over to this side."

My heartbeat throbbed in my ears. "Right." I panted. I'd almost died. Holy shit. I'd nearly just fallen down the side of the mountain. "Not that way. Of course. Not that way."

He cupped my cheeks in his hands. I stared into his dark eyes as his aura flowed over me. It was beautiful—bright and pure, like a sunny day. He was so strong. So kind. Being with him was like being surrounded by sunlight. I never wanted the touch to end. "Deep breath."

I followed his order and took a shuddering inhale.

"Good." He let out a long breath, too. "You're doing fine. Just watch where you're going. I'm not as young as I look, remember? You almost gave me a heart attack."

I nodded. "Right. I'll be more careful." He really was making me lose my concentration. One smile and I almost fell off a mountain.

WE SPENT the next few hours huffing it up the mountain. Or at least I was huffing. Lucas made carrying two packs look easy. If he didn't have a leg up from being a wolf, I would've felt bad. But as it was, I didn't. Even with the two packs, he was slowing down for me.

"Let's take a break."

"A break?"

"Yes." He kicked a log and stared at it for a second.

*What on earth...*

"Sit there."

I followed his command before I knew what I was doing, and boy did sitting feel good. I hadn't realized how tired I was already.

Lucas set down the packs and dug around in his. "Here you go."

He handed me a plastic bag filled with some sort of jerky. "What is it?" After yesterday with the guinea pigs, I needed to know exactly what I was eating.

"Beef jerky."

*Thank goodness.* I took a piece and chewed. "How much farther do you think?"

"We'll get to the mine right before the sun sets."

I nearly choked. My feet were already killing me, and it was just past midday.

"That's why it's important to take breaks. I don't want to have to carry you back to the van."

I thought he was joking until I saw his face. "Could you?"

"What? Carry you back? Yes." He handed me a water bottle. "With the packs, it'd be cumbersome. But yes."

That was pretty damned impressive. I knew my pack weighed at least fifty pounds. His was just as big, if not bigger. And then add me? "How much can you carry?"

"Let's just say a lot."

I laughed. "Well, all the same, I think I'm going to be fine."

"Of course you are. You just need a little bit of time to heal up." He paused. "I've been meaning to ask you something."

I looked up at him, shielding the sun with my hand. "What?"

"After all this is over, what do you want to do? What are your plans?"

I knew what he was getting at. He wanted more from me. He wanted there to be an *us*. So, it made sense that he'd ask. But I didn't have a great answer for him. "I don't really know. I've been stuck on the compound for so long..." I stood up, brushing off the back of my pants. "I always dreamed that if I left, I'd go to college. Travel as much as I could." I shrugged. "And maybe go to some concerts."

"Concerts, huh?" He took the water bottle back from me. "What kind?"

"Symphonies for sure. But besides classical, I'm not sure. I guess I'll see whatever comes into the town where I end up."

He took a long drink before picking up the packs. "And what do you want to study?"

What didn't I want to study? "Everything."

"Everything?" He bumped his shoulder into mine. "That's ambitious."

"I guess. I just want to know more. See more. I feel like my life has been so confined. So limited and controlled. I know I might not get to everything I want, but I figure if I shoot for the stars, I might just land on the moon."

"College and travel then."

"Yeah."

I hoped that wasn't a bad thing. If he was Alpha that meant he'd have to stick around here. Would I also be stuck here if I was with him? It wasn't that I didn't like Peru, but I'd been so confined—especially the last few years—that being tied anywhere wasn't in the least bit appealing.

Could I really give up my dreams for a guy?

I wasn't sure that I could. I'd given everything up for everyone in my life. I'd blackened my soul and was still paying the price to make up for that. Now that I finally had hope on the horizon, I couldn't just abandon my plans to be mated with some pack Alpha.

Even if that Alpha was Mr. July.

"A thirst for knowledge is never a bad thing," he said, breaking me out of my thoughts. "Neither is travel. It tells me that you're wise."

I hoped when he found out that I wasn't keen on giving either up, he'd still be supportive. Otherwise...

I made a face, trying to break myself out of my suddenly

181

gloomy thoughts. "I'm not wise. I barely know anything besides what the coven taught me."

"Which was..."

I sighed. "Nothing good."

"That's not true. You helped your brother with magic." He moved a branch out of the way, and motioned me past.

"If I hadn't learned about my magic then Luciana wouldn't have been able to use it. And Raphael wouldn't have needed my help in the first place. So, nothing good." Fathers Valentine and Albert came to my mind. "It seems like the people practicing black magic outweigh those practicing white by an impossible number."

He grunted. "No. I don't believe that at all."

I stopped walking for a second. "You don't?"

"No. I think you've seen far too much evil for someone your age. It's set an impression on you, but you have to separate yourself from it. Your magic is strong and good. You just need to let yourself shine." He reached for my hand. "Aim for the stars, Claudia. If anyone can reach them, it's you."

THE SUN WAS SETTING over the mountain, spreading a mixture of oranges and pinks across the sky. It looked as if the clouds were on fire.

Lucas stopped in a clearing and set down the backpacks. "We'll set up camp here for the night. The mine is just a couple hours away."

I wrung my hands together. "We're so close and we're going to stop?"

"It'll get dark fast. If you twist your ankle on the way, then I really will have to carry you back to the van." He pulled a tent out of his pack. He gave the fabric a shake and it popped up, almost on its own. "We're going as fast as we can. You told Raphael to hang in, and he will. But if you ended up hurt again and we couldn't complete the journey, he'd be in trouble."

Lucas was right, but that didn't help. I rolled my shoulders, trying to release the tension in my back. Being so close yet not actually there was frustrating. I wanted to get there.

I tapped my fingers against my leg as I contemplated going on without Lucas. He'd catch up, eventually.

"You're making me nervous with all that tapping."

I sighed. Realistically, I couldn't go anywhere without him. I'd probably just get lost.

I sat down on the dirt as Lucas built a fire. He set rocks around the perimeter so the flames wouldn't spread, and then placed some dried leaves under a teepee of sticks. I laughed when he got out a lighter.

He glanced over at me, his eyebrows raised high. "You thought I was going to rub two sticks together?"

I winced. "Kind of. I mean, the way you were going about it —" I waved to the fire. "It seemed like two sticks was the next logical step."

He chuckled. "No. I abandoned that method a long time ago. This is much faster." When he was finished, he went back to his pack. "I didn't bring anything to cook for dinner, but I did manage this." He tossed a small plastic bag.

I somehow managed to catch it. "Marshmallows?"

"I heard Americans really love them for camping."

"Not that I've done much camping, but you heard right." I set down the bag. "So, a healthy dinner of beef jerky and marsh-mallows. Is that enough for you?"

He shrugged. "Don't worry about me. I can go wolf and hunt my own food."

My mouth dropped open. "You'd eat it raw? Something furry?"

"Yup. My wolf doesn't mind too much."

I shuddered. "Yuck."

"You might like a furry, newly killed animal."

I full on gagged. "Nope. Not going to happen."

"Don't knock it 'til—"

Suddenly Lucas and the campfire disappeared.

All I saw instead was the darkening forest. A massive tree stood in front of me, with a large knot in its center.

"Luc—" Before I could get out the words, hands with thin, cold fingers wrapped around my throat.

"Careful little one," a deep voice said as the hands tightened just enough to terrify me. "Mustn't move. Mustn't speak. Or Gobble will take care of you."

I froze as I realized what had happened.

This was a fey.

I'd been kidnapped by the fey.

# CHAPTER EIGHTEEN

A WOLF HOWLED in the distance, and I hoped that meant that Lucas would be here soon. If that was Lucas at all...

*Please be Lucas.*

The hands released me and I collapsed to the ground. I whirled to face the thing as I tried to catch my breath.

In the fading light, I could see the creature's face—long and narrow with a pointy chin and thin lips. It stared with big, round eyes the lightest shade of blue I'd ever seen. The silver hair that fell in curls to its chin was tucked behind slightly pointed ears. His tall blue-and-green wings rippled behind him.

His aura was like a sapphire, glittering with silver speckles. Not quite as pretty as Cosette's, but still beautiful.

"Little you looks tasty," he said, flashing sharp fangs.

I scrabbled backward on the leaves, trying to put some distance between us.

*Please don't let him mean that literally.* Maybe he meant tasty in that I was nice.

That was a possibility, wasn't it?

The wolf howled again, this time closer, but I didn't dare turn toward the sound.

He wore only a tattered loincloth. If he'd have been tiny—mouse-size—I would've thought he was just a creepy little fairy.

No such luck. He was big. Lanky. Tall. He wasn't thick with muscle, but he was completely lean. My throat throbbed where he'd grabbed me.

He crouched in front of me, bringing his face close to mine. I didn't dare move out of fear that he'd strike out. Instead, I waited and watched. Hoping I could cast a defensive spell faster than he could attack.

"What brings such a tasty treat to these parts?"

*Oh God. He really did mean to eat me.*

I swallowed. "I'm looking for white mages—"

"None in these parts. Not for a long time. Just underhill."

He slurped his lips and my breaths started to rasp. If I didn't calm down, I was going to start hyperventilating.

Fey didn't eat people. Cosette had never—

*Cosette.* I'd almost forgotten. Time to play the only card I had. "I'm friends with a fey. You must've heard of her."

"Who then?"

"Cosette Argent."

A bright flash burst and suddenly the creature was tiny—or what I imagined was normal fairy-size. It flitted around my head before hovering in front of my face. "You're the witchy witch she likes." His voice was high-pitched now. A tiny squeaking thing.

*Thank God.* Cosette hadn't let me down. I was going to owe her one, and whatever she wanted in return, I'd give it. "Yes. She said she'd tell your people I was coming and that I might need your help."

The creature snarled. Somehow, even tiny, his teeth were terrifying. "Fey don't help witches."

I shoved my fear down. Showing it would only make me seem weak—like I was prey. "Cosette helps witches and she's fey." I said it before I realized the implications. I hoped I didn't get her into too much trouble.

Another flash of light burst and he was full-size again. "This is not agreeable to me."

I wasn't sure what to say. Should I apologize? "Where am I?"

"Not far from your wolf mate."

I nearly laughed. "He's not my mate."

He tilted his head to the side. "Are you sure?"

"I think I'd know if we were bonded." Wouldn't I? Maybe it was possible, but it certainly hadn't happened yet. "How did you get me here?"

"I have the gift of travel." He disappeared without a sound. One second he was there and the next, he wasn't. "I go where I want."

I screeched when his voice came from right behind me.

He grabbed my shoulder hard. "That sound is very disagreeable."

I cleared my throat. *Don't show your fear, Claudia.* "I apologize. You frightened me."

He let me go, and I was sure I'd have his fingerprints as bruises by morning. "I like being frightening." He grinned, showing his row of sharp teeth. That together with the look in his eye... He was doing a fantastic job of being frightening.

I was wondering if running would be a good idea after all, when a snarl tore through the dark.

A wolf leapt between us. His back faced me as he snarled at the fey creature.

It didn't take a second for the fight to start. I crab-crawled backward to get out of their way until I hit a tree. They moved faster than I could track, turning into blurs of aura—Lucas' bright light yellow and Gobble's glittering blue and silver. Their snarls and cries broke the quiet of the night. I froze for a moment, watching in awe.

But what was I doing? I needed to stop them.

"Stop!" I yelled. I stood and put the force of my will and magic into my voice. "Stop fighting. Right now." It wasn't a spell per se, but the words would carry my power if I believed they would.

The two separated, breathing hard as they stared each other down. The wolf transformed to human, and suddenly I was staring at Lucas.

A totally naked Lucas.

I covered my eyes with a hand. "You're naked!"

"Yes. That's usually what happens when I shift." I would've had to be deaf to miss the humor in his voice.

"I just... Where are your clothes?"

The fey clacked his tongue. "Little tasty is a prude."

*The nerve of that little...* "I'm not a prude!" But I still didn't lower my hand.

Well, maybe I was a little bit, but I didn't need to hear it from him.

"I'll shift back in a bit," Lucas said before addressing the fey. "What's your name, fey one?"

"I don't share my name." His words were so haughty, I almost lowered my hand. I was sure he was making some sort of awful face.

He was smart, though. If words had power, names were infinitely stronger. I'd read that true names were precious things among the fey. It could make one become a slave to another.

"Then what shall I call you?" Lucas asked.

"Gobble."

I couldn't suppress a wince. That was both creepy and appropriate.

"Fine. Gobble. Why did you take her from me?"

"She seemed tasty."

"Enough with the tasty thing." It gave me the creepy-crawlies.

"She's not food and you know it. She was under my protection." Lucas' growl echoed across the mountain. "Or are you willingly and knowingly violating our pact?"

Pact? The wolves and fey had a pact?

"No! I didn't break a pact! I didn't know she was your mate."

"You did and you took her from me. If you don't leave us be, the pack will bring this matter to your prince."

Gobble sputtered words in a language I didn't know. It favored voiceless dental fricative and sibilant sounds. When he finally started speaking English again, his voice was wheedling. "She said you were looking for the mages. They've not been here in many years, but I remember where they were. I can help along the way."

I doubted his intentions were anything but selfish, but if he had the gift of travel... "We might need him."

"Take us there directly if you're so eager to help." Lucas' words were a half-growl.

"Lazy wolf. You must do some of it on your own."

"Her brother is dying. Time is something we don't have."

"Then it's good that I can keep you from getting lost."

Lucas growled again. "I'm going to shift, Claudia. You can take your hand down in a second, but don't stray far from me. Understand?"

"I didn't stray in the first place." I muttered the words, not that Lucas would appreciate the distinction.

Something brushed against my legs and I lowered my hand. Lucas stood in front of me in his wolf form, speckled black and brown. Maybe I should've been cautious, but he looked so soft.

Before I could stop myself, I was brushing my fingers through his fur.

I knew that wolves didn't purr, but Lucas came close, making a deep rumbling sound at the back of his throat.

As we walked back to our campsite, Gobble flitted around us in his little pixie form. I couldn't stop thinking about Gobble identifying me as Lucas' mate. I hadn't let myself think about it too much, but what did that really mean? Was I really considering turning?

If I didn't, what would that mean for Lucas? Would he end up being like Muraco? Alone for centuries because his mate chose not to risk being bitten? Could I do that to him?

Did I even want to be mated to a wolf in the first place? It was a serious decision that needed a lot of thought. Mates didn't divorce, as far as I knew. It was a serious commitment and if the mess with Matt had proven anything to me it was that rushing in didn't work.

Then again, comparing Matt and Lucas was impossible. They didn't compare. Not in any way. I trusted Lucas.

But was I ready to commit to more than that?

Lost in my thoughts, I almost tripped over a root, but Lucas was there before I could fall, pushing against me with his fur.

"Thanks." I brushed a hand against his head and he made a rumbling noise. I didn't speak wolf, but I could guess what he meant. "I'm fine. Just a little tired."

It was way more complicated than I could handle right now. The long day of hiking through the mountain, the stress of worrying over Raphael, and now this fey kidnapping added up to a whole bunch of exhaustion.

When we got back to the tent, I crawled straight inside. There was a blanket, and I spread it over my body, not caring about changing. Lucas butted inside in his wolf form and settled down half on top of me. He rested his head on my stomach.

I knew that this wasn't a big dog—that it was Lucas—but my brain was too tired to register it or care anymore. I scratched behind his ears and closed my eyes.

"Good boy," I said, as I fell asleep.

I felt a wet lick against my cheek just before darkness took hold of me, but I couldn't move enough to do anything about it if I wanted to.

# CHAPTER NINETEEN

I WOKE to the sound of Lucas' voice. The sun was just breaking over the horizon. Rays of sunlight cut through the leaves, making it seem like God was shining light down on the mountain. My back ached from sleeping on the hard ground and I wished there was a hot shower in my future, but that wasn't happening. Probably not until I was back with Raphael.

That thought jolted me all the rest of the way awake.

No time to waste. I threw off the blanket and got up. I didn't remember taking off my shoes, but they were lined up in front of the tent. I slipped them on and double knotted the laces.

"Ready to go?" I asked.

Lucas nodded. "I'll pack our gear." He handed me a protein bar as he brushed past. His fingers lingered on mine for a just a second before he started folding up the tent.

He was always doing that. Giving me lingering touches. More and more. I watched his back as he moved, enjoying the view a little. I quickly ran my fingers through my hair before redoing my braid, and then dug into the protein bar.

The crumbly texture made me thirsty. I grabbed a water

bottle from the side pocket of Lucas' pack, and took a long drink. "It's cold."

"I went to the falls to fill up. They're not far."

I nodded, but my stomach soured. What about parasites? If I got some kind of worm from this... I stared down at the bottle in disgust.

He chuckled. "Don't worry, city girl. I purified the water. It's safe to drink."

Easy for him to say. "I didn't grow up in the city, but we had clean running water." I took another careful sip, then almost gasped when it hit my tongue. It might be the best tasting water I'd ever had.

I quickly inhaled the rest of the protein bar and drank some more water before putting the bottle away. I stretched, and my ribs still ached. It was bearable, but if I thought about it too much—about Matt—the anger would overwhelm me.

Gobble had shifted back in his tiny form and he sat in the tree above the tent, watching us move around. It made me nervous when he stayed quiet like that.

The sound of Lucas zipping up the backpack caught my attention. "All right. Let's go," he said as he slipped the first one on his back. "The mine is this way." He slipped the other one across his chest and started walking.

Gobble flitted down from the tree and settled on my shoulder. The image of tiny little teeth tearing into my ear raced across my mind, and I stiffened.

Lucas spun toward me. "Why are you—" He didn't have to finish his question. "Get off of her. She doesn't like you sitting there."

"Sure the tasty does," his tiny voice screeched in my ear.

Lucas' eyes flashed bright. "And she doesn't like you calling her the tasty," he said, with a low rumble in his voice.

They started arguing back and forth as we walked.

The day had just begun and I was getting a headache already.

LUCAS HAD BEEN dead-on when he said it would take two hours to get to the mine. We stopped for a rest when we arrived. Weeds and branches covered up most of the entrance, blocking it from view. Without the map to tell us where to stop, we might've walked by it a million times and never seen it. It was too dark to see all the way inside, but a set of rusted and broken cart tracks ended at what looked like the mouth of a very long cave.

Lucas reached into his bag, grabbing out two flashlights. I took one, thankful for it. I hadn't thought to bring one. It was rare that I found someone more prepared than I was. I kind of admired that quality in Lucas. It was nice.

As we stepped inside, the air grew thick and heavy. It smelled stale and earthy, like no one had entered in a good long while. Spider webs ran down from the corners of the braced walls, and I moved to walk behind Lucas.

He glanced back at me. "Don't like spiders, huh?"

"Does anyone like them?"

Gobble flew in front of my face. "I like them just fine. Tasty," he squeaked.

"Right." That didn't surprise me in the least.

One of the branches off this tunnel exited to a secret valley between the mountains, but I had no idea which part or how we were supposed to find the right path. The map didn't show anything about the inside of the mine. My only lead was magic. The mages' auras had stuck to the map. If they'd used the mine to access their temple, then it stood to reason that there would be more traces of pure white to follow. I just had to find them.

We moved past a line of five rickety mine carts. The metal bits were rusted and the wood looked like it might disintegrate if we breathed too hard.

"Hop in," Lucas said when he reached the last one.

I stared from him to the cart and back again. "In that?"

"Yes." When I didn't move, he continued. "It'll be faster. You just tell me when you see the aura you're looking for, and we'll head that way."

I knocked my fist against the side of the car. It didn't collapse, but I still wasn't convinced. "Is this safe?"

Lucas blew out a breath. "Honestly, I'm not sure." He placed the backpacks in the cart before hopping in with one graceful move.

Yeah. I wasn't going to be able to get in it without making a fool of myself.

"There are miles of tunnels down here. We've got to narrow it down or it could take days."

I closed my eyes and thought of Raphael. Every time I did, he felt farther away. Our twindar used to bind us tight. If he was hurt or feeling something strongly, I could feel it, too. That had faded over the past few days and I didn't think it was because of the distance. Now, my sense of him was almost gone. Thinking about what could happen to him made stabbing pain shoot through my chest.

"Fine," I said. "Let's get this over with."

Lucas leaned down to grasp me around the waist and then easily lifted me into the cart. It shouldn't have been a surprise or anything to overreact to, but it made me feel safe. Protected. Even in this rickety thing.

Gobble flitted over to sit on my shoulder, but this time I didn't stiffen. I was too worried about what was going to happen as Lucas started pumping the lever on the car. Slowly, we all rolled forward.

"Let me know as soon as you want to stop or if we need to take a turn." Ahead of us, the tunnel split in three directions. "Like now. Which way?" Lucas asked.

"I don't know."

"Come on, Claudia. Which way?"

"I don't know. Gobble? Do you know?"

"You want Gobble's help?" He flitted in front of me to grin with those sharp teeth and I suddenly felt hesitant. From what Cosette said, I shouldn't make a deal with him. Not unless I really, really, really needed it. I wasn't that desperate. Not yet, at least.

"You can do this, Claudia. Trust yourself."

But I didn't. I couldn't see any auras at all. It was all darkness ahead.

I moved the flashlight around, trying to see anything else, and then I realized I was an idiot. I couldn't see anything past the beam of light.

I clicked it off. Once the glare was gone, I could see a faint glow somewhere ahead. "To the right." I clicked the flashlight back on, and Lucas hit the lever for the right tunnel.

"Good work."

I breathed out a sigh. "Thanks."

The next hour was more of the same. We moved from tunnel to tunnel, taking twists and turns. Then our cart started picking up speed as we went down an incline.

We hit a bump and gained some air. My feet landed on the cart floor with a jarring thud. "Slow it down. You're going too fast."

"I know," Lucas said.

A dip was coming up ahead of us—at least I hoped it was a dip. The closer we got, it looked like it was more drop-off than dip. I couldn't see any tracks beyond it.

Oh my God. The tracks were ending. We were going to fall. And who knew how far down we'd fall. It could be miles.

We could die.

I grabbed Lucas' arm. "Lucas."

"I see it."

"See what? The tracks freaking disappear!" My fingers dug into his skin. "Lucas! Stop the car. Now. Right now. We're going too fast and that dip is way too steep. We'll fly off the track."

"I know. The brake is broken, and we're going too fast to jump."

A cold sweat broke out across my brow. "You didn't check the brake?" Why hadn't *I* thought to check the brake?

"No. I didn't check the brake."

We sped closer and I finally got a good look. The dark spot ahead was a giant cave. The tracks ended over the yawning hole. "Oh my God. We're going to die." I gripped him tighter, bracing for whatever impact we were headed for.

Gobble screeched and dug his nails into my shoulder. Then he let go, flitting off. Leaving us both to our fate.

I huddled down in the bottom of the cart, hoping for something to hold on to, but there was nothing.

"Hold on to me." Lucas threw his body over mine, as we fell down. I wrapped my arms and legs around him as I screamed so loud my throat ached. And then I screamed some more.

It felt like we fell forever before we hit the ground. Somehow Lucas timed it, changing our positions so I landed on top of him. He grunted as we hit the bottom of the cave, but he didn't make another noise.

Our breaths still came fast as the cart slowed down. But we were alive.

I pulled back enough to see Lucas' face. "Are you okay?" I asked as I cupped his cheek in my hand.

Lucas leaned into my touch. "I've survived much worse," he

said as he wrapped my braid around his hand and then raised his mouth to meet mine.

At first, the kiss was a soft brush of lips, but it slowly turned into more. My body heated, and I tightened my arms around him. He felt safe. Good. And I wanted more. His tongue touched mine and I moaned, unable to stop myself. And not caring in the least. He growled and twisted my braid tighter, as he devoured me. I ran my hand under the back of his shirt, and his muscles tightened. I wanted to be closer, but—

Gobble's tiny hand swatted my cheek. "Stop messing about and look around."

I pulled away from Lucas, completely out of breath. I'd only been kissed once before and it didn't count. Not really. Daniel and I had been bored and I wanted to know what it was like.

The thing about growing up with everyone on the compound was that they all started to feel like family.

But Lucas, he was an unknown. Someone new. And it wasn't just the newness that was affecting me. It was everything about him. Even with all the reasons I had to pull away, I couldn't stop my feelings from growing.

I stared at him, not knowing what to do or say as he quietly watched me. And then I started laughing.

I wasn't sure why. Maybe it was the ridiculousness of the situation. I'd thought I was going to die. Then I was kissing the hottest guy I'd ever seen. The guy I wanted more than anything, who was slowly becoming everything to me. It was absurd, but I would've kept kissing him if not for the creepy little Tinkerbell hitting me.

Yes. Absurd was the right word. My life had taken a turn for the completely absurd.

Using the lip of the cart, I slowly hoisted myself up and Lucas followed suit. I started to climb out, but he stopped me, grabbing my hand. He moved his other hand to my cheek and slid his thumb along my skin.

Something intense burned in his eyes and I wasn't sure what to say. What was really between us? Before I could decide, the look was gone and he was lifting me up and out of the cart.

"I think we'll be walking from here," Lucas said.

I laughed. "No kidding. I feel like living out the rest of my life, thank you very much." I watched him as he grabbed up the backpacks again, and I was kind of in awe.

At first, he'd been Mr. July to me. Just a pretty face.

He'd proven he was so much more than that. Lucas was kind and caring. Patient and protective. Yet not overbearing.

Was perfection a wolf thing? Watching Dastien and Donovan, I'd thought they were each a fluke. But now I wasn't so sure.

Because Lucas was pretty perfect. At least to me he was.

"Look at all the pretties!" Gobble said.

For the first time, I really looked at where we'd landed. We stood at the edge of a huge cavern. I could see the tracks that we'd fallen from, but in the dark, I couldn't see where the ceiling of the cave was. I turned in a circle, taking it all in. Every surface sparkled. It was like giant diamonds encrusted the rock walls, like we'd landed inside a massive geode.

"Flashlight," I said. Lucas handed me one. Wherever I shined the light, it glittered with purples and blues. "Wow." I walked to the closest wall and touched one of the crystals. As soon as my fingertip pressed its cool surface, it started to glow pure white. "Have you ever seen anything so beautiful before?" My voice came out in an awed whisper. If just one crystal looked this amazing...

Could the rest light up like this?

I took a second to form a rhyme and then let out a deep exhale, allowing my magic to flow outward with the breath.

There wasn't much left, but I hoped it would be enough. *"Aura strong and bright. Power good and right. Show us pure white light."*

It was as if I'd flipped a switch. The light caught like fire, spreading from crystal to crystal until the whole massive cavern was lit and glowing with a bright white aura.

I clicked off my flashlight and turned in a circle again. The cavern went up at least three or four stories, and crystals glowed all the way to the distant ceiling.

I touched one, running my finger along the sharp edges. Some of them were huge, thicker than Lucas' thigh muscle. Little ones, the size of my pinky, stuck out between them. They were all piled on top of each other, until it was impossible to see the cave wall. Their energy was so strong it made my fingertips tingle. "What are these?"

"Magic," Gobble said. Then he wrinkled his nose in a little scowl. "Maybe you aren't a witch."

This time *I* swatted at *him*. "I *am* a witch. I've just never heard of crystals like these before. Ones that store aura and magical power, but something about them..." My eyes widened as I realized. "That lady from the market. She was wearing one around her neck."

"You're right. That one was much smaller, but they're the same." Lucas touched a nearby crystal and it turned from white to amber. The same color amber as his aura. Interesting, but I wasn't sure what it meant.

"Do you..." It could be total sacrilege to ask this, but... "Do you think it'd be okay for me to take one? Just one of the little ones. I'm pretty sure the white mages somehow stored their magic inside, and—"

"This could be what helps Raphael," Lucas finished for me.

I smiled, relieved that he understood.

"Sure. Let me see what I can do."

I nodded. He was much stronger than I was and would have a much easier time getting a crystal free.

Lucas reached for a crystal the thickness of my thumb. If he could break it off, it would be easy enough to carry.

As soon as he touched it, the crystal fell into his palm. He turned to me, mouth hanging open. "I didn't have to do anything."

I took the crystal from him. As soon as it was in my palm, its aura changed to ice blue. "Weird."

"Is it okay?" Lucas asked.

I put it in my pocket—not wanting it getting lost in my purse. "Yes. Thank you. I'm sure it's great."

"Which way?"

I looked around the cave. "I don't know."

"What does your gut say?"

I laughed. "My gut has no clue." There was so much white aura here, that I couldn't see anything beyond it. "Gobble. Do you know the way?"

"Of course I know the way." He sounded offended that I would even ask.

"And?"

"Oh. You're asking for a favor. That will cost you, tasty. What will you give me?"

I sighed. Nope. Not there yet.

I spun around, counting five different chambers we could go through. I needed just enough magic to give us a direction. *"Eenie. Meenie. Miney. Mo. Show us all the way to go."* All of a sudden, the light in the cavern died.

I sucked in a breath. Was I empty? Finally drained of magic? "I'm sorry. I—" I froze as a line of light appeared in the crystal.

The glow moved in a straight path from us like ancient streetlights, pointing down the third corridor on the left.

*Thank God.*

I grinned at Lucas. "That way seems good."

He laughed. "So I see. Let's go."

Gobble landed on my shoulder, and the three of us headed deeper into the mine, following the path that had been left for us.

I was exhausted. Using magic took energy from me. My well was almost totally empty and I needed time to rest and build it up again. I wasn't sure when I'd have the time.

Having Lucas next to me gave me the energy to keep going, even if all I wanted to do was crash.

"You doing okay?" he asked, almost as if he could sense my exhaustion.

I wasn't okay. Not yet. But I was one step closer. "Getting there," I said as his hand found mine.

# CHAPTER TWENTY

AS WE MOVED FARTHER into the mine, crystals dotted the walls. They weren't as thick or as dense as they were in the main cavern, but they were there. About two-thirds up the tunnel wall, a waving line of them gave off a pure white light. It wasn't a totally straight line, since the crystals were more organic than orderly, but they guided us and gave us just enough light to see.

We followed the glowing path through the tunnels carved out long ago by miners, taking countless twists and turns. Time wore on, and my shirt was nearly soaked through. The mines were hot and—even with the pretty crystals—more than a little oppressive. I grew desperate to find the exit to the valley.

After a while, the tunnels started to rise again and my muscles burned as we worked our way uphill. I took that as a good sign. We had to be getting closer to the temple.

"Do you smell that?" Lucas said as we turned a corner.

All I could smell was dirt, dirt, and more dirt. "No." But if the wolves could smell emotions, then they had a way better sense of smell than I did. "What do you smell?"

"Fresh air. It was there and then gone."

"Weird. Where did it come from?"

"I don't know."

Gobble giggled from his perch on my shoulder, but I ignored him. He'd been doing that off and on. I couldn't worry about what was amusing him. I wanted to tell him to go away, but if I got desperate enough, I'd give him whatever bargain he was after.

We rounded a turn, and I slammed into Lucas. He'd stopped walking. "What's wrong?" I asked as I stepped around him. As soon as I had a better view, the problem was clear. There were no more glowing crystals. The walls in the next cavern were all dirt and stone. Nothing glowed.

My heart sped as I noticed four tunnels leading off from where we'd stopped. If we kept going and didn't pick the right one, we'd be in big trouble. There was no telling where they led and we didn't have the supplies or the time to be stuck down here for days.

Not to mention that the thought of being lost in these mines made it feel like the walls were closing in on me.

"Can you see anything?" Lucas asked.

"No. I..." I searched for any hint of an aura ahead of us, but couldn't see anything. I chewed my lip as I tried to decide which route to take, but none of them felt right. "We had to have missed something. We should backtrack."

I wasn't sure where we'd gone wrong, but something had changed. Why would it lead us into a dark chamber with four equally possible routes?

It didn't matter. I spun around and started walking back.

As we walked back toward the glowing crystals, they started flickering. Then, one by one, they went out.

"Are you seeing this?" I asked as I forced my already aching legs to walking faster.

"Yeah."

The lights started glittering faster and faster. If we lost the path... It was too complicated to remember. Too dark. We'd be lost.

"Run." I took off, following the flickering lights, trying to stay ahead of them, but the faster I ran, the faster they died. As they started to outpace me, I finally skidded to a stop, gasping for breath. "We're lost."

"We're not lost." Lucas had gotten farther than I had, but he quickly moved back to me.

I scowled at him as he turned on his flashlight. "Do you know where we are?"

"Not exactly, no. But I can scent our way back to the entrance. So, we're not lost."

The breath I'd been holding left my lungs. Living the rest of my life wandering these tunnels until I died of dehydration sounded like a special kind of hell.

Gobble giggled again. This time I was paying attention.

"What do you know?" I angled my head to the side so I could get a good look at him.

"Witches and wolves all distracted by lights and not paying attention." He rolled his big blue eyes. "I'll only tell if you pay back the favor. Not helping for free."

But he'd already said enough. We'd missed something. The exit?

I grasped Lucas' sleeve. "We're idiots."

Lucas narrowed his gaze. "We are?"

"Yeah." I laughed. "We really are. Where did you smell that fresh air?"

Lucas chuckled. "We *are* idiots. That's where the exit is."

"Exactly. Can you get us back there?"

Lucas nodded. "Sure can. Stay a few steps behind me so I can scent it."

"You got it."

I let him pass by me and waited for a count of five before following. After a short few minutes, he stopped.

"It's here." He ran the light up and down the tunnel walls, but no break or gap was visible. Even the ceiling looked solid.

"We're missing something," I said.

"Can you see anything? Any auras?"

I shook my head. "Just a faint residual glow from the crystals. Nothing that points the way."

"Okay." He squatted down and scratched a little groove in the floor to prop up the flashlight. "Our eyes aren't seeing anything, but maybe our hands will. You take that wall." He pointed behind me. "I'll take this one."

I turned and crouched down to start at the bottom. I ran my hands along the crystals, not caring if the sharp edges nicked my skin. They stuck out at odd angles, growing out of each other in clusters, but there were no seams or holes. I couldn't find a break. Not anywhere.

"Are you sure we're in the right spot?" I asked.

"We're in the right spot." His voice had a hint of growl in it.

I turned to find him squatting on the ground, staring at the wall. "Sorry. I wasn't trying to—"

"I'm not angry at you. I'm just frustrated." He quickly stood and glared at Gobble. "And he's not helping. He knows how to make this door appear." Lucas tried to flick the fey, but his wings zipped into motion and he zoomed off my shoulder.

"Not my fault you're stupid."

Lucas' aura was usually so toned down that I didn't see it unless I focused. Alphas—like Teresa and Dastien—glowed much brighter than other wolves. Apparently Lucas could turn his off and on. In a flash, he lowered the floodgates and I had to blink to adjust to the blinding halo of gold and white.

Gobble shrieked and fled to hide between the crystals on

the wall. "Pack Alpha means nothing to me, wolf. You can't force me."

Lucas moved fast, snatching a little arm in his fingers, but Gobble disappeared—reappearing behind Lucas.

Lucas howled as the little beastie bit down on his ear.

I wanted to wring both of their necks. "Stop it. Neither of you is helping anything."

I turned back to the wall, ignoring those two yahoos. I crossed my arms and stared it down. There had to be something —some clue that would tell me what to do next. I stuck my finger in my mouth and pulled it out, holding it in the air to see if I could feel a breeze.

It was there. Faint but there. In front of me. I felt along the wall again, but there wasn't a hinge or handle or anything. I pushed with all my might. Nothing budged.

"Push with me," I said to Lucas.

He joined in and, again, nothing.

"It's here. I know it." God. I was so bad at rhyming. I wished my magic pulled me in a different direction, but belief gave my spells power, and somewhere along the line I'd started believing in rhymes. *"Door from here to there, give way. Let in this wolf, witch, and fey."* The magic built as I said the words. For a second after, nothing happened. I held my breath, waiting for something. Anything.

Then a creak echoed through the tunnel. It started off softly and slowly grew louder.

I reached out, needing something to hold on to as I waited for the exit to appear, and Lucas grabbed my hand tightly.

*Oh my God. My heart raced. I found it. I actually found it.*

Slowly, a crack formed between the crystals. It wasn't a straight line. Instead, it followed the curvature of each individual crystal. Finally, the outline became visible.

This was it.

The door opened barely an inch, and then all was quiet.

I let go of Lucas' hand and pushed.

This time it swung open like it weighed nothing.

A breeze felt cool along my skin. There was a long staircase upward, but I could already see the pinks and oranges of the setting sun. I grinned. "We did it."

"*You* did it," Lucas said as he put his arm around my shoulder. His dark eyes sparkled in the light. "You did it."

"I did, huh?"

"The tasty is no fun. No fun at all," Gobble said before flying up into the sunlight. He wasn't getting his deal from me. Not yet. And if all continued to go well, maybe not ever.

"Go on." Lucas gave me a little push forward.

I started up the stairs. Excitement that we'd finally made it this far made my achy muscles a little bit more bearable. We hadn't stopped much, but Lucas had occasionally handed me a bar to eat, some jerky, or a bit of dried fruit. I'd taken it and kept going. The urgency to help Raphael had never died down. Even with the exhaustion, I'd been so focused on finding the way that I hadn't realized how much time had passed. "I can't believe it's been a full day."

Lucas shook his head. "For a bit, I thought we might be sleeping in there."

That was a terrifying thought. I never thought of myself as claustrophobic, but being deep in those tunnels had tested me nearly beyond my endurance. I wiped my sweaty forehead on my damp T-shirt. "Well, it's a good thing we don't have to."

When we finally stepped out and onto the grass, I was beyond tired. My thigh muscles quivered from the strain.

"We should set up camp and take a look at the map. See if we can figure out which way the temple is from here, and we'll get started at first light."

I knew we had to wait, but that didn't help the pressure bearing down on me. I couldn't feel Raphael at all anymore. He was beyond our twindar and I had no cell reception to check on him. "Let's get set up then."

"I know you want to keep going, but wandering around in the dark isn't a good idea."

"I don't want to wander. I want to go straight there." If I didn't keep making progress, I'd start to think about the consequences, and that would do nothing but paralyze me with fear.

"I promised you that I'd get you to him in time, and I mean to keep that promise. Okay?"

I nodded, but I wasn't sure how he could really promise that.

Lucas started walking, looking for a good place to pop the tent.

"You found the way," Gobble said as he reappeared and settled down on my shoulder.

"No thanks to you."

He made an unimpressed noise. "Not my job to do it for you."

That was debatable, but at least I didn't owe him anything. Being bound to an evil witch was bad enough.

Lucas set down our packs in a small break in the forest. "This is enough room for the tent and a fire." He took out the tent and started setting it up.

I sat down on a fallen log and slipped off my shoes. My feet had swollen from all the walking, but by the grace of God I'd managed not to get blisters. I worked my thumbs into my arches as the sky turned dark and stars appeared. As I sat there, I realized I really had to pee.

The thought annoyed me. Camping was not at all in my comfort zone.

Somehow, I managed to put my shoes back on. I made sure I

still had some tissues from in my purse and checked my cell phone. The battery was dying, but one bar appeared before going away. It kept flashing in and out—which would do me no good—but I wanted to keep it with me at all times. Just in case. "I'm going to go..." I motioned with my hands.

"Holler if you get lost on your way back," Lucas said.

I started off to find a bit of privacy, making sure I was far enough that I'd avoid any embarrassment because of his Were hearing.

When I started back to the campsite, a glow caught my eye. Something... Just a little ways off from us. I'd thought I was able see because of the moonlight, but this was so much more than that. The aura was a pearlescent white.

I couldn't help but investigate. I made my way through the forest, breaking branches as I went but not caring. The closer I got, the faster I went.

"Where are you going?" Lucas said suddenly from behind me.

I let out a high-pitched scream before I could stop myself. My heartbeat echoed in my ears. I hadn't heard him—hadn't known he was following me at all.

He gripped my waist as I took a few deep breaths, trying to calm down. It took me a few seconds to find my voice again. "You scared the living daylights out of me," I finally managed to say.

"You scared me when you wandered off, so we're even." He studied me. "What are you seeing?"

I twisted out of his grasp and pointed ahead. "Something really bright is just up there. I wanted to see what it was." It wasn't far, just on top of a small hill.

"And you didn't come get me?"

I shrugged. "I didn't think of it. I had to see what that was. It could be the temple." I glanced around. "Where's Gobble?"

"How should I know? One second he was there, and the next, gone. I expect he'll be back, but I'm glad to be rid of him for now."

"He's not that bad."

He growled softly.

"Come on." I kept walking toward the glow, stepping around trees and plants as I moved through the forest. It was weird being able to see this well at night, but I liked it. Made things much easier.

A thick curtain of moss hung down from a tree branch. As I moved it out of the way, the temple came into view.

I gasped as I took in the overgrown stone structure made of perfectly cut square blocks of stone. Just like some of the Incan ruins I'd seen in passing. A small steeple cut into the night sky. And the most beautiful part of all: The windows on either side of the door glowed with a pure bright light.

I nearly laughed. It didn't feel real. I'd hoped, but I wasn't sure that anything would come of this. But now I knew. The map had been right. I had a real chance of saving Raphael. Everything might turn out okay.

"That's it. We found it." I took off running for the entrance.

"Wait." Lucas caught up and jerked me to a stop. "Some-one's been here."

I froze. "What do you mean?" We'd asked so many villagers, and no one had even the smallest story about the mages or their temple. So how could anyone have been here?

"Here." He pointed to a broken branch and some trampled grass. "Tracks."

I couldn't make out a footprint. "Couldn't that have been a bear or something?"

"No. Those are human tracks."

There was no way that was possible. "I thought no one knew the way."

Lucas squatted to sniff the supposed track. "Human. They smell familiar, but not." He stood up. "We have to be careful. No running. You stay behind me."

Maybe people had been here recently, but that didn't change what I needed to do. "I don't need to be protected. I have plenty of magic of my own." I brushed past him and closed the distance to the temple.

As soon as I stepped inside, the most foul smell ever hit me. I covered my mouth and nose as I gagged.

The temple's entry was one massive room. Along the far wall, double doors led off to elsewhere. An altar made of three huge slabs of stone stood between us and the corridor. A bowl of fire burned on its surface.

I stepped toward the altar. "What is that—" I stopped myself. I didn't need to ask the question. I knew that smell. Only one thing was that disgusting.

"Vampires," Lucas spat the word.

Standing in front of the walls, frozen like statues, were vampires.

Hundreds of them.

"Oh God." They weren't moving, and if they were really alive, they would've attacked by now. But if something changed, we were toast. There was no way we could fight this many. I didn't have enough magic left. And no matter how strong an Alpha Lucas was, he was only one wolf.

"Whatever you do, don't move," Lucas whispered. "You could set them off."

"Oh *God*." My throat was suddenly tight. I took in the room with wide eyes, trying to come up with something—anything—that could help us.

What was I supposed to do now? Whatever I needed was surely inside this temple, but one wrong step and we'd both be worm food.

Just the two of us against an army of vampires... We didn't stand a chance.

# CHAPTER TWENTY-ONE

"WHY WOULD the white mages have vampires in here?" My voice was tight with fear, as I stood there, taking in the surroundings. There had to be hundreds of them.

"I'm not sure. They're frozen now by some sort of spell, but I don't know what—if anything—might release them." His aura flared bright as he paused. "Maybe we don't meet the criteria. Maybe you have to do something the mages wouldn't like to set them off. Or practice evil magic? Or maybe if one of us steps on the wrong tile, they'll swarm. It could be anything."

Perfect. Nothing was ever easy. Not for me, at least. "You don't have to come in with me."

"Like hell I don't." His voice was a little more gravelly than normal. His wolf must not like being in here. "Where you go, I go."

I turned slowly, not wanting to set off the vampires, and faced him. "This could be really dumb. I don't want to be responsible for your death. You're a pack Alpha. You have more than just some witch on a quest to worry about."

"You're not just some witch." The gravelly tone was getting thicker.

He stared me down until I looked away. If he wanted to go in, there wasn't any way I could stop him. And part of me was relieved. I didn't want to go in there alone. But the rest of me wanted him safe. I didn't want my mess to cause anyone else any more harm. "Fine." I held my breath as I took one step, and then another.

A fine coating of dust covered the floor. It kicked up in the air as I walked, tickling my nose. The walls might've had something on them, but I couldn't see past the vampires. I was doing my best not to look at them. I passed by one, and glanced at it quickly. Its strawlike hair and half-rotted body gave me the creeps. It wore all black with a long, frayed duster that touched the ground.

I stood close enough that it could have reached out and grabbed me. I held my breath as I stepped past, focusing on the floor, but nothing happened. Maybe this wasn't going to be so bad? "Let's head to the next room."

Lucas motioned me forward. "You lead the way."

I wiped my hands on my pants. "Okay." I took even, measured steps, half expecting the vampires to charge as I walked around the altar.

As I made it closer to the doors on the other side of the room, I started to breathe a little easier. If there was a booby trap, we hadn't set it off yet. We had a ways to go before getting out of here, but maybe Lucas and I didn't meet the mages' criteria for enemies.

Lucas had to help me push the carved wooden doors open. They weighed a ton, and once they got moving there was no stopping them. I winced as they slammed into the walls, and then glanced back at the room, but as far as I could tell none of the vampires had moved.

I sent Lucas a wide-eyed look, but he just shrugged. "Seems okay," he said.

It did seem okay. *So far, so good.* I focused on moving forward, even when all instincts told me to turn and run. I didn't like vampires—not one bit—and the smell was only getting worse.

I glanced over at Lucas and he gave me a small nod as we started walking down the passage.

"Any clue what you're looking for?" Lucas whispered to me.

"Not really," I whispered back. "At least I'm not sure. I figure whatever I need will glow a lot. Or something."

The hallway was lined with rows of vampires two and three deep. All frozen.

"How did the white mages capture so many of them? There's got to be hundreds," I said. Under other circumstances, I might've been able to analyze the magic, but even if I wasn't totally exhausted, I had no intention of casting a thing in here unless the worst happened.

"I don't know. The magic that's holding them must be strong. I wonder if we could replicate that." He paused. "Although, why keep them around when we can kill them and be rid of them for good?"

No kidding. "Right. They're not exactly the type I'd want guarding my house. They'd just as soon eat me as protect me."

"Plus, the smell is horrible."

"It's bad for me. Must be even worse for you."

He grunted. "Nearly unbearable."

Poor guy. We kept moving forward at a steady, even pace. I held my hands out, ready to cast a protection ward just in case we triggered some vampire release lever.

The hallway ended in a set of downward stairs. Crystals—the same as from the mines—lit the stairwell as it twisted down. I was slightly dizzy by the time we reached the bottom. There was another long passage leading back the other direction. At the end was another set of huge doors. Whatever was behind those doors was directly underneath the altar upstairs.

Things of extreme importance were typically placed under altars for protection, but also because whatever magic was performed on the altar would drift down and imbue the object with residual magic. The longer the object rested under the altar, the stronger it became.

That told me that what I wanted had to be behind those doors.

The smell of dirt and dust was stronger here, but there were no vampires stationed along the hall. Instead there were bones— thousands of them—piled to the ceiling. All of them gave off a slight glow.

They were separated by bone type. The little ones near the base of the stairwell had to be toes. At the end, surrounding the doorway, were skulls.

I rolled my shoulders to ease the tension in them. It was probably weird, but I felt a little more relaxed around the bones. They wouldn't suddenly start moving and trying to eat me. At least I didn't think they would.

I glanced back at Lucas. "This is a crypt."

"Yes. It used to be pretty typical for the temples and churches in the area."

This could actually be perfect. "One of my cousin's books said that the bones of the ancients could be used in defense against demons. This could be exactly what we're looking for."

"So, we can just grab some of these and get out of here? Great. Let's do it." He moved to grab the closest fibula, but I managed to stop him before he touched it.

"Wait. It can't be just any ancient. It has to be someone really holy. A saint." I licked my lips as I took in the bones. "They should be glowing more."

"I thought all of these mages were saints."

"I guess not. To be sainted, the body would have to be preserved. There would still be flesh on the bones. Dried flesh, but still." I looked at the bones assembled into neat, categorized piles. "These all are dried bones. No flesh. They wouldn't have taken them apart if they were saints."

Lucas made a face. "Sometimes you witches are disturbing."

I sighed. "It's gross if you think about it, but I try not to. Especially when it's magic that I really, really need—like something to save my brother." I punched Lucas in the shoulder. "And you eat furry, bloody, still-warm animals."

"So do all carnivores. But taking bones from a preserved mage..." He waved his hand around. "Let's find the right bones and get out before the vampires wake up."

"I wonder if they can wake up. Maybe they're just for show."

He started walking. "I don't intend to stay down here long enough to find out."

I caught up to him. "If the altar is upstairs, it stands to reason they'd rest the holiest of their sect below. In that room there," I pointed to the end of the passage. "And hopefully, the aura will tell me what's best to take with me."

"Makes sense."

We closed the distance to another set of wooden doors. This time, we were careful to open them slowly.

As soon as we saw inside, Lucas let out a string of curses. "You can't be serious."

The altar matched the one above except for its occupant. A body dressed in white robes. The figure held a bouquet of dried flowers and an athame. A ring of fire surrounded the stone, burning two feet high. The glow of the mage overpowered even the light of the fire. But that wasn't what really caught my eye.

The walls were stacked deep with vampires. Not just two or three. But in some areas, five and six.

The fire helped burn off some of the smell, but even then it was a lot. My gut urged me to leave. Run. But I couldn't. I needed to get to that altar.

Lucas growled and grabbed my arm, pulling me behind him. "I don't want either of us to go into that room. Not one bit."

Neither did I, but I didn't have a ton of options. I patted his hand and he let go. "You can stay here." I started to step past him. "But I need to go in."

He pushed the long sleeves of his T-shirt up to his elbows. "Like hell you're going in there alone." He stepped through the doorway. "Let's do this fast."

We paused as we reached the fire. Sweat rolled down my hairline and I brushed it away. "Can you lift me over?"

"Can't you put it out with magic?"

Something in my gut told me that was a really bad idea. This time, I wasn't going to ignore that instinct.

I glanced around the room again, and then at the fire. "I think that's the booby trap part. Any magic done in this space could make the vampires wake."

"How do you know?"

"I don't know for sure, but I have a feeling."

He grunted and then grasped my waist. "I'm going to have to throw you, okay? I don't want you to get burned."

That seemed like the best plan. "Okay."

"On three." He counted down, and then I was airborne for a split second.

I came down on the stone floor hard.

"You okay?"

My ribs ached and my feet throbbed, but nothing was broken. I stood up and brushed myself off. "Fine."

The mage on the altar looked to be asleep. The purity of his soul had saved his body, perfectly preserving it. His eyes were closed, with both arms crossed over his chest. Long white hair cascaded over his shoulders, braided in thin sections. The only thing that told me he was dead was the dried out, leathery look of his skin—and the fact that he wasn't breathing.

I reached out to him with shaking hands. I didn't want to touch him. Disturbing him felt wrong. Only the thought of saving Raphael kept me moving forward.

What was I supposed to take?

I wondered if I could get away with taking a little hair. Hair was used in a lot of spells. It could be enough for Raphael.

But what if it wasn't enough?

I didn't travel all this way to come up short.

"Hurry up. All these vampires staring at me…"

"They're frozen. They're not staring at you, Lucas."

"No, princess. Their eyes have been following us the whole time."

I spun around. "Shut the fuck up." I slapped a hand over my mouth. I'd never said that word out loud before. Fear was getting the better of me.

His lips were pressed into a thin line. "I'm not joking. Watch their eyes."

He took two steps to the side. Then two more. I watched the vampire behind Lucas. It was slight, but its eyes tracked the motion.

A shiver rolled down my spine. "This is bad."

"I know. Get what you need and get back over here."

He didn't have to tell me twice. "I'm sorry for disturbing you, but you'll be stopping a very evil witch. Thank you for your gift." I grabbed a handful of the mage's long white braids and pulled. They slipped easily out of his dried scalp. I wrapped them in a knot and placed them in my purse next to my cell phone.

Then I noticed the ring on his hand. It was a thick band of silver with a large ruby in the middle. The aura glowed white around the ring, but the ruby had a different aura. It was a hundred shades of red, separate yet all together at the same time. It took me a second to get the ring over his thick, gnarled knuckles. I put that into my purse, too.

Now, I just needed a bone. But what? It had to be something small—something I could take in my purse—but something that held a lot of power.

A hand. That was the implement that we used the most when practicing magic. If I could dislodge his hand...

My stomach rolled at the thought, but I had to try. I hoped it would be enough. I grasped the mage's hand like I was going to shake it. The whole thing fell off at the wrist.

I screeched and jumped back, nearly dropping it.

"Calm down!" Lucas shouted.

"Sorry." My heart was racing. "Sorry. I just..." I turned toward him to show him. "I have some hair, his ring, and a hand. I think I'm done here. That's all I need to—"

When I turned all the way around, my stomach dropped.

Father Valentine stood in the passage.

Lucas had been right. Someone had been here before. Someone really bad.

Father Valentine waved his hand in a spell-like motion.

"No!" I finally found my voice. I pointed behind Lucas. "Stop him! Now!"

Lucas lunged, but he was too late. The fire was out in an instant and the doors swung shut with a deafening thud.

We were alone. In the dark.

With at least a few hundred vampires.

# CHAPTER TWENTY-TWO

"FIRE BURNING BRIGHT. *Show me your light.*" My magic sped out, but I could feel how weak it was. How weak *I* was.

*Not now.* If my power failed...

The fire around the altar flared again.

The vampires were slowly starting to move. Turning their heads slightly. A few tensed their arms just a little.

The magic holding them in place was fading as Lucas pounded on the door. "It's stuck. I can't get it open."

"Get over here!" Vampires didn't like fire. "Jump onto the altar. The fire will keep them away."

Lucas frantically looked around, and then ran toward me. He leapt over the fire, sliding to a stop at my side.

"Get under," he said, practically shoving me down.

"One sec." I hopped back up and grabbed the athame before crawling under the stone slab. Having some weapon—even a small one—made me feel a little better.

Lucas slid under with me. "The fire won't keep them for long. They're blood starved. What do we do now?"

He was asking me? "I don't know." Maybe if I had more magic, I could do something. But I couldn't. I'd been drained for so long... I was below empty. "I don't have enough energy to do anything helpful." It was miraculous enough that I'd gotten the fire burning again.

"I can't fight all of them. There are hundreds."

I swallowed as the truth hit me. We were going to die. And so was my brother.

A tear rolled down my cheek. "I'm sorry I got you mixed up in this."

Lucas brushed away the tear. "I'm not giving up yet."

"There's no giving up. Just reality. We're going to die." Sweat broke out along my skin, and I brushed it away on my shirt. As I moved, I saw my hands shaking.

Okay. I needed a way out of this. Something. Anything.

I dug through the contents of my purse. The ring. I put it on my thumb and felt the hum of its power against mine. *"With the power of this ring, I let the mages' power sing. Destroy the evil in this room, so that the good in here can bloom."* I focused all my will and energy on letting those words ring true, but I didn't feel anything. Not even a little bit of magic stirred inside me.

I waited, holding my breath. Hoping for a miracle.

But none came.

Beyond the flames, the vampires edged closer, moving faster by the moment. My breath came in tiny gasps as I watched them. We were running out of time, and I didn't have anything to make a spell with. Just some hair, bones, the ring, and the crystal. But what could I do with them? One vampire would be hard enough to manage, but this many?

There had to be something. I just needed to think.

*Come on, Claudia. Think.*

"We need to bond." Lucas' words cut through my panicked thoughts.

All the air was forced from me like I was punched in the

gut. "What?" Was he totally crazy? We'd known each other for days. Both of us came with a whole heap of baggage.

"Think about it," he said as he scooted closer. "You'll have all the pack magic at your beck and call. We've mixed so much with the *brujos* that we've got power to spare, but my Alpha powers are useless here. I don't have the ability to harness any kind of magic that would help, but you do. If we bond, you'll have access to all of it."

Just like that? He couldn't be thinking this through. I swallowed. "But... But it's not a full moon. And we can't do the ceremony here."

"That's all for show." He scooted closer, reaching for my hands. He looked calm, with a small smile on his face. "It's trappings, just like a lot of magic. You like to rhyme when you do a spell, but you don't need it to access your magic."

He was right. Holy moly. He was freaking right.

"You just need to accept the bond."

This was insane. I couldn't do this. Not right now. Not here. "But how do you know you want to be tied to me? You don't even know me."

He squeezed my hands. "I knew you were my other half the second I saw you. The more I got to know you, the stronger that pull was. I know all about your past. About your parents. About your brother and the coven. I know everything you've sacrificed. And what I don't know, I'll learn."

"But... I don't know you. I don't even know how old you are."

His small smile spread into a full-on grin. "It doesn't matter right now. What you don't know, you'll learn, too. But we don't have a lot of time." His grin faded, and he leaned forward. "I know this is scary. It's not ideal. But I want to live. And I want to spend my life with you, Claudia de Santos."

It felt as if a thousand butterflies took off in my stomach, and for a second everything paused.

*He wanted to spend his life with me?*

A vampire reached through the fire. I screeched and jerked away from it. The hand caught fire and turned to ash.

Lucas' hand guided my face back to his. How was he so calm right now? "Do you trust me?"

I did. I knew that much. "Yes."

*Holy moly. Was I actually going to do this?*

I cleared my throat. "But I don't know if I want to be a wolf."

He raised a brow. "Do you mind being mated to one?"

I shook my head. "I don't think so." If the wolf was Mr. July, I was in.

"Well then, hand me the ceremonial blade."

I handed it to him as another vampire tried to go through the fire and burned instead.

I ducked down in front of Lucas. "What now?"

He took the sharp knife and cut across his left palm. "Now you."

I took the athame from him but paused, holding it over my left hand. "Won't this turn me into a wolf?"

"No. It has to be my saliva directly into your bloodstream."

Did that even make sense?

"Make the cut. Do it quickly. Mine's already healing."

Crap. I didn't have any more time. If I wanted to live—and I really did—I had to do this. And if I was honest with myself, I wanted it, too.

I counted to three and slashed the knife across my palm. Before I could do anything else, he grasped my left hand in his.

"What's mine is yours and yours is mine. From earth to air to fire to water. Moon and sun. I will be yours to the end of time."

I gasped as his aura rolled over mine. All I could see was gold. I felt his aura. I'd been thinking that it was sunlight, but it really was like the sun. Warm. Kind. He had this deep well of patience and respect for others that I wasn't sure I had. It was beautiful.

My mother had always told me to look for a good man. I never really knew what she meant, but I did now. Lucas was a good man. A really good, tenderhearted, strong man.

And then I felt it. The pack. Each bond running from him to the various members. Hundreds of them. Like little tendrils, reaching out across a great space. They were all moving. Running through the forest. They were following the bond with their Alpha. It overrode whatever magic was hiding this valley. I could almost feel the wind brushing against their fur as they headed straight for us.

But they wouldn't get here in time.

"Knowing what I have to offer, will you accept me and this bond?"

He was quiet, not even breathing, as he waited for me to answer. I almost didn't. Feeling what he felt—knowing how strong and good he was—I didn't feel worthy. But I wanted to be.

"Yes."

It was as if a tether wrapped around my heart. I could almost feel it pulling my soul out of my body as his soul wrapped around me.

Then something snapped so loud I could almost hear it break.

The oath to Luciana. Her anger rolled at me, but fell short. I was free of her. After years, it was over. Just like that.

I wanted to cry and laugh. The relief I felt was so strong that for a moment it was as if I were weightless.

Then the pressure of the mate bond increased. My breaths

came in quick pants. It was too much. He was too much. All this power. I couldn't—

"With these words the bond is complete. I share all my power with my mate."

It rushed at me. Filling me up. The empty well was now overflowing.

I blinked a few times as his aura faded a little from view.

A hand reached through the fire, yanking on my braid. For a second, I slid away from Lucas, but he tightened his grip on my hand. Moving fast, he threw the athame across the fire.

The vampire screamed and let go of my hair.

I had to do something. Now.

Lucas pulled on my hand until I was sitting on his lap. My legs wrapped around his waist. Our left hands were still grasped together, trapped between our bodies.

I couldn't think enough to rhyme, but I didn't need it. I had more power—more magic—at the tip of my fingers than I'd ever had before.

"Burn." I pictured the vampires drowning in flames. Turning to ash.

Screams filled the chamber.

The magic swelled through our bond and I grabbed it. "Burn. All of the evil in this temple. Burn." The magic flowed out of me. It didn't feel like my magic. It felt like Lucas. Like the pack. Like ancient witches. But it didn't matter. It was working. The cries of the vampires told me that.

I kept repeating the command until it was quiet. Until I felt the magic expanding beyond this room. Going upstairs. Turning every undead monster to nothing more than a pile of ash.

Sweat rolled down my back, and even with all that added magic, I felt drained.

I leaned back from Lucas. "Are they all dead?" My voice was hoarse.

"I think so." He leaned back against the leg of the altar. "I can't hear any of them moving. How about putting out the fire?"

I nodded. My throat was sore, so instead of saying it aloud I closed my eyes and pictured the fire going out. When I opened my eyes, it was done.

Sweat made Lucas' hair look spiky instead of messy. I ran my hand through it, and he closed his eyes, leaning into the touch.

*That feels nice.*

I heard Lucas' voice in my head and froze.

Lucas opened his eyes. "What?"

"I heard you."

He raised an eyebrow.

"In my head. I heard you."

"Of course you did. You're my mate, princess."

"I thought you weren't going to call me that anymore. It's still a little condescending."

"It's not meant to be." He ran his thumb down my cheek. "A very long time ago, I was once a prince. And that would make you—my mate and wife—a..."

My jaw dropped, and I sat there for a second, stunned. "But you called me that when you first met me." He couldn't have known then that he wanted to be my mate. He couldn't possibly have known. "I remember distinctly you calling me princess and being annoyed about it."

He nodded slowly, not looking away from me, and I could feel what he felt when he saw me that first time. He really had liked me—more than liked me—from the beginning. I couldn't be anything other than shocked. I'd been attracted to him, but the idea of spending my life with him had seemed so far-fetched at the time.

Only now it was a reality.

Holy moly. I was bonded—more than married—to a freaking wolf.

I felt his amusement at the direction my thoughts had taken, and instead of weirding me out, it made me feel a little more comfortable. I wasn't sure why, but even if part of me thought this whole thing was nuts, another part of me was thrilled. And knowing that he'd felt this way all along... It made me more secure. Like it was okay to want this—safe to feel like this—because he wanted it just as badly.

Being in his head was odd. Teresa had visions and slipped into people's minds all the time, but I never had. I almost felt like an intruder, but I couldn't help it. I wanted to know more.

"Why didn't you say something sooner?"

"When Muraco called to tell me you were coming, he mentioned that mating with a wolf could rid you of your oath. Even though you were tied to someone against your will, you wouldn't take a mate to get out of it. I took that to mean you didn't like Weres. But when I saw you, I knew. When the others heard what I called you, they knew, too. But I wanted to give you a little time to get used to this. If we hadn't been trapped, I would've given you a lot more time."

It was true. I'd said that I didn't want to bond with a wolf, but he wasn't just any wolf. He was my wolf.

I leaned forward slowly. Even though I was still a little bit unsure, I couldn't stop myself from kissing him. The second our lips touched, it was almost too much. I could feel everything he was feeling, and it only made my feelings—love and lust and everything in between—that much stronger.

When we finally pulled apart, he rested his forehead against mine.

I looked into his dark brown eyes and smiled. "Thank you."

"For what?"

"For being you. I..." I wanted to say that I loved him, but I was scared. My heart was pounding. It was almost like I was jumping off the highest cliff.

"I know you do. I can wait for the words." He paused. "Just because we hit fast-forward here doesn't mean that we have to skip all the other steps. We have time. Lots of it." He picked me up off his lap and placed me in front of him, and I missed being so close to him. "We should get out of here before those *brujos* come back."

*Raphael.* What was I thinking, wasting time like this? We had to go.

I took Lucas' hand when he reached down for me.

The room was a ruin of smoking ash. The smell was horrible, but it was better than being dead. The only thing left untouched by all the grime was the saint. He rested there, still perfectly preserved. Only missing a hand, some hair, and a few accessories.

I reached down and put the hand into my purse. At the last second, I spotted the knife in a pile of ash across the room and grabbed it. The knife had our blood on it, and I wasn't leaving a drop of it behind.

Lucas made a face at the hand sticking out of my purse. "Witches," he said with a laugh.

"Without magic, we'd be dead right now."

"True enough, princess. True enough."

We stepped over piles of ash and rot on our way out. By the time we reached the exit, I was more than ready to be outside. The cool mountain air flowed over my skin as Lucas pushed open the door, and I breathed a sigh of relief. Now, all I had to do was get to San Jose and somehow heal Raphael.

I was enjoying the air so much that I didn't notice Lucas had stopped walking until I was jerked to a stop. "What?"

Lucas growled, looking ahead of us, and I turned. All I

could see was forest. But I knew Lucas had much better night vision than I did.

I stepped back to stand next to him as we waited.

*The brujos are still here,* Lucas said in my head.

*What?* I tried answering back the same way.

*There. In front of us. They'll be here in a second.*

They? My stomach knotted as I took in the severity of that word. It sounded like more than just one of those creepy *brujos*. *Just Father Valentine?* I asked.

*No. All of them.*

# CHAPTER TWENTY-THREE

TEN MEN DRESSED in black robes stepped into view in a wall of black and red aura that made my heart beat faster. Father Valentine's white hair made him stand out.

*The pack isn't far, Lucas said, his voice was deep and gravelly. His wolf was close. But if they attack, I'm going to switch forms. Don't be scared. I'm going to try to keep him away from you—stall until the pack gets here—but keep the knife handy.*

I felt along his pack's bonds, and the other wolves wouldn't be here. Not soon enough. I reached into my purse, feeling for the cool metal and gripping it tightly. *Okay.*

"You surprise me," Father Valentine said. "I didn't expect you to get out alive."

We needed more time. "Why did you do it?" Not that it mattered, but if I was going to stall, I might as well ask him something relevant. "I wasn't doing anything to bother you. I would've taken what I needed from the temple and left. You never would've seen me again."

Father Valentine grinned, and I took a step back. "I would've thought you'd have figured it out by now."

Figured it out? I'd missed something. What was it?

The only reason he might not want me dead was if he was working with Luciana. "You taught her?"

He spread out his hands. "Who else?"

It made sense. Their auras weren't the same exactly, but they both had a heavy dose of black in them.

Matt stepped around Father Valentine and a small gasp slipped free.

I hadn't seen him since he attacked me. I hadn't really had time to think about it. Everything had been a rush the past couple of days. I would've thought anger was going to be my first reaction to him. But it wasn't.

I saw Matt, and all I felt was fear. It was powerful—making my whole body shake with tremors. I wrapped my arms around myself.

*I'm here with you,* Lucas said, as he stepped in front of me, blocking Matt.

"You're not still upset, are you, Claudia?" I ground my teeth at the sound of my name—*Clod*-ia—coming from him. "You don't use your powers for yourself. I need them. So, you might as well give them to me."

Give them? *Give* them? I'd given everything I had to everyone else. I knew what giving felt like. No. He'd tried to *take* them from me. And failed.

I stepped beside Lucas. I needed to be strong, not cowering behind him, or else I'd never feel strong and safe again. "I'm not giving you anything."

Matt stepped closer, and the moonlight hit his face, revealing a cold look in his eyes. There was something wrong with him—with the color of his skin. It was too gray. I scanned him, trying to figure out what else was making my skin crawl, and I kept coming back to his eyes.

Matt had never been a nice guy. He was always rude, even

when he'd been trying to win me over. But this was different. The way he looked at me...

It was the way Luciana looked at me. Like a thing instead of a person.

His aura was the same as it always was—pink and gray—and I wondered if this was a side of him that had always been there or if it was new. A real change. If so, it wasn't for the better.

"I need to go, Matt. I have somewhere to be. Let's not turn this into a fight." I had zero faith that we'd get out of here without at least some kind of a fight, but I had to try. This was a waste of time. A very dangerous waste of time.

Matt spat on the ground. "If you won't give me what I want, I'll take it from you. In case you missed it, you're outnumbered."

I focused on the bond that linked Lucas and me together, and felt for his pack again. The wolves were closer. Minutes away. If I kept him talking a little bit longer, then maybe they'd get here before—

Everything happened all at once.

Matt moved his fingers.

Lucas shifted.

Father Valentine started muttering a spell.

I made a quick knot in the air, matching the ends. The magic heated against my skin. With the protection spell in place, I felt better, but there wasn't any time to waste.

Lucas knocked against me as a flash zipped by, narrowly missing me.

Fire.

What was with today and fire?

The smell of sulfur burned my nose.

Dread crawled up my spine, and I focused on drawing as much magic as I could through Lucas.

The priests had formed a circle. Lucas ran at it, but hit an invisible barrier. He flew back a few feet and skidded across the ground.

Matt ran at me. His lips were moving, but I couldn't hear what he was saying.

I pulled on the pack magic to fuel what little I had of my own. *"I block your spell. I bind you well. It's you I'll quell."*

He was still running at me.

No. This wasn't what was supposed to happen. The spell should've worked by now.

I dropped to the ground, wrapping my arms around my head as I braced for impact, but it never came. Instead, I felt a breeze against my back as something flew over me.

I looked up to see a wolf I didn't know standing on top of Matt. His muzzle nearly touched Matt's face as he snarled.

Matt tried to move, but the wolf snapped his teeth a hair's breadth above Matt's neck.

The smell of sulfur grew stronger as the *brujos'* chanting got louder.

The pack was starting to arrive, but in time for what? If the *brujos* raised a demon, we were dead.

I'd only just found the white mages. There hadn't been enough time to figure out how to banish or kill demons yet.

Something started burning my thigh.

I yelped, as I tried to figure out what it was. Nothing was touching me.

*My pocket.*

I dropped the athame and turned my pocket inside out. The burning disappeared as the crystal fell to the ground, glowing blindingly bright.

What on earth...

I carefully picked it up, but it didn't burn me. Not anymore.

I didn't have the words for a spell. Didn't have the rhymes. I couldn't think. But I needed to break that circle. And it had to be done before the demon rose.

*"Break the circle."* I paused and held the crystal above my head. The wolves started running at the circle, but each one flew back with a whimper. *"Break the circle."* I pictured the circle breaking apart, but nothing happened. The priests didn't move. The wolves weren't giving up. Some were swatting at it with their sharp claws. Some running against it. Their golden auras clashed against the dark, shimmering barrier, but it wouldn't budge. *"Break! Break! Break!"*

My voice burned from screaming. My chest heaved as I pushed magic and will toward the circle, but nothing was working. I was failing.

Lucas nudged my side. "What do I do? This isn't working," I said as I ran my fingers through his fur.

His muzzle nudged me. *Run. Break. Now.*

I looked down at his dark face. Apparently his wolf didn't speak in full sentences. "You ran at it and nothing happened except getting knocked on your behind." I waved my hand at the wolves. "Look at them. They're all trying."

He nudged me forward.

"Fine." It was better than nothing.

I took a step toward the *brujos* and the crystal grew brighter. Another step. Brighter. Another. Same thing.

Okay. Lucas knew something I didn't.

I started running. Full out. When I hit circle, I passed right through it and stopped in the center. I'd gotten through, but they still held their circle.

Lucas' panic hit me, but I blocked it out. The wolves howled and started rushing the barrier, but none got through.

It was just me stuck in there. Surrounded by the *brujos* and whatever they were trying to conjure.

I blinked as I tried to catch up with what was going on. I

wanted to run back outside, but if I didn't stop the *brujos* then who would?

Their magic passed over me in a wave of energy that sent me reeling. I knocked into something on my way to the ground.

The men stood around me. Their arms stretched above their heads, hands touching as they chanted. Their eyes glowing red as they stared down at me, half-tranced.

Something bristly scratched my side and I screamed.

I wasn't alone in the center anymore. I was too late. They'd raised a demon.

I crab-crawled back until I hit the legs of one of the mages. I didn't dare look at the thing. Its energy alone made my skin crawl and the thick scent of sulfur made bile rise in my throat.

Something bright and glowing caught my eye. The crystal. I'd dropped it when I fell, but it was here, inside the circle, with me. It lay on the ground inches away from where the demon was crawling out of the underworld.

I didn't want to get any closer to it, but I had to. I needed that crystal. It was the only weapon I had here.

Shaking, I got up on my knees and took a breath. My heart pounded in my ears as I flung myself toward the crystal.

As soon as I had it, I gripped it tight and stabbed it into the demon's hand. *"Back to hell where you belong."*

An explosion broke the night as soon as the crystal touched flesh.

I flew back, knocking into the *brujos,* finally breaking their circle. A cry rang out, raising all the hair on my arms. The portal slammed shut, cutting off the demon's arm at the joint. Blackish-green goo oozed from it, and even though I was trying not to look, I could still see it twitching and moving on its own.

Everything was quiet for a second before spells started flying. The wolves tore into the *brujos*. Snarls and cries of pain bombarded me.

I crawled away from the demon's arm and then stood up slowly, taking in the surroundings. As I turned, I came face to face with Matt.

*How did he get away from that wolf?*

He raised his fist and I jumped back. I moved my fingers quickly through the air. The spell ignited and Matt stumbled back a few steps.

A wave of pain came through the bond as a spell hit Lucas. He wasn't paying attention to the *brujo* in front of him as he tried to get to me.

*Be careful! I shouted at him through the bond. I can take care of myself.*

Lucas fought two more *brujos*, still trying to get to me, but Matt was coming at me again.

*Where's the athame?* I'd dropped it over to the right. I searched the ground, trying to spot the metal.

A spell rolled by overhead, lighting the night, and I saw it.

Matt's fingers flicked, and a burst of flame flew at me. I threw myself to the ground. Just a few feet away.

Matt closed the distance between us. "The *brujos* have taught me a lot."

If I did a spell now, he'd just counter it. I needed a weapon. He wouldn't expect me to use anything other than magic to fight him.

I scooted back a few inches as he stepped toward me. "I don't need their help to drain you. Not anymore," he said.

If I had more time, I'd ask what was going on with his coven that was making him resort to this, but it didn't matter. Not anymore. It needed to end. Now.

I scooted back a little more, reaching my hand back as I watched Matt's mouth move. He wasn't saying the words aloud, but he didn't need to. He just had to believe that they'd work and back it with enough magic.

I kept scooting back until my fingers brushed something metal.

Finally.

I had one shot at this. Any second he could end the spell, and I might not be fast enough to dodge it.

A wolf howled, and I felt Lucas' anger. He'd spotted us. I could feel him through our bond but he wasn't going to get here in time. The *brujos* had separated us, focusing on Lucas, for just this reason. They wanted my power. Like everyone else.

In one move I grasped the athame's handle, sat up, and slashed its tip across Matt's leg.

He kicked my ribs and I heard a crunch before the sickening wave of pain registered. I couldn't breathe, but if I didn't move I'd be as good as dead.

I kicked his leg, and he fell on top of me. I tried to roll him off, but he weighed too much.

His eyes were red, like the other *brujos* were. Almost like he was in a trance, his lips kept moving. He was going to finish the spell.

I had the knife in my hand. All I had to do was stab him, and it would be over. I raised it up and closed my eyes.

*God, forgive me.*

Before I moved the knife downward, the weight on me was gone. Matt screamed.

I opened my eyes to see Lucas snarling at Matt. He had Matt pinned, claws out and digging into Matt's chest.

I sat up, feeling the ache in my chest. If I wanted to say anything to Matt, now was the time. But there wasn't anything to say really.

For a second, I almost asked Lucas not to kill him. To give him another chance. But Matt's eyes flashed red again as his lips moved. In my heart, I knew he wouldn't give up. Not ever. He'd follow me every day of my life, sinking deeper and deeper into evil. Putting my friends and family in danger. I'd let evil hold sway over me for too long already.

"Do it."

Death wasn't a pretty thing.

I wanted to say that I stood there with Lucas, and I did, but I looked away. I hadn't been in a fight until recently, and I hoped that after all of this was over—after Luciana was defeated or dead—I wouldn't have another one ever again.

I took in the surrounding carnage. Three wolves were on the ground. I wasn't sure if they were dead, but they weren't moving. There were two *brujos* down, too. The rest had fled. The sounds of the fight grew farther away as the wolves gave chase.

Then I heard it. A familiar noise that was so out of place it took a second for it to register.

Raphael's ringtone.

I had reception? How did I have reception out here?

*Stop questioning it and move, Claudia.* If Adrian was calling, it wasn't good.

I raced to where I'd dropped my things. The ringing stopped just as I reached the phone.

*No!*

It started ringing again. I flipped the phone open. "Adrian."

"Thank God. I've been calling you for hours. Haven't been able to get through."

"Sorry. I'm in the mountains. Cell coverage is bad. How is he?" I squeezed my eyes shut, hoping that the worst hadn't happened. Not yet. I needed just a little more time.

"It's bad. You need to get here. Like now. We had to tie him to the bed because he kept trying to attack us. The drugs aren't working on him at all. And...he...he smells like he's rotting. He's got hours at best."

I swallowed. "I'll be there." I closed the phone. This didn't feel real. None of this felt real. I was dreaming. Some awful nightmare. It couldn't be—

Two arms wrapped around me and I leaned into the warmth. "What am I going to do?"

"I have an idea." Lucas' voice rumbled against my back.

So did I. Oh my God. So did I.

I shoved the athame into my purse and cradled it to my chest. One glance at Lucas told me he was back in his running pants, minus the shirt and shoes. Good enough.

"Gobble!" I stood up and turned in a circle as I yelled. "Gobble! Come here now. I'm ready to make a deal."

He flashed in front of me in his tiny form. "Yes, tasty. You ready now?"

I nodded as I linked my fingers with Lucas'. "I need to go to San Jose. Hotel Jesus de la Luz."

Gobble whistled. "That's a far trip. It will cost you."

"What are your terms?"

"I will need a favor from you one day soon." His pale blue eyes glinted. "That's when you will have to pay."

I wanted to say yes right then, but Cosette had warned me. That was too vague. I had to be more specific. "I won't do anything bad or evil. I won't kill or hurt anyone. You can't hurt or kill me. Or anyone that I love. You cannot steal my magic or bind me to anyone."

Lucas cleared his throat.

"And where I go, Lucas goes. Whatever you ask me to do can't go against the pact you have with the wolves." Not that I knew what the pact entailed, but I was pretty sure it would cover the worst Gobble could think of. I took a breath. *Anything else?* I asked Lucas through our bond.

*No. That's about all we have time for.*

"Do we have a deal?" I asked Gobble. I held my breath.

Gobble disappeared and I nearly cried out. But then I heard

his voice behind my ear. "You've got a deal." It was his deeper voice. He was full-size again. "Close your eyes, tasty and her wolf."

I did what I was told. A loud pop sounded in my ears, and then the quiet forest was replaced by the sounds and smells of the city.

I opened my eyes and looked up at the sign on the building in front of us.

In big red letters. Hotel Jesus de la Luz.

We were here. If I didn't know better, I would've thanked Gobble. I would've offered him anything he wanted. Because I was here.

I just hoped I was in time.

# CHAPTER TWENTY-FOUR

"LET'S GO."

I raced inside the hotel. Adrian's text said they were in room 304. I wasn't paying attention to the gaudy gold, hot pink, and black decor. I didn't answer the woman at the front desk when she called out to me. All I wanted was my brother.

I saw a sign that pointed to the stairs and started running. Lucas kept pace beside me as I took the steps two at a time.

When we hit the third landing, I raced into the hallway.

Lucas grabbed my arm. "This way."

We sprinted down the hall in the other direction.

I pounded on the door with a gold plate that read 304.

Adrian gaped at us. "How in the hell did you get here so fast?"

I pushed past him, not answering. There were four doors. It was a suite. "Which way? Where is he?"

"Here." Adrian led the way, hurrying through the room.

I froze in the doorway.

What was on the bed wasn't my brother.

His rattling breath had gotten much louder. And the smell. I covered my nose. "Raphael?"

He cackled. "Hey, little sis. Come on over here. Give your big brother a kiss."

My stomach rolled. His voice... What he said... That wasn't him. That wasn't my brother.

A tear rolled down my cheek, and I swept it away. I couldn't let myself think that I was too late, but the closer I got, the worse the smell was.

"We've tried everything," Shane said. I turned to see him standing in the corner across the room. He crossed his tattooed arms as he looked away from Raphael. "The healing chant helped for a little bit, but..."

"I knew it wouldn't last forever." I walked to the bed. Adrian hadn't been lying. Raphael's skin was gray, and a few patches looked gangrenous. What caught me off guard were his eyes. They were solid black. Not even a speck of white was visible.

But he was still breathing. Which meant I wasn't too late. I had to hang on to that, because looking at my twin right now made me want to sob.

I reached into my purse, for what felt like the millionth time in the last few hours, and placed everything on the bedside table.

"What do you have?" Beth asked, as she came up behind me.

I blew out a breath. "I have the hair and hand of a sainted mage. I also have his ring and an athame. And a small magic-infused white crystal—but it's burnt out." There wasn't even a tiny glow from it anymore. It looked gray instead of white. "What to do with it all... I don't have the time—not to mention the supplies—to do any real potions with the hair. But..." I untangled the tiny braids and pulled one free. "I guess I'm going to wing it."

I turned to Raphael. His arms and legs were tied down, so he couldn't do anything to me, but he started hissing and cussing as I came at him with the braid. I wrapped it around his wrist four times before I tied it off. As I wound it, I said the Lord's Prayer. The white aura cut through the muddy color of my brother's aura, revealing a little sliver of his normal bright blue and purple.

Raphael started screaming. "You stupid fucking bitch. How dare you try to bind me?"

I ignored him. This wasn't my brother. Not really.

The mage had been wearing the ring, which probably meant that it had some protection abilities. I was glad I was wearing it. I was going to have to touch my brother, and I didn't want the demon to jump into me.

"What are you going to do now?" Lucas asked.

I stared down at what was left. The hand. The athame. The crystal. "I don't..." I swallowed down the fear that was choking me. My hands shook as I reached toward the nightstand again.

I grabbed the pinky finger and broke off the tip of it. The bone was brittle and white. I turned to Beth. "Do you have a mortar and pestle?"

She nodded.

"Sage. Cloves. And cinnamon. And holy oil or water, if you have it."

"I have everything but the oil or water."

It would have to work. "Shane, will you—"

"Boil water. On it."

I turned to Lucas, hands shaking.

"No matter what happens, I'll be here for you," he told me.

A tear rolled down my cheek, and I brushed it away. I could do this.

Shane and Beth returned, and I ground the bone down to dust. I wished there was time for me to steep the tea, but I couldn't. I poured the mixture into a little glass cup.

This would work. It had to.

I started to climb onto the bed, and Raphael started thrashing. He was tied down, but if he didn't stop, I was going to spill the brew. "Hold him."

Adrian, Lucas, Beth, and Shane each grabbed a limb.

I reached over my brother. "I love you, Raphael. I'm sorry. Please forgive me."

"I hate you, you fucking cunt whore. You're sleeping with the fucking dogs now. You're nothing but—"

I pinched his nose, and his mouth opened. I poured the brew down his throat. He sputtered, choking. His mouth started foaming. At first the foam was white, and then it turned into black sludge.

I slid off the bed, stepping back until I hit the wall, hardly breathing.

Raphael started convulsing and I couldn't hold back the tears. I sobbed and crumpled to the floor. Lucas' arms came around me, but I couldn't look away from my brother. He wasn't breathing anymore.

I'd killed him. He was dying. And it was my fault. I killed him.

My breaths came so fast that I almost threw up.

"Calm down, Claudia." Even Lucas' soothing voice couldn't keep me from losing it. "Breathe. Breathe. Slower. Slow it down, princess."

I tried to follow his orders, but my heart was shattering into a million tiny pieces and I didn't think there was enough glue in the whole world to put it right.

Raphael let out a scream, and I froze. At first it was raspy and had too much texture to it—like it was more than one voice. And then it changed. It was his voice. And then he started coughing as a white light filled the room.

I blinked as my eyes adjusted to the light.

I scrambled over and looked into his eyes. They were clearing. His skin was less gray.

Shane leaned closer, studying my brother. "He's back."

Adrian, Beth, Lucas, and another wolf I'd never met before came around the bed, all looking down at him.

"It's okay," Lucas said as he ran his hand up and down my back. "I think he's going to be okay."

I was too scared to look. I kept staring straight ahead. Not glancing down at all. I blinked back the tears. The others started moving around the room. I heard them cutting my brother free, but I still couldn't look.

"Cloud?" Raphael grasped my hand. "You can look at me now."

I blinked a few more times before looking down. My legs gave way as I started crying again. I rested my head on the edge of the bed, and Raphael's arms came around me. "I thought you were going to die. I thought that was it. It was like losing a piece of my soul. We're twins. You're me and I'm you. You can't die."

"I'm not going to die. I'm okay."

I wiped my face and looked at him. And then punched him. "Don't ever scare me like that again. I swear. I don't... You can't... Just. No."

He smiled. "I'll do my best."

I stood up and leaned over him, giving him a hug. I held on to him a little too long and Raphael laughed. "Hey, Cloud?"

"What?" I mumbled against his chest.

"You smell."

I started laughing. Hard. It felt good. I'd been so panicked. Ever since z-Daniel bit him, I hadn't relaxed.

When I caught my breath, I sank down to the floor, exhausted.

Shane cleared his throat. "You bonded with this wolf?"

"Lucas..." Oh shit. I'd never learned his last name. I'd just mated to a guy whose last name I didn't even know. What was wrong with me?

"Reyes," he said for me.

"You paid for my hotel room?"

He raised a brow. "Yes. I'm the pack Alpha."

I shook my head. It made sense. I just never put it together.

Shane cleared his throat again. "That means you broke your oath with Luciana."

Oh God. I'd practically forgotten about that. I wasn't tied to her anymore. My magic was my own again. "Yeah." A grin spread across my face. "Yeah, I did."

"So, Beth, Raphael, and the others can take an oath to you. You're stronger than Luciana. I know you are."

No. Nope. No way. "I don't want to be a coven leader. I don't want to be part of a coven at all. I've had enough of that for one lifetime."

"It could be temporary," Beth said. "Just until this is over and we join a new coven."

"I don't know..." Even temporarily, I wasn't sure how I felt about it. I hadn't even tasted freedom yet, and now I was tying myself down.

I'd already tied myself to Lucas, but Mr. July was worth it. But anything more...

"Do it," Raphael said. "Then she can't use us to get back at you anymore."

"You'll still have your freedom," Lucas said. "I'll make sure you travel and take all the courses they offer at whatever college you choose. I won't let you give up your dreams."

"Please," Beth said. "I don't want to be tied to her anymore."

I clenched my fists at my side. Every part of me rebelled against this. "But not a blood oath. Just the normal one."

Beth gave me a sharp nod. "Fine."

"By Claudia de Santos before whom this sanctuary is holy,"

Beth, Raphael, and Shane said the words as one. "I will be true and faithful, and love all which she loves and shun all which she shuns, according to the laws of God, magic, and the order of the world. Nor will I ever with will or action, through word or deed, do anything which is unpleasing to her, on the condition that she will hold to me as I shall deserve it, and that she will perform everything as it was in our agreement when I submitted myself to her and chose her will."

As they finished, I felt the oath tighten like a noose around my neck, binding me to them and them to me. It wasn't that I couldn't bear it—I just didn't want it. I didn't want the responsibility that came with it.

The magic snapped into place, and if I'd been bone tired before, now I felt half-dead.

The phone rang, and Adrian left to answer.

I made my escape to the bathroom. I needed to wash my face. To take a breath.

When I came out, Adrian was waiting for me. "St. Ailbe's has been attacked again. We've got to get there. Can you get us back there like you got here?"

I shook my head. "Not without making another bargain with a fey. I think one—"

"You made a bargain with a fey!" Raphael yelled from his bed. "You bonded with a wolf and made a bargain with a fey? What were you thinking? Why would you do this?"

Well, I guessed he was feeling a little better. "I did what I had to in order to get back here in time."

Before he could speak up again, Lucas bent over and picked me up. "We need a place to shower and sleep, clothes, and food."

Adrian grabbed a key. "Take my room. It's next door. I'll order room service for you and then get to work on arranging flights for us all."

"I'll grab some clothes for you." Shane moved past us. "You're bigger than me, but I'm the closest fit." Shane was built thick and very tall. Adrian was cut and tallish, like all the wolves, but Lucas was at least a few inches taller and much more built.

"I'll find some things for you, Claudia." Beth hurried out of the room.

I rested my head on Lucas' shoulder. I felt him walking, but my eyes were heavy. Everyone was safe and alive. It would take my brother a bit to recover, but he would. The oath was broken, and everyone was safe from Luciana for now. My job was done. I could finally rest.

And so I let the darkness take me.

# CHAPTER TWENTY-FIVE

I WOKE to the sounds of people talking and the smell of food. My stomach rumbled and I sat up.

The talking stopped.

I rubbed my eyes and saw Lucas and Adrian staring at me over a pile of food. "What time is it?"

"Ten in the morning," Adrian said.

"What time did we get here?"

"Two. You've been asleep for eight hours."

I fell back against the pillows. "I could sleep for another twelve."

Adrian snorted. "No kidding. How many days did you stay awake before you left for Peru?"

"Uh." I scratched my head as I thought. "I think I got two or three hours the first few nights at St. Ailbe's. Then I pretty much stayed awake for three days straight. Although I passed out in the infirmary for a couple hours. So..."

"And how did you sleep now?" Lucas asked.

I thought about it for a second. "Like the dead. It was amazing. Best night of sleep I've had in years." I felt Lucas' pleasure at that and smiled. This whole thing was new, but it was nice knowing that my sleeping well made him happy.

I struggled to sit up again. "I'm going to shower. Save some food for me?" I didn't wait for an answer. I went into the bathroom and started the water. Some of Beth's clothes lay on the counter. In the rush to get here, I'd left my backpack in the forest. I guessed all those clothes were history. What a waste.

The water was perfectly steamy. I scrubbed myself from head to toe before getting out and brushing my teeth. It was a crappy hotel toothbrush, but I didn't care. Running water was a treat I now appreciated in a whole new way.

I got dressed in the yoga pants and tank that Beth had loaned me. She was taller and thinner than me, but the clothes fit well enough. I finger-combed my hair and then left it. My body was still too tired to bother with a braid.

When I stepped outside, Adrian was gone. A new tray of food was in his place, with silver covers keeping it warm. I poured myself a cup of coffee, holding it with both hands as I settled into the chair. I pulled my feet up, and sighed. This was the life.

"Feeling better?" Lucas asked.

That was a giant understatement. "There's not much that coffee and a hot shower can't fix." We were quiet for a second, and for the first time it was a little awkward. I wasn't sure how to be his mate. Or what he expected. And I wasn't sure what I wanted from him either.

"I didn't know what you'd want for breakfast, so I got a bunch of things."

I took a breath, letting go of all that worry.

This was Lucas. My Lucas. I knew him. He was kind and generous and thoughtful.

He still made me nervous though. No one had the right to be so handsome.

I set down my coffee and busied myself with uncovering the dishes. Eggs, bacon, toast, potatoes, roasted tomatoes, yogurt, granola, a bowl of fruit, and a basket of pastries. I laughed. "You really did get everything."

He shrugged, and if I didn't know any better, I would've thought his cheeks had a little more color. But Lucas wouldn't blush. Would he? "Better safe than sorry," he said.

I met his gaze. Those twin dark pools. I bit my lip as I considered him. I hadn't known him long—days really—but he'd hooked me from the beginning. "Thank you." I took a bite of fruit. "So, what's next? What did I miss?"

He crossed his arms over his chest, and I couldn't help but stare at the shirt that was stretched so thin over his biceps I was half-convinced it'd rip any second. "Your brother is doing better. Adrian has us all booked on an afternoon flight to Texas."

"You're coming?" I almost winced. That came out wrong. I wanted him to come, but I wasn't sure if he wanted to. Or if he was even able to. He had a pack to take care of, and I... Well, I had at least one more fight ahead of me.

"Of course I'm coming." He frowned. "Do you not want me to come?"

"No. I want you to come. I just thought—you have a pack and responsibilities and I know we're mated—"

"I was wondering if you caught that." He grinned, and my cheeks caught fire.

"I did catch that." I cleared my throat. "But I don't really know what it is that it means... What you want and everything. I don't know what I'm supposed to do or what's expected of me."

His shoulders relaxed, and I felt his relief through the bond. "Don't worry. There's nothing expected except for you to just be you. We jumped into the deep end, and it's going to take time for us to settle into who we are as a couple." He grinned and I couldn't help the blush that spread across my face. "I know I said it before, but we were rushed and I want you to know that I wasn't planning on doing it this way. I wanted to get to know you. For you to get to know me. To consider your options. But..." He shrugged. "So, now, where you go, I go. We'll take this as fast or as slow as you want, but as for what I want—I want to be with you."

Now it was my turn to be relieved. "I want you to be with me, too."

"Okay, then. So we go to Texas and deal with this woman. And then we can travel a bit."

Travel? I had a million questions, starting with where? But I didn't want to get my hopes up. Not yet. "What about your pack?"

"The pack is fine."

"But what about those mages?"

"The pack is taking care of it. Don't worry."

But I was worrying. I'd done so many things wrong, and I wanted to make sure that I got this right. "But you have—"

"I'd give up the pack if I thought it was a problem."

I snapped my mouth shut. *He would?*

"I've been the Alpha there for a very, very long time. I've got a good second, and he'll keep things going. I haven't had time for myself in... Well, let's just say it's due. So, I'm taking time with my new mate. Honeymoons are traditional for humans. We'll just take a long one. Maybe a few years. Okay?"

Years? That sounded crazy, but also pretty amazing. "Okay. But what about work?"

He raised an eyebrow. "You want to work? Doing what?"

I started fidgeting with my napkin. "Not me. You. Don't you have a job, or...?"

His smile was back. "Haven't for a very long time. I don't need to work. I have lots of sound investments."

I opened and closed my mouth a few times, unsure of what to say to that. "So, we travel?"

He tilted his head to the side as he stared at me. "Where do you want to go?"

Everywhere. Anywhere. I didn't really care. "I don't know. I never thought I'd be able to."

"Well, think about it. But breakfast first." He pointed to my plate.

I played with my food for a second before looking at him.

"What?" He drew out the word with a smirk.

"I was just thinking..." I shook my head. "No. It's embarrassing."

"You don't have to be embarrassed. Just ask."

I knew how I felt about him. I'd been attracted to him at once. And then he was nice. And fun. I loved his laugh and his smile. I liked how polite he was to everyone. Well, except Gobble. But he was kind. Warm. And his aura... It was so him. Warm like sunlight. Being around him was like spending the day tanning by the pool. But did he love me? No one had ever said that to me. Raphael wasn't much for those kinds of words, and my parents... Well, they weren't the best at being parents. "I was just wondering—"

All of a sudden the bond opened, and I could feel everything Lucas was feeling. Everything he was thinking. I knew it all. Could feel it all as if his emotions were my own.

It was so powerful, what he felt. So...

So much. It was like wrapping myself in a warm blanket.

It was love.

Oh my God. He wasn't just saying that. He really loved me.

"You thought I didn't? That I'd want to mate with the first witch I came across?"

It seemed ridiculous when he put it that way. "No. I just... I don't know what I thought."

"I waited a long time for you. Many, many decades. Longer than that."

I laughed. "How old are you?" I stuck my fork in a hunk of melon.

"I'll wait until you're not so young before I tell you. I don't want you to get spooked."

"Are you as old as Donovan?" I asked as I waved the fruit in the air and then took a bite.

He settled back in his chair and crossed his arms. "Older."

That didn't make sense. "But you look younger."

He laughed. "I can't wait to tell him you said so."

I paused. "But then why aren't you one of the Seven?"

Lucas gave me the most wicked look. "I don't like to play by the rules."

Holy moly. How did I not know he was a bad boy at heart?

No. I must've misunderstood.

Lucas motioned to the food. "Eat. And then you can take a nap before the flight. I didn't realize how exhausted you were. You didn't move the entire time you slept."

I rubbed my eyes. "It's the first time I've been able to actually sleep without the fear of Luciana draining me. I did okay in Peru—I was far enough away—but I was—"

"Restless. I thought it was because I was with you."

I shook my head. "Not at all. I was just afraid to close my eyes."

"Ah. I see." Lucas stood and walked to my chair, reaching a hand out to me. It seemed natural to reach back to him.

He pulled me down on the bed and tucked me against him so I could rest my head on his chest. Then he pressed a kiss to my forehead. "Sleep. I'll watch over you."

I got comfortable, resting half on him, my arm across his stomach. He ran his fingers up and down my arm. For the first time in longer than I could remember, I felt safe. Comfortable. Not panicked.

Complete.

WE MET in the lobby a few hours later. Adrian was already there, chatting with Shane and Beth. We were just waiting for Raphael and the wolf I still hadn't met yet.

After the nap, Lucas ordered more food, and I felt infinitely better. As I sat down, I was glad we hadn't stayed here longer. The couch was a fuzzy zebra print with hot pink and neon green pillows. The coffee table was chrome and glass. Actually everything was either black and white, neon colored, or chrome. There were so many shiny surfaces that the hotel must spend a fortune on cleaners.

What I didn't understand at all was the hot pink deer head hanging over the mantel.

*It's a little much, don't you think?*

Lucas nodded. *It's hideous.*

*Right?*

We both started laughing, and Adrian moaned. "Not you, too."

"Sorry," I said.

I felt Raphael coming down the hall before I saw him. Twindar was back. I stood up. "Hey," I said as I gave him a hug. His skin tone was still a little off, but he looked like himself now. "You look better."

"Feel much better. Thank you."

"Anything for you."

Raphael turned to Lucas, sizing him up. "I hear you're mated to my sister now."

Lucas stood tall, meeting Raphael's stare down head on. "I

would've liked to have met you before we bonded, but we found ourselves in a bit of situation and Claudia needed the added power boost." He held out his hand. "It's nice to finally meet you. I hope you know that I'll do everything I can to make sure your sister is happy and well taken care of."

"Are you going to make her change?"

I choked on air at the blunt question. Before I could say it was none of his business, Lucas spoke up. "Never. If she wants to change, that's up to her. She's my mate either way." He didn't even bristle at my brother's sharp tone.

Raphael crossed his arms. "None of this forced biting like the guy my cousin hooked up with."

"Absolutely not." Lucas looked to me. "What Dastien did was wrong. He knows it. He was young and couldn't control the urge. But I'm not young. Okay?"

I nodded. My life was complicated enough without being a wolf, and for once I wanted to think things through before jumping in. For the time being, it was enough to just be me.

"Let's go," Adrian said. "Don't want to miss the flight. Tessa is freaking out. She thinks Luciana is up to something."

I sighed. "She's always up to something."

"Well, this time it's extra bad."

When it came to Luciana, it was always bad. "You got the stuff?"

Raphael held up a small gym bag. "Although how we're going to get a shriveled hand past security..."

I winced. "We'll figure it out." Lucas ran his fingers down my arm, until he reached my hand, twining our fingers together. "Let's get this over with," I said.

"And then on to the next chapter," Lucas said. "Maybe we can pick up a travel book in the airport?"

I grinned up at him. "That would be amazing."

As we left, I knew that we had some big things to do before

we got to have our time together, but I was aiming for the stars. And I'd be more than happy with the moon. It was fitting, too. I'd have the moon and the wolf.

As we got into the taxi, I leaned against Lucas.

"Everything okay?"

I looked up at him. "Everything's just fine."

He pressed his lips against mine, and I melted. When he pulled away, I leaned against him again. "Yup. Everything's just fine."

Tessa and Dastien return in ***Alpha Unleashed***,
Book Five of the Alpha Girls Series.

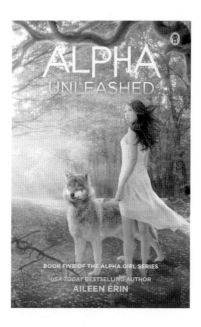

## From *USA Today* Bestselling Author Aileen Erin

Tessa McCaide has had it ***up to here*** with supernaturals.
Luciana may have failed to steal Tessa's magic, but she's just
getting started on her crusade for magical domination. If her
demonic summoning isn't stopped, it could mean the end of
everything.

Tessa's pack, including her mate Dastien, are ready to fight, but
the ragtag group of shifters and witches are no match for
Luciana's power. A little help (and ancient Inca mojo) from
Tessa's *bruja* cousin, Claudia, may give the side of good a

chance if she can make it home in time, but stopping the war is no longer an option.

When witches and werewolves fight, no one wins. **Only time will tell who will still be standing after the last spell is cast.**

Now available from *USA Today* Bestselling Author, Aileen Erin
*Off Planet*, Book One of the Aunare Chronicles.

In an all-too-plausible future where corporate conglomerates have left the world's governments in shambles, anyone with means has left the polluted Earth for the promise of a better life on a SpaceTech owned colony among the stars.

Maité Martinez is the daughter of an Earther Latina and a powerful Aunare man, an alien race that SpaceTech sees as a threat to their dominion. When tensions turn violent, Maité finds herself trapped on Earth and forced into hiding.

**For over ten years, Maité has stayed hidden, but every minute Maité stays on Earth is one closer to getting caught.**

She's lived on the streets. Gone hungry. And found a way to fight through it all. But one night, while waitressing in a greasy diner, a customer gets handsy with her. She reacts without thinking.

**Covered in blood, Maité runs, but it's not long before SpaceTech finds her...**

Arrested and forced into dangerous work detail on a volcano planet, Maité waits for SpaceTech to make their move against the Aunare. She knows that if she can't somehow find a way to stop them, there will be an interstellar war big enough to end all life in the universe.

# INK MONSTER
# NEWSLETTER

## STAY UP-TO-DATE WITH EVERYTHING AILEEN IS WORKING ON -- INCLUDING SPECIAL SALES, BEHIND-THE-SCENES CONTENT, AND MONTHLY GIVEAWAYS!

SUBSCRIBERS ARE AUTOMATICALLY ENTERED INTO MONTHLY GIVEAWAYS FOR SIGNED COPIES AND MORE!

Subscribe at: https://www.aileenerin.com/subscribe

# ACKNOWLEDGMENTS

To all my readers, you asked for Claudia's story and you got it! I'm hoping to expand to other characters, too. Anyone want a Meredith book? ;)

Thank you to everyone who read this book. I wrote it during a particularly difficult time in my life. For a while, I wasn't sure if I'd get it done in time, but somehow I did.

I needed some cheerleaders to get through it.

Lola Dodge: I wouldn't have finished if it wasn't for you believing in me. Thank you for all the random Skype sessions and speedy edits. I'm always so thankful that we got paired together all those years ago. Best crit partner ever. If it wasn't official before, it surely is now. You're stuck with me forever.

To all of the lovely ladies at INscribe: Thank you for everything that you do. Ink Monster couldn't have come this far without you!

To the lovely Kristi Latcham: Thank you for all of your support and proofing! You're the best mother-in-law a girl could ask for. We've been through the wringer the last six months, but the light is ahead.

To my family and friends: Thank you for all of your support. It's been a rough few months, and I couldn't have gotten through without you all.

Last, but most importantly, to my husband: You are my everything. Thank you for carrying me through this hard time. Thank you for being supportive through thick and thin. For believing in me, even when I didn't believe in myself. I love you more than words could ever express. A lifetime with you won't be enough.

**Aileen Erin** is half-Irish, half-Mexican, and 100% nerd—from Star Wars (prequels don't count) to Star Trek (TNG FTW), she geeks out on Tolkien's linguistics, and has a severe fascination with the supernatural. Aileen has a BS in Radio-TV-Film from the University of Texas at Austin, and an MFA in Writing Popular Fiction from Seton Hill University. She lives with her husband and daughter in Texas and spends her days doing her favorite things: reading books, creating worlds, and kicking ass.

For more information and updates about Aileen and her books, go to: www.aileenerin.com

Or check her out on:

facebook.com/aelatcham

twitter.com/aileen_erin

instagram.com/aileenerin

bookbub.com/authors/aileen-erin